CHICAGO PUBLIC LIBRARY
CONRAD SULZER REGIONAL LIBRARY
4455 LINCOLN AVE.
CHICAGO, ILLINOIS 60625

FIC
MACMILLA

Chicago Public Library

W9-BWG-269

SULZER

Village of a million spirits : a no

AUG - - 1999

VILLAGE OF A MILLION SPIRITS

VILLAGE OF A MILLION SPIRITS

A NOVEL OF THE TREBLINKA UPRISING

Ian MacMillan

STEERFORTH PRESS
SOUTH ROYALTON, VERMONT

Copyright © 1999 by Ian MacMillan

ALL RIGHTS RESERVED

For information about permission to reproduce
selections from this book, write to:
Steerforth Press L.C., P.O. Box 70, South Royalton, Vermont 05068

Library of Congress Cataloging-in-Publication Data
MacMillan, Ian T.
Village of a million spirits : a novel of the Treblinka uprising /
Ian MacMillan.
p.   cm.
ISBN 1-883642-84-1 (alk. paper)
1. World War, 1939–1945 — Prisoners and prisons, German — Fiction.
2. Holocaust, Jewish (1939–1945) — Poland — Fiction.
3. World War, 1939–1945 — Atrocities — Fiction.
4. Treblinka (Concentration camp) — Fiction.   I. Title.
PS3563.A318955V54   1999
813'.54 — dc21   99–18847
                                                      CIP

Manufactured in the United States of America

SECOND PRINTING

R0129395685

CHICAGO PUBLIC LIBRARY
CONRAD SULZER REGIONAL LIBRARY
4455 LINCOLN AVE.
CHICAGO, ILLINOIS 60625

FOREWORD

Village of a Million Spirits deals with World War II in Middle Europe, balancing history and fiction by using a verifiable historical context as a stage on which fictional characters act and fictional events occur.

In Village of a Million Spirits the major events are verifiable: It is true that an officer named Max Bielas was killed by an Argentine inmate named Meir Berliner, but this event is seen obliquely through the eyes of a fictional Ukrainian guard. It is true that after a long winter lull during which no transports and therefore no food or valuables had arrived at Treblinka, Deputy Commandant Kurt Franz (The Doll) announced that the trains would roll again, bringing on a sustained cheer from the starving workers. These events are all seen through the eyes of fictional characters.

The real heroes of Treblinka — the engineer Galewski, Zhelo Bloch, Rudolph Masarek — are presented obliquely and at a distance, leaving the points of view to fictional inmates counted among those who were lucky enough to survive the transports but were not as consequential to Treblinka's fate as the heroes mentioned above.

The estimates of the number of people killed at Treblinka range from 600,000 to 1.2 million. The discrepancy in figures is itself evidence of the secrecy of the camp and the scarcity of written records of the reported forty survivors (and the many perpetrators) willing to discuss it. Survivors' accounts of events at Treblinka tend to contradict each other in certain respects but are generally consistent in presenting a broad picture of the year of the camp's existence. But the estimation of the number of dead may be the most horrible of all the "inconsistencies." In this case, to use an obscene euphemism, the "margin of error" comes to 600,000.

The various motivations for the perpetration of this crime are obviously complicated, but the core of the crime was genocide. It is often thought of as an aberration from a half century ago, but on a smaller scale it has continued to happen since, and is, as you know if you're tuned in to the news, still happening.

One last point: The crime that was committed more than fifty years ago has not yet been "completed." Historical revisionists demand proof that it happened, and rest their case because they feel that "objective" proof cannot be provided to their satisfaction. This is the last part of a process that began with denial of human rights, went through theft of wealth, then murder. Now the last act is the attempt to deny that these people ever existed, thereby robbing them of their identity, and their relatives and friends and descendants and us of the opportunity to acknowledge their existence and honor their memory.

OUTSIDE THE PERIMETER FENCE, TREBLINKA

AUGUST 2, 1943

Only a year ago, she remembers, when they first heard the train whistles, she and Michal Balicki from the village were here on this bed of brown pine needles, looking out of the pine grove at the new camp only a few hundred meters away, and he explained to her that just beyond that fence inside those low buildings whose rooftops you could just barely see, they killed Jews every day and took all their money. Then he put his hand on her and said, the Jews from Russia sacrifice gentile children and drink their blood, did you know that?

And now Magda Nowak waits as she has come to wait every day for the past month, watching the air between her and the fence boil up from the ground. In the distance, the camp rises from a mirage, a horizontal strip of molten silver, wisps of smoke hanging in the air above it. Back then, a year ago, it was Michal with his hands on her, Michal with his hot anxious force, and then because her father ordered, it was Anatoly, with his uniform smelling of sulfur and she thought death, because he was in the camp with them every day, as much a prisoner as the Jews even though he came out every day leading the work crews, his rifle hanging from his shoulder. And now, in the intense heat, the dreaming daytime stillness of the woods, she waits, her fingers intertwined under her enormous belly inside which the pulsing, ticklish surges of the baby increase, causing a breathless electrical throbbing to worm up into her chest and down into her legs. Surely this week it will be born and Anatoly is in there, as much a prisoner as the Jews.

She thinks, *death camp*. Camp of death. In his awkward West Ukrainian accent Anatoly called it a factory. We make death — that is our industry. She saw the trains from the woods, fifty, sixty cars each, every day, with the square-shouldered Germans sitting on top, their guns cradled in their arms. No one can do anything about it, the thousand or so workers, the guards like Anatoly, no one. When they caught Anatoly stealing they punished him by cutting off his finger. They are all slaves and the Germans are their masters, and they make death every day. When Anatoly could take making death no more he came out leading the men and then did not go back, and she tries to fix the time. June, two months ago. He had money, a gun, clothes, and he hid in the woods. He was supposed to meet her so that they could leave the country but never did. He was probably back in the camp, and she thinks, he is in there, under that guard tower somewhere wearing his uniform and smelling of sulfur and making death, standing there with his rifle and his weary sad-eyed look, his huge ears bright red in the sun. She smiles, thinking of his ears.

The heat settles on her in a somnolent, downward sweep, like dizziness, and she moves closer to the edge of the pines so as to get a better view of the camp. They are burning something there. Here the radiated heat from the unshaded ground a meter away presses against her like heat radiating from a stove. Usually there are workers out cutting wood, forked sticks Anatoly calls them, but today it must be too hot. Come out, Anatoly, she thinks, and see the birth of your child.

She should walk home. As her mother had arranged, the midwife is due to visit, to look at her. She imagines a nurse dressed in some sort of a medical uniform, a competent village woman who will show her how to have her baby. In the meantime she should help her mother in the kitchen, or her father out in the fields. They no longer want her. Her father's face became more and more sour as her belly grew and she could see what he wanted to say in his eyes. None of the guards would want a sow like you. Thousands of Jews come every day, all of them rich, and every day the guards come out with their pockets bulging with money looking for a little relaxation, and look at you. Other men sell their daughters for gold coins, jewels, and those girls are not so stupid as to get pregnant. They are not so stupid as to become infatuated with a dish-eared idiot like Anatoly, who cannot distinguish gold plate from gold, glass from diamond. Day by day as regular as a clock the trains come loaded with Jews, and each time he heard the whistle, his face slowly dropped — yes, thousands upon thousands, and look at you. She hates her father because he just does not understand. She is seventeen, old enough to know what she wants. The baby is hers and she wants it, as does Anatoly, who told her they would go to the Ukraine and get away from the death. If only he would come out, if they would once again let him watch the work crews in the woods so he could leave. But the Germans are the ones to decide, and no one can do anything about what they decide. And if they decide that he cannot come out, then the baby will have no father and will be born deformed, or dead. She is sure of that.

[3]

The wisps of smoke are heavier, and she squints, feeling beads of sweat run down between her breasts. She looks down at her bare feet, pine needles stuck to them by sweat. They are swollen so that none of the veins are visible, and they hurt, as if the stretching skin cannot contain the pressure, the bones cannot bear the great weight.

She is about to turn to go across the kilometer of brush and rye fields to her house when a huge billow of black smoke mushrooms upward from the camp, and inside of it flashes a tongue of dark orange fire, and then she both hears and feels the dense *whoosh* of an explosion. Cracking sounds reach her — gunfire, she thinks, and she is suddenly frightened. Something has happened in there. She turns, and feels a wrenching in her side, from moving too fast, and as she waits for the pain to recede, she realizes that it expands and begins twisting itself under her rib cage in a slow cramp that makes sweat bead on her forehead and arms. As the cramp drives itself downward she looks once again at the camp, and the billow of smoke has been replaced by a huge fire that shoots sparks into the hot air, and now another mushroom of smoke ruptures upward, and tongues of flame appear in other places. She remains immobilized by the cramp, which has now died out under her stomach, leaving her weak-kneed and shaky.

The sounds of gunfire reach her again, dreamlike in the dense, scorched air. Anatoly. What if he were hurt? But she must get home. She moves into the pines, and feels her legs wet. She looks down at her feet and realizes that she has wet herself, reaches down and touches the liquid on the inside of her leg. She rubs it between her thumb and fingers, her hands shaking. It is a clear, slippery liquid, not urine.

There is another explosion, then the faint sounds of people yelling, and the rapid pulse of a machine gun. Who could be doing that? Why would the camp be burning? She should not be here. As she tries to walk her legs do not obey her. They

[4]

shake so badly that she can barely keep her balance. She must get home. She should not be seeing this.

She feels another cramp begin to expand high in her rib cage, like a pair of powerful hands inside her squeezing downward so that she finds it hard to breathe. More of that liquid runs down her legs. She laces her fingers under her belly, and turns to look back at the burning camp. Across the brush and dry grass she sees dark, wriggling specks, and as her eyes adjust to the distance, the forms of running men materialize rising from the silvery mirage, liquefied in the shimmering heat. Three, four of them, no, a dozen. More than a dozen. Then it appears to be sixty or seventy, a line of shapes enlarging in a molten undulation. They are not wearing uniforms. She stumbles into the pines, breathless with fright, her arms and legs numb. There, hanging onto the brittle branch of a pine tree, she feels the hands squeezing downward, so that she cannot move. The men coming are not soldiers — they are Jews, and they have apparently broken out of the camp. What had the farmers and villagers called them? The evil ones, the devils, the blood drinkers? That is not possible — no one leaves the camp unless the Germans let them leave. She holds on to the branch, trying to breathe, aware that those men have broken loose and are running toward her, the nightmare that so many of the people living here have dreaded since they first heard the train whistles.

At the end of the lane through the rye is the slightly elevated rail bed, topped by a bright silver strip. As he walks toward it, the sound of his own steps on the parched, rocky dirt comes in *whoosh*ing thumps to his ears. He will not go back to the school because she yelled at him in class, you, Janusz Siedlecki, you are a dunce! And they laughed, their laughter a hollow echoing punctuated by bursts that sounded like a hammer on a pail.

Out by the track, up on the rail bed, he sees the land sweep away into the distant haze, the heat shimmering over the rye, with a line of trees on the horizon, gray translucent cones. He wets the end of his index finger and touches the track, and the wet spot vanishes in less than a second, the diminishing heat from his skin's contact on the searing metal buzzing like sluggish, fading electricity.

They laughed at him because he lived inside his head, all his life. His mother poured oil in his ears, they irrigated his ears with water, but it never worked. Then his father would become angry at him for being deaf and order him to his room, where he would remain alone with an old encyclopedia, with which he bored himself into exhaustion. He was always assumed to be partially deaf, but on those strange occasions when it vanished by some miracle — after playing so hard that he became drenched with sweat, or perhaps after swimming — he would experience two hours, sometimes half a day, of a bizarre auditory lucidity that would frighten him. The world was a constant gabbling of sounds, snappings, tinklings, far-off moans, vibrations of sound so mysterious that he could never identify their source, and he wondered if deafness was somehow preferable. Then he would recede once again into that world of a perpetual roaring paced by the *whoosh*ing sound of the beating of his own heart. When his parents were arrested he did what he thought his father would do: He used a bow saw to cut stove wood, which on weekends they had always sold by the wagonload in Warsaw, thirty kilometers to the south of their little town. He waited for his father to come back, to pick up where they had left off, but he never did.

There is a subtle vibration in the ground, perhaps a wagon coming, and he turns. There is no wagon. The lane through the rye vanishes into brush, beyond which is the village. To the left, up the track, a line of gray smoke advancing, billowed into the air above the track and then stilled, creating a fuzzy, curved snake that hangs in the air, fading in density as it recedes into the horizon.

He sees the dense black shape of the engine emerge in a slow, rocking advance from between trees, the black smoke shooting from the stack in a rapid pulse like an elevated heartbeat, and now he feels it in the air, a series of soft shocks on the skin of his face. The engine sweeps in a slight curve, and low on the side he can now see a pair of knees, and above them the barrel of a rifle. He backs up into the lane, then moves into the rye and lies down at the edge of it facing the tracks, feeling the rye stalks crackling in a dry brittle settling under his shirt, and the dusty tassels tickling his forearms.

He feels the engine in the hot ground, and parts the rye. The engine approaches at little more than the speed of a man walking, looming above him on the left, and the pulsing roar echoes in his ears. Then it passes, and the soldier sitting on the step appears to be asleep, his head to the side. As the first car passes, the scorched, salty odor of smoke from underneath the train flows down across his face, and he smells the grating, metallic friction of metal on metal, the rail bending downward as each wheel passes over it, and in the ground he feels the crunching of the gravel under the ties. He counts, four, five, six, and then stops, because the cars are moving too slowly for him to count. Some of the cars have little window holes crisscrossed by barbed wire, and on the lower frames of these windows he sees fingers, knuckles, and behind them in the darkness in some of the windows the brief glint of wire-rimmed glasses. A trainload of woodcutters and farmers.

His father had jumped at the sound of a German voice. Hearing is a weakness — it makes the body react. Because the deaf cannot react to sound they achieve a kind of invisibility.

After a while it is as if he has watched the train for hours, although he knows it is only minutes. The rail bends, gravel crunches in the ground, the white fingers and knuckles pass. Finally four empty cars pass, the doors open so that they flash squares of pale sky, one after another, from the other side.

The train's last car passes, and rocks slowly down the track. He stands up, wipes the dirt from his trousers and shirt. The smells and sounds have given him a dull headache, and he feels groggy and weak, as if the train has hypnotized him. The heat hammers down on his head and shoulders, radiates out of the ground, and he places his hand on the top of his head. His hair is hot. Above him the fat gray snake remains suspended, and curves, hovering over the tracks sweeping away in the boiling haze.

A man standing at the railway car wall, his face mashed against the slit between two planks, announces that he sees bare countryside, thatch houses, well sweeps, and fields of rye. A bright slice of light cuts down his face, and Yzak Berilman can see his eye moving inside it. Berilman stands jammed in the corner of the railway car with his hands bracing his body away from the splintered planking of the wall, jouncing to the jerking movement of the train that carries him farther and farther away from his canvas, brushes, from the rich, olive-oil smell of the pigments laid carefully on the easel lip, their heads pointing upward at him like a line of tiny cannons. Between his shoes is the box that holds what he could save of his smaller canvases and paints, his mother's silver, and the little daguerreotypes inside the brown imitation-leather boxes, each with a little brass clasp — his ancestors, those stern, emaciated faces with the pale, bleached eyes, images that when tipped to the light go negative in a strange, ghostlike metamorphosis.

The rocking of the train pushes old Meir Goldwicht against him in soft, heavy surges, and he holds himself steady, trying to ignore the heat and the thirst and the sour smell of Goldwicht's coat and that desperation all of the rest seem to be captured by. Why should they all assume they will die? he thinks, and sees again the unfinished canvas, a rectangular window into a field under a blue sky, given depth by a broken wagon wheel in the left foreground. How long he had worked on how far inward toward the rusted hub each spoke should be broken, so crucial to the little rectangular world's being that part was.

Goldwicht now comes into profile, and in the drooping eye and nose and in the secret whispering motion of his lips Yzak Berilman sees the fear and the shame and regret, if only I could have bathed before this, if only I had time to rescue a few of the larger things before they —

The window has been stamped into rag. The sky and wagon and field once bent are rag, and on the floor the oils became gaudy swipes under their heavy boots. Head bowed, Berilman watched the ransacking of his father's house, seeing at times his own warped reflection in the high polish of those boots.

"Pine trees," someone calls. The whispering voices float in the foul air, and he envisions pine trees, the black-green of their darker recesses and the bristling cones of their shapes, absolute verticality so perfectly contrasting the tipping of the land no matter what the degree of pitch — so special a symmetry that they could have been hung from string.

The train lurches off its straight momentum, making Meir Goldwicht's back press against him, and he offsets the weight as if pushing himself off the ground from the palms of his hands. Then the pressure relaxes, leaving Goldwicht plumb.

"Some sort of a siding," Goldwicht says to him. He imagines a pair of tracks moving in a closing V so that two sets become one. "Perhaps we will change trains. The trip has been too short for a relocation."

Whispered prayers float, slide along the wall toward Yzak Berilman. He smells the oil on his hands. Now, if he were at home, he would put down his brush, stretch and groan feigning fatigue, and make his way past his mother to the toilet where inside the smell of raw, dry planking and feces and urine and lime he would peek through the crack of the door and abuse himself, superimposing upon the darkness the image of Sofia Kuron, only a hundred meters away helping her mother in the kitchen, her buttocks and their shape — lean, Botticelli, visible even through the colorful curtain of her dress below the off-white blouse open at the top because of the August heat and superimposed upon the door she lies dress up and blouse down staring away from him in awe and shame but forcefully, involuntarily pulling him down as in the smell of oils he couples with her, not as his father did, seen years ago grinning and making his mother a laughing toy, like monkeys they were, until he had to look away, no, a dignified, serious coupling. That is how it would be. When he smells the oil on his hands, nine o'clock or nine-thirty. Each morning. Later, at the fabric window — he thinks geometry, labors over the color of the negative spaces, lets the spokes alone.

Where he goes he will show them how he paints. The man in the black uniform about to strike sees the painting and stops his hand.

Goldwicht's muscular inflation forces him closer to the wall. He braces himself, studying the tiny overlapping of weathered wood, grain like sheets of water flowing one over the other over the other. The officer in the black uniform, his hand up stopped halfway through the swing, studies the painting. The spokes capture his imagination — radiating in different lengths from the hub they impress upon his imagination the inescapable sense of being. The officer's hand moves just perceptibly into an involuntary salute. He cannot say anything because he must maintain a secrecy about his respect for the otherworldly being of the painting. And Yzak, his hand on the painting so as to establish beyond doubt his authorship, must show no recognition of this silent and subtle complicity.

The train slows.

"This is Malkinia Station," Goldwicht says. The name has snaked through the plane of heads, whispered as a question, a speculation. Malkinia Station. The train grinds to a shuddering stop, and Yzak Berilman feels it moving in his feet, which clasp the box of his mother's silver and the pictures. Here tracks will merge and the train will continue east, the voices say, yes, toward newly conquered Russia, where he will be introduced to a room where light will enter creating columns of bright dust swirling in tiny cyclonic eddies. The officer in black will order him to make these windows, some perhaps for the officer's house and some perhaps for public buildings, it doesn't matter, but to go to Russia and stand before the easel there, to bring to the godless and barbaric land the windows of being. He stands before the easel and blocks out in pencil the shape of a synagogue, or perhaps a soldier advancing from a pit, his arm outstretched in the direction of his enemy in a heroic pose. He had been taught all about their art, about how moronic it is, how hulkingly overromantic, how carefully fashioned to pander to the basest tastes. But he has to please the officer in black, and if perhaps Sofia Kuron were to join him for her own safety he would — "It is not unusual at all — many of the great works are representations of the nude female" — paint her form, seeing in the jiggling liquidity of the soft flesh above the left breast the rapid pulsing of her heart, so awed is she at her own nudity and at the studious, objective probing of his eyes as they travel over her form, feeling to her amoebic in the completeness of their touch. She does not know, cannot know, that in looking at her he looks through her, at pulsing organs, branching veins, oozing membranes, long, circuitous tunnels. "Do not be afraid." And so comes alive the beautiful flesh, made three-dimensional inside the window.

The railway car lurches with a sharp, metallic jolt, and begins moving again, opposite from before. "Malkinia Station," Mr. Goldwicht says. "We are not going toward Bialystock. We are going south."

Yzak Berilman's parents and grandmother are in the next car forward. Sofia Kuron? The next after that. He stares at the worn planking of the wall.

Relocation is a simple matter, he thinks. Each person to his own expertise. In the creation of a new Europe the Germans need people to populate their conquered lands and to sing in different ways the praises of the conquerors.

Sofia would have no other choice. "This pose is merely a celebration of the human form." He stands, brush in hand, his mind captured by an almost violent conflict between desire and artistic objectivity, a state that is the height of experience. The appreciation of the swelling breasts, hips, the dark, curly hair disappearing so defensively between her thighs, and the awed, almost shocked look on her face — they must both lose control —

"Oh!" Goldwicht grunts, toppling against him. He holds an old man Berilman does not recognize, and the old man's eyes are closed. "He has fainted," Goldwicht says. Others turn and attempt to help the old man, who is unable to fall to the floor because he is crowded into a standing position.

The man's face slides at Berilman, and the mouth is slack, the eyes glazed, the lips strangely pale as if someone has smeared chalk on them. Then the face vanishes, the upper body having been heaved into a standing position by Goldwicht and another man. "My God," Goldwicht says. "He may be dead."

Dead. His mouth suddenly fills with the taste of metal, and his heart begins to thump. If any person can die on a train, then all persons can die on the train. But no. "Relocation."

"What?"

"Is the man all right?"

"I don't know. He just bounces there — look."

He stands, his head bobbing.

"Why is the train going south?"

"I don't know," Goldwicht says. "Perhaps Pinsk? In the marshes, and why not? We shall be pioneers."

He studies Goldwicht's face. Obese and florid, but not unlike certain Greek faces. Handsome, in a way. With the correct light, one could picture him as a jester.

The train slows again.

He must thank his father. Pioneers. His father once walked into his room and glanced quickly at a painting, and then stopped, seemingly amazed. Could its quality have shocked him? Then he said, I remember spending years being skeptical about life — I remember thinking that it was easy enough to see no use in it, for those of us who are not religious, who have lost our form where God is concerned. The understanding was crushing, that there was indeed no use in life. I thought that. Until you were born. After you were one and a half or two, I would awaken before dawn troubled by the sensation that I had heard something — I would rise, and listen, and hear my son in his crib whispering, carrying on a strange conversation with the darkness. I tell you it was like overhearing some arcane ceremony. Every morning. I had thought that there was no use in life until then. After that I stopped thinking about it.

The train shudders, nearly at a walking pace now. The whispers snake through the plane of heads. Another siding? A change of trains. Why south? Pinsk? Perhaps.

He will thank his father.

The train grinds to a stop, and as if it had been sliding past him all this time, the smell of the people seems to move across his nose, a rich combination of sweat, fear, sour breath, and gas. He feels the vibration of metal against metal — they are doing something. Again, a metallic thump.

Goldwicht's face is now held in a mask of suspicious doubt.

The train lurches in an explosion of sound and a single, violent shock, so that the crowd surges as one, producing a gasping that trails off into a series of whispered questions.

The slow rocking of the train makes Berilman stare again at the splintered planking of the railway car wall. *If she would allow him* — After his eyes had engulfed her like a smoke, she would become more accepting of the —

"If anything we go straight to the south," Goldwicht says.

Accepting of the very normalcy of it. Which would lead to his closing the door. Would you mind if I closed the door? In her eyes he would see the surprise and question. The door? In the almost-blinding sunlight he would approach. *If she would* — Blinding sunlight. Perhaps a droplet of abashed sweat between the breasts, a trembling of desire when he looked at her, the tarpaulin she sat on stained a little with old paint, swipes from his brushes. The sun would be almost too bright, so that each touch would produce so clear a depression in her flesh that only his artistic curiosity would keep him from fainting — and perhaps the brightness itself, the ancient Russian light would hypnotize her into raising her hands to him in a dreamlike motion as he, a kind of conspirator, paused and —

The train slows. The whispers that move like smoke through the car solidify — buildings, barbed wire. Chimneys. The train produces a grating metallic shudder and then a morose shriek, and the crowd surges forward, advancing against the stopped car.

When the door slides open, light as harsh as exploding electricity invades the dusty air in a blinding forty-five–degree angle shaft, and heads drop into it leaving swirling eddies of dust in the air. He hears yelling — *"Alle Hieraus! Idioten!"* and then the sound of frightened voices. Berilman's eyes adjust, and beyond the shaft of light he sees a train station, with signs suspended from a wire.

He begins seeing space around him as people drop into the light. The older ones are helped by the stronger men who jumped out first. Berilman picks up the box, feeling the weight of the objects inside tipping, and makes his way behind Goldwicht toward the light. His mother's silver is on one side, his paints, rolled up canvases, brushes, knives, and various bottles of thinner and so on are on the other side. Hence the lack of balance, he thinks. There is more yelling outside, and as he waits for the space to enlarge he feels the swelling of a kind of globe around him, in which everything that ever happened to him happens at this moment, the sensation of the fullness of disembarkation, that with him stand every member of his family, of Sofia Kuron's family, all families he has ever known. Now the railroad car is open only for him.

His mouth feels numb and dry. Getting down from the car he feels hollow, airy, almost blind. The guards are tall, not German — they have Slavic faces. Russians. Off there, one German officer in black. Berilman's mind pulls in on itself in something like the reverse of magnification, perception through the wrong end of a telescope. He is roughly jostled by one of the guards, and the box almost tips from his hands.

The crowd from the car is locked in a frightened silence by something — over there, one man who has spoken now bleeds from the forehead. The guards indicate that they should leave their bundles and walk over there. The men and boys to one side and the women and girls to the other.

Berilman falls into line with the others. He cannot see his father or mother. He cannot see Sofia Kuron. Goldwicht is five men ahead of him. Now he begins to perceive the surroundings. The signs refer to what the travelers should do with their luggage. Ahead the men are being ordered to undress, and to pile their clothes and belongings together. Berilman feels the prickling of shame suffuse his skin. He turns and looks behind. Inside the crowd of men he cannot see the women and girls. Forward.

"How do I get this back?" he asks. "How do we —"

No one listens. They are taking off their clothes. One guard holds up two shoes, indicates to them that they should tie the laces together to keep them in pairs.

Ahead, beyond the undressing men, he sees a narrow sort of hallway made out of fencing intertwined with evergreen branches. "How will I get this back?" He does not know what to do with the box. He puts it down and begins undressing.

Then he is awake — it is as if he had been sleeping up until now, and pulling off his trousers he studies the ground under him, concrete, with a little sandy soil advancing over it like a windswept wave from the desert. He tangles his trousers on his shoes, and squats down to undo the laces. Carefully he ties his shoes together by the laces, using the same knot he uses to tie up rolled canvases. Then he rises and holds the shoes up to indicate to the guard that —

He lies on his back. Over him stands a guard, smiling down at him, his head framed by clouds. A line of pain crosses Berilman's back, where the cane hit him. He struggles to his feet to continue removing his trousers. Ahead men are already being pushed down the strange, evergreen-lined lane. The guards are shouting, but he cannot understand what they say — his mind has gone to sleep again.

Naked, he lines up behind other men and finds himself studying moles and odd hairs on the back of the man in front of him. The men continue forward toward the lane in jerky steps. Berilman realizes that he is holding both hands over his genitals as he moves forward, as other men are doing. Then they are walking faster, and the man in front of him turns, and in profile Berilman sees the ashen shock on his face. "They are killing us," the man says. "They are killing us, they are killing us." Berilman looks ahead, but the lane twists so that he cannot see their destination. He slows down. "The box," he says. "How will I get the box back?"

"God save us," the man in front says. They pass a guard who threatens them with a shovel. Berilman ducks and moves on, becoming breathless.

"Did you get a ticket?" Berilman asks the man. He should have received a ticket for the box. Ahead he sees the men stopped, crowded around the narrow door of a low building. Only one man can go in at a time. There is a guard near it with a dog, an Alsatian that snarls at the men.

"Order!" a guard yells in Polish. "No talking!" Berilman sidles up to the man in front of him, thinking that he can avoid the dog if he positions the man between him and it. The dog tugs at its leash, rising up, its forelegs waving at the men's naked hips and thighs. Another guard at the door is hitting men with a wooden cane, one by one as they go inside, as if he is counting. He has a strange, irritated grin on his face. Berilman feels his bowels churn — he is afraid he will void them on the ground. He tightens his buttocks and grits his teeth, his skin burning with fear and shame.

"The box," he whispers. "How am I going to —" The pressure in his bowels is so great that he feels it coming, and at the moment he thinks it might, gas escapes, and he feels a little decrease in the pressure. He is closer to the door now, and the guard continues to hit each man entering the building. The breeze changes, and an odor sweeps past, salty and metallic and thick, of either cooking or carrion, and then it vanishes like an invisible object that had just passed by on wheels.

Ahead the repetition of sloping shoulders and backs of heads narrows, until Berilman himself approaches the small doorway, and he ducks in quickly so that the guard caning the men misses his head and the cane slips almost painlessly down his back, lubricated by his sweat.

The ceiling is low, and Berilman's eyes adjust to the near blackness of the room. He slides along the wall, his hand feeling tiles, which go from the floor to halfway up the wall. Now he sees the water jets on the ceiling, and shudders at the thought that it will certainly be cold when it comes out, so he stays near the wall, imagining that at least one side of his body might remain warm once it starts.

There is a window, a little rectangle smudged by fingerprints and skin grease. He stops there, now becoming aware of the din of voices around him. "We're dying here, they're killing us!" And what seems like Goldwicht's voice: "Almighty God protect us! Please I beg save us!"

"We'll get our stuff later," Berilman says. The men continue to press into the room, and he is pushed against the little window — the glass is warmer than the tiles. He struggles against another man to turn his face to the window. It is at shoulder level, and he dips his head and looks out. Ground, to the left black officer's boots, straight out, the side of a building, under that a fuel can covered with oily dust.

He is crushed against the wall. Something is wrong with the man next to him. He begins to slide downward, and Berilman feels his body sliding against his side, his limp hand wedged between Berilman's stomach and the man's hip. Embarrassed, Berilman frees his hands to hold the man up, and finds himself face to face with him. The man's face is slack, and fluid dribbles from his mouth. His eyes are glazed and turned up into his head.

Berilman's perception becomes dreamlike with a grotesque two-dimensionality, and his throat constricts into a nauseating lump. "I must leave now," he says. "Excuse me, but I must get out of here." He cannot move. He forces his body around so that he can see the window, and again is afraid that he will void his bowels. *The shower will take care of that*, he thinks, understanding that his expected mortification will be only temporary. The wave of claustrophobic fright has passed, and he sees beyond the shoulder of the unconscious man the continued inward pressing of naked bodies, bright, almost bluish-white in the slanting column of light in the tiny doorway. "That's enough!" he yells, but his voice dies in the yelling and cursing of the other men. They are all yelling, praying, fighting for space.

The increasing heat becomes suffocating. The unconscious man's head lolls on his shoulder, so that his bristly chin irritates Berilman's skin. With a sudden strength fed by disgust at his physical contact with the man, he shoves him away, so that he wedges between two other men, one of whom wails at the low ceiling of the room, his face twisted with horror and fatalistic dread. The room darkens.

The door has been closed, and Berilman waits, looking at the faint reflection from the little fixtures in the ceiling. He feels a vibration coming in through the slippery floor. Something is being drawn up — it is in the air, a kind of shifting, so that the foul heat wafts across his face. "Gas!" someone yells from the center of the room. "It's gas, and —" Berilman's head is driven to the wall with such force that sickening points of light sweep across his vision, and there is a sudden shock of pressure in his ears and nasal cavity. He cannot breathe — the pressure of the bodies is so great, and the yelling so loud, that he feels on the border of consciousness. Then the yelling dies down, because the air has stopped moving. Again he feels the vibration of something in the floor, and his chest is constricted by a series of convulsive sobs. There is a moment of dead silence while everyone waits.

The room's air moves again, and inside the renewed din of the yelling and fighting he hears an engine of a large truck of some sort. The pain from the blow to his head pulses at him through the powerful thumping of his heart. Men in the middle of the room are now fighting each other and screaming with throat-ripping shrieks, and then coughing. He smells it — a rich, salty, sulfurous odor that he tastes as rusted metal in his mouth. Exhaust fumes. The air is filled with exhaust fumes. Berilman fights to turn himself back to the little window, and crushed against the wall, he slides along the tiles until he sees through the glass, and there, on the other side, is a man looking in, his face crossed with an expression of wonder and awe. Berilman cannot move away from the face, which is too close.

He is now breathing rapidly, accepting the harsh, salty taste of the air. It sears his throat and he feels vomit rising. He holds it back, feeling his chest constrict with strange, inward convulsions, and fights to make space between himself and the wall so that he can get more air. When he does so, his elbows crushed against the tiles, he breathes in huge gasps of the metallic air, and his eyes flood, his nose begins to run, and he tries to speak: "I am — I am —" The rusted metal taste makes its way down his throat, and he heaves from his stomach, feeling hot fluid rolling over his chin. Now his body feels as if it will explode, and the bodies of the men pressing him against the wall begin to slide downward, as if he is rising. His throat feels as if it is closing, and then he fights those pushing against him, clawing at their faces, shoulders, hair, needing the space to get his breath, but they push harder at him. He strains against them, now breathing rapidly and shallowly, because he is full of air and can get no more, so full that he feels his bowels explode downward, and even that provides no space for more air. He is full of air and can get no more, and he claws at the flesh of the other men until he feels his nails breaking.

He tries to scream for them to get away, but his throat is closed, even though he still breathes. The salty air is now a liquid in his mouth, a liquid filling his mouth, from his throat, and the pain in his chest is so great that his body must circle it, must relax around it. He relaxes, and again sees the face in the little window, framed by light, the window dirtied by grease.

They are locked so tightly in their embrace that he feels their bones crushing against each other, Berilman gripping her so tightly that he can see only the side of her head, their flesh so powerfully one that both of them must explode away from the contact, penetrated so powerfully and so deeply that he has crushed her bones and she is gripping him so tightly that his flesh is destroyed by her power, and then, as one, they both explode from the bases of their shattered spines, while above, in the stark, frightening blue of the sky, dark birds circle in beautiful sweeping arcs.

Dizzy and blinking, I pull myself away from the dirty glass of the viewing window. The diesel engine vibrates the ground, and in this lull after the madness of the run to the chamber, the sun seems altogether too bright, and reality too sharp-edged and visually lucid to make sense, considering the amount of schnapps I have already had. It will make classifying and evaluating their trinkets even more difficult.

I should be home or at the front. How Petra laughed at my being a part of this, and at the childishness of our uniforms, insignia, stupid formalities. We're raising a nation from its knees, I told her. The ludicrous pomp of the SS is necessary. But this much? she asked, and laughed until tears filled her eyes. That was all right. I would remove my clothes and she hers, and in the ashy moonlight coming in through the window I would enter her while she looked toward the door open a crack, to hear if the boy would awaken.

Here I take furtive looks at the women standing in line at the beginning of the tube. They have dimples above their buttocks. The younger ones — I lie in bed at night thinking of them with their pale skin and long black hair. I could if I needed to, but deliberately, almost mechanically I think of Petra with the pale blonde hair and heavy breasts. Would it be the same? In the Undressing Barracks guards looking for valuables force them to spread their legs, and I sneak a look and wonder. We all do, officers and guards, with an expression of secrecy and embarrassment that we might be caught showing our curiosity. Regardless of everything, we remain captivated like dreamers in an alternate world.

The dizziness is gone. That big Ukrainian Ivan is now looking in through the window.

Last night we were drunk as usual. Weyrauch leaned forward in his chair and said, "Voss, are you listening?" I nodded. "That we have captured Rostov is important," he said, a little like a pompous teacher satisfied with his student's attention. "We crossed the Don too, at a place so unpronounceable that it makes me dizzy. I memorized it. Tsymlyanskaya."

Then I noticed that the ring finger on his left hand was missing, all the way down. "Tsymlyanskaya," I said, adopting an attitude of scholarly thoughtfulness, knowing I was doing so — I was holding on to normalcy, mental balance. As on every other day I had seen thousands living become thousands dead. "Say, what happened to your finger there?"

He said, "When I was a child I climbed a fence, and I was wearing a little silver ring my mother gave me. The ring caught on the thick wire at the top of the fence and I fell. It stripped all the flesh off, leaving a bone as thin as a twig."

I winced in vicarious pain. In fact for a moment my drunkenness vanished like smoke blown away by wind. It was an awful thing. "My God," I said. "That's awful."

"I remember how it stung. The finger was no more than a red twig. And on top of the fence there was the ring, stretched with the plump flesh hanging there like a rolled-up sock. I remember how it stung."

We had our boots up on the table. Comrades. Weyrauch drank, leaned back. But having your finger stripped like that — I couldn't get the horror of it out of my mind.

"Think of it, Rostov, like a ripe plum."

"I hear things are going badly."

"No, the Russians have squandered too much at Kursk."

"How old were you when you lost your finger?"

A silly question.

I walk across the dry dirt toward the German barracks, thinking of more schnapps. I see off by the Undressing Barracks that leads to the tube the suspicious movement of guards. One of them peeks around the building corner at me and smiles in a strange, obsequious grin that signals forbidden activity. I know what they are doing. They have kept out a girl, a twelve- or thirteen-year-old who could not hide her beauty. I saw them, studying the naked women and discussing whom they should pick. Why do they pick them so young? My heart flutters — their excess makes me nervous. I saw them yesterday after one of the transports. They took a girl into their barracks and I made the mistake of peeking in the window and saw two of them pinning her on her back on a bunk while one of them worked between her legs and another drank vodka and watched. The guards were laughing and pushing a cane into the girl. I know it is forbidden, but I want to write some of this down. I know I can be court-martialed or worse if I am caught. Could I forget this? With the alcohol, probably.

I walk. I walk deliberately, trying to look normal. Now they are all busy in the sorting square, under that mountain of clothes.

"This is not —" What? What did you suppose it was supposed to be? A work camp like the one just down the dirt road? We will not leave here alive. How can they let us? This is not the euthanasia program and it is not mass executions of hostiles. This is not Minsk or Dragobich or Lvov. This is not the ransacking of their shabby little houses in search of artifacts, watches, jewelry, gold.

The barracks buildings bounce before me — drunkenness makes things bounce, because the eyes are slow, and the ground tips and jerks with each step. I should write all this down.

I must either drink or vomit. Then I remember: Your specialty is not death, but the recovery of property of the Reich.

Weyrauch is not a bad sort, or Bielas, except for his obsession for pretty boys. He doesn't hide it, in fact watches the unloading of the trains with happy, almost simpering anticipation. He keeps them in a little barracks building in our birch grove. And Deputy Commandant Franz, Schneck, Liebner? They are different. It is killing they look forward to with happy anticipation. Liebner drinks with us. He is grossly overweight, and he has piggish habits, and an irritating attitude of loftiness that in a way belittles by exaggeration our very Aryan identity. I saw him and a couple of his young friends kill prisoners, and he did it with a look of thoughtful experimentation as he aimed at the stomach of one prostrate and begging prisoner and shot him there, just to see how the prisoner would react and also how he himself would feel doing it. Liebner is an adolescent in a man's clothing. There is always that question of why it is we who are here. Either it is a special responsibility, or it is that we are misfits. I should be home or at the front.

I will write that my jaw aches. Probably the tension. The vision of the naked people being driven along the narrow path enclosed by barbed wire woven with the branches of evergreens: It was not that they were naked, or that they were ugly somehow, made ugly by their hunched, stinking resignation. It was not that they were being struck by wooden clubs or whips. It was the knowledge of where they were going. The extremity of it is such that one can make no true analysis of it. We keep our verbal consideration of the obvious reality of it oblique by being direct: When it is windy and dry cover the engine. This grit will do damage, and how would it be to have the thing malfunction? I am getting more and more annoyed at how much contraband there is here. The Shaulises and the Ukrainians are an ignorant lot, but they know how to steal. Why can't they keep this place clean? And then there are people like Weyrauch, who will stop and look with helpful sympathy at an injured worker — what happened to you? Shouldn't you get that wound looked at? Absurd. Any worker walking around with an obvious wound is routinely liquidated.

The barracks building tips and jiggles in my dream vision. There, on the ground, a fountain pen dusted by the yellow, sandy earth. The pen appears to have gold fittings around its green tube. Valueless, but I should pick it up.

I know the feeling. The work with the *Einsatzgruppen* produced such an effect, so that, after unwittingly witnessing the shootings, I would find that my jaw ached. I was supposed to be in their houses, feeling under furniture surfaces for their valuables, studying the layout of loose floorboards, checking root houses, sheds, odd hiding places behind chimneys. I was supposed to locate their marriage rings, bridal belts, kiddush cups, their money and watches and heirlooms. I was not supposed to watch as the soldiers made them take their clothes off and then shot them in the backs of their necks. By the thousands. It is as if I remember each and every face now, with a detestable lucidity. Those on the front are lucky.

The engine they use is from a captured Russian tank. I felt it in the ground when the exhaust was pumped into the low building. I was invited for a look through the viewing window. Have a look, *Untersturmfuhrer* Voss? You never come out to inspect our system. You're always over there looking at their trinkets. Have a look? The elegant sadist Schneck, taunting me with my squeamishness. He would be a good fellow but for his obvious enjoyment of this place.

No more transports today. On the ground, a folded piece of sheet music. Why?

School in Oberkassel. Across the river is Dusseldorf. A pale-haired child of twelve sits at the desk of Herr Dulpers, and the child is in awe of the man's magnificent, benevolent masculinity. The piano teacher is one of Oberkassel's more famous men. He compliments the child on the expertise of his rendition of Chopin. Yes, it is not improbable that you will one day be a musician of note.

The man leans over close to the boy and wags his finger — those who work hard succeed, no? And staring into that benevolent smile the boy has creeping into his awareness the speculative desire to gather saliva in the front of his mouth and spit directly into the man's face. The boy nods respectfully, but feels the involuntary movement of his tongue, which manipulates saliva along toward his lips. Then he begins to experience the horrible recognition that he will not be able to resist. At the moment when it will happen, the man is uttering another sentence, which to the boy is incomprehensible, as if garbled out in a dream or in another language. The boy saves himself only a second before doing it — he turns away and grips his mouth. Is something wrong? Herr Dulpers asks. No, the boy says. Only a sneeze.

Why on earth would you remember something like that?

Before me stand the barracks. But the pen. Perhaps I should go get the pen. Turning produces a dizzying sensation, and I must steady myself before walking. I might leave gold, jewelry, banknotes, but I will not leave a pen.

Sometimes when I was standing next to my mother or father or sister I would have that sudden urge to strike them over the head with whatever I was holding. It would be a hammer, a garden tool, a bottle. I would have to step away to keep myself from doing it.

Now ahead of me jounces the corner of the Undressing Barracks. Standing there with his shoulder-slung rifle behind him a Ukrainian guard observes something happening on the ground by the building's base. Yes, it is the continuing rape of the girl. The guard has on his face a look of awe and resignation, because I can have him shot if I want to. But the pen — where is it? The ground is bright, dry, dusted by footprints and littered here and there with little objects: a hairclasp, a piece of ribbon, over there a spool of thread. But why thread? Do those women think there is any use for thread here?

I cannot find the pen. For some reason this brings tears to my eyes, and it is as if I will burst from grief. My knees threaten to buckle. My uniform feels too tight, my underclothes oily, irritating. The guard backs away from the activity at the building base, and now I see it, the rhythmic surging of a pair of buttocks on either side of which are pale, children's legs bent at the knees. It is as if she has been crushed under a rock. In a short, involuntary moment of prurient curiosity I step to the side to see her.

Then I look at the guard, and wipe my eyes. He has large, red ears, so large that he looks like some genetic freak, like some absurd cartoon from a children's book: a taxi with its doors open, an elephant in disguise. I will burst forth with laughter, but I am afraid that in my drunkenness I will fall down. And I cannot find the pen.

Inside the heat's yellow buzzing I see him. He is too drunk to know what is happening. Voss is his name. On the ground her eyes are rolling back into her head — Vlodya is saddened by her whimpering, and whispers sympathetically to her.

The officer leaves, looking around at the ground. He has lost something. Beyond where he stood I see the walking dead, the forked sticks, shoulders hunched, carrying clothes, bundles, valuables. You must empty yourself for this. Of all of them

I hate the Lithuanians most, because they don't need to be empty for this. They love this — one said to me in gestures, a point to the fly of his trousers, a circle with the thumb and forefinger of the other hand — do you want to put it in her before she's gone? He had specks of blood on his boots. Vlodya said yes. For the Lithuanians God has no eyes — they don't care. I hate them most of all.

I see Germans by the barracks — in the yellow they stand talking like gentlemen, or businessmen, having no eyes for this.

I used to scythe wheat. The rhythm of the swing, the blade separating half a meter a stroke, is a heart beating. Pigs would watch from the fence by the thatch shack. Every day I went out over the vast, sad landscape of my birthplace, always imagining that just beyond the limit of my vision lay bright cities, electricity, sleek automobiles.

The smell hangs in the boiled air like a jelly. The smell carries the virus of death into me — there is no escape. You must empty in order to absorb the smell. Beyond the wire the woods stand dark and clean, the pine smell like a jelly too all around. In the woods you can't smell it. The breath of maggots. Soon now, and we lead men into the woods until sundown.

That man. His daughter is fresh, he said. Just bring a little gold, a handful of zlotys, and you can have her for fifteen minutes. The money and the gold watch and a pair of little glasses on a golden stick hang there in my pocket, drawing one side of my trousers down.

Ever waited at a train station for fifteen minutes? he asked me. When he smiled he showed gaps where teeth should be. Some of the remaining teeth were brownish-black stumps, and his gums looked diseased. I'll even bring vodka. You can get a lot of her in fifteen minutes.

At home I saw the Germans, their tanks and trucks and cars and cannons new, smelling of petrol and oil. At home we waved flags, we tied kerchiefs around their necks, we set rich tables for them. I could see that the girls wanted them, that in their faces was a secret, elaborate fantasy of making love with them. I could smell their excitement, their sexual heat. I was only seventeen then, jealous of how they wanted the Germans. I even saw them, girls I knew, doing it with the Germans. I walked past a haystack. Two of the Germans were fucking my cousin, one going at it, the other watching where they joined.

But you shot that boy for looking at your ears. A sickening wave of heat rushes through me like water into a sponge. The forked sticks of the *Tarnungskommando* gather by the barracks, ready to come my way. We will go to the woods and gather branches for the tube. The money and gold weigh in my pocket. It makes no difference what she looks like, as long as she is not too fat or too skinny. I will open her and empty myself. It is as if it is already on the way, hovering like water traveling up a pipe.

With a short piece of birch Vlodya prods the forked sticks, and they march this way. We will pass the garage and storehouse and the office and walk out the main gate and turn right to the vegetable fields and then the woods. She will be there waiting, and in the smell of evergreens I will open her and empty myself.

We walk. The loot in my pocket weighs, and I keep an eye out for the Germans. I could be shot. The heaviest is the watch, gold with a hinged cover carved with flowers and other geometric designs. Out the main gate, past the Spanish Horses lined up in precise order. The steel antitank barrier is two lines of horses deep. The woods loom dark and smelling of evergreens.

I see the farmer, and see that he is also visible to the watchtower in the vegetable field, so I wave him back with short jerks of my hand. Behind me Vlodya plods along next to the weary forked sticks, two of whom pull a two-wheeled cart that creaks and moans in the afternoon sunlight.

"You're going to buy yourself a fuck?" Vlodya asks. "Why don't you take it free?"

"I want a Pole."

"You don't like Jews? I like Jews. I like to make them squeal."

"Watch for me, will you? I'll be gone a half an hour."

Walking, I remember the boy. I hated being assigned to the train station in Siedlce because I had to help the grandmothers and the children up into the cars. I hated it because I knew where they were going. I hated having to be a part of it, but that turned on itself so that the boy looking at me made me aware of the ears and I raised the rifle without thinking and shot him in the face before he could even change his expression away from that look of surprise that seeing the ears always brings out, and he went back in a harsh snap with the pink mist of brain and blood and hair flung out behind him spattering children who looked down at their clothes, eyes wide with wonder at how that got there.

The Polish farmer is in the evergreens, and I work my way toward him, sliding myself between two of them so that the hard branches scrape my uniform leaving white marks where they scrape. I do not see the girl.

When Poles speak Russian they flatten everything and hiss too much because their language hisses.

"A hard day's work, to be sure," he says to me. "I've just the remedy — now she's not that experienced, so you'll just have to tell her what to do. And she doesn't speak a word of Russian."

"That will be all right."

I pull the watch and zlotys and the little gold eyeglasses out of my pocket. The man's mouth drops open, and he gasps.

"My word," he whispers. "This is a — what is that word? Lorgnette, yes, that's it. And the watch. Does it work?"

"I think so." I hand him the gold and currency. He seems surprised, as if he thought I would barter with him.

"Yes," he says, "this way."

I follow him past more trees to a little open space, beyond which I see a thatch shack, perhaps a livestock shelter. "She's in there," he says.

I take a few steps, and then pause. The rifle. I take it from my shoulder and then sling it with the strap across my chest, to show that I do not mean to draw it. I expect some sort of arousal, but it does not come.

I lean into the shack, and wait until my eyes adjust. She sits back from the middle of it, wearing a peasant blouse and a long skirt. Her feet are bare. She speaks a short, breathless sentence.

"I do not understand." I slip the rifle off and lie it down on the dry, dusty chaff.

"Magda," she says, her hand on her chest. She beckons me in. She is attractive, with wheat-colored hair and a chubby face. I step inside, and have to keep my head lowered because of the low ceiling. She gestures me down, and I kneel.

The expression on her face is strange, as if she is a cautious worker trying to please her employer. She sits with her knees peeking out from under the bright skirt.

I feel nothing. It is as if I am nervous, but that is not it. I feel pulled in, shrunken, empty and dead.

She cocks her head, and I see that she has looked at the ears. I take the fabric of the blouse in my hands and lift, and she wriggles as it slides over her head. Her breasts bounce there, and I hold them, feeling her heartbeat, as fast and shallow as that of a rabbit. Her breasts are covered with a sheen of cool sweat. I know she is looking at me. The me who knows she is looking is ignored by the me who shakes her breasts.

I feel nothing. She whispers, and I shrug.

I push her back on her elbows and pull up the skirt. She is wearing no underclothes. I separate her legs and look, then touch it with my right hand, but I feel nothing, and lean back up on my knees.

[34]

She whispers a question.

"That over there is a factory of death," I say. She nods, then sits back up, her face crossed with an expression of awe and fright. "There they gas old women and little babies, they beat little boys to death with shovels, hack their arms off with the edges of shovels."

She whispers a short sentence.

"They rape girls younger than you are, and then take them to a place they call the Hospital and shoot them into a ditch. They hang people upside down until they die. They like all of this. They get drunk and they go out and look for people to torture and kill."

She nods quickly.

"But mostly they push people naked into gas chambers and kill them that way, thousands every day. In the process of course they take their money and valuables. We steal some of these valuables so that we can pay for girls like you."

She holds the blouse against her chest.

"I shot a boy who looked at my ears," I say.

She nods.

"It was simple — he looked at my ears and I shot him. In Siedlce. I did it because the impulse hit me. It is strange in a way, that here we can do whatever our impulses tell us to do. Say, if Vlodya wants to get himself a fuck, he pulls a pretty girl out of the line and takes her either behind the Undressing Barracks or to his bunk, and then he does whatever he wants to do. Only the Germans would stop him, if they had the impulse to, but they don't care. Then when Vlodya is finished he takes the girl over to the Hospital. Then he says, 'H'm, what shall I do now? Eat perhaps.' The Germans don't care. After all it's hot, and a lot of the time they stay in their barracks and drink. The deputy commandant — he comes out to shoot people and keep order, but otherwise we just follow our impulses." I look at her. I can see her rabbit's heartbeat in the base of her throat.

[35]

"I will go now," I say. I pick up the rifle and sling it over my shoulder and get up. She sits there on her knees. "Thank you," I say, and leave. The sunlight hurts my eyes, and I see the farmer standing over at the other side of the little clearing. He nods enthusiastically as if to say, see what I told you? See what I told you? Fifteen minutes.

"I'll come again in a couple of days," I tell him.

"She's a grand little tart, wouldn't you say? Let me know what you want her to do. I'll have her do anything you'd like."

I leave him there, and listen to the woods for the sounds of the axes. I hear the sound coiling through the evergreens, and walk into it. What will I do? I don't know. Even shame is dead — it hardly even prickles the skin. I think of the tart and now feel the beginning of something swelling me just a little, so that it feels like something jouncing in a pocket. I think, should I kill one of the forked sticks to make things right? The sensation of expectation races upward into my trunk. I can kill one of the forked sticks.

As we walk, and I watch them dragging the cartload of branches through the copper light of sundown, I feel the moist coolness through the fabric of the uniform. Ahead Treblinka camp rests, squat and dark and weary, deflated back to its mysterious, whispering rest.

When he aimed I hunched and closed my eyes. Then he shouldered the rifle again and walked back toward the camp. We followed, listening to the wheels hissing in the dirt. My hands are sticky with pinesap. Schrhafta! they say. Are you going insane? But I will not wash it off. I will leave it on my hands, blackened patches of the sharp fragrance that wards off the smell of the corpses and the exhaust fumes. I will sleep with my hands closed, and they will be glued together in the morning so that I will have to peel them apart while, whipped or beaten with sticks, we are driven out to the portable kitchen for our potato soup. In the smell of the sap wafting off my hands I will work all day, unloading boxcars and helping the aged to the landing, carrying luggage and prettying up the tube to the gas chamber, and all day the smell will ward off the odor of the bodies and the fumes, and then, toward evening, they will push us to the woods again and I will cut pine boughs and I will hold the branches until the amber sap sticks to my skin so that, walking back and hearing the whispering wheels, the smell of death and the beating and bullets and hunger will all be held off by the amber smell. Odor is the object that smells in suspension — a kind of fog composed of minuscule shreds of the object that smells. When you smell a corpse, you breathe the rotted flesh into your lungs. The smell of pinesap is a suspension of tiny amber spheres of sap, like millions of tiny planets.

You next to me smell like a corpse. The guard there with his rifle smells like gunsmoke. David Schrhafta smells like a pine tree. Once I smelled like polished leather. My father and I worked all day cutting and punching out leather in the sharp fragrance of polish and soap, and even now my eyes stop on belts, straps around suitcases, shoes. Always I wonder, is it ours? They shot him outside the shop. And it was a train ride for me. And now David Schrhafta smells like a pine tree.

The camp rises in silhouette and the guard, walking, disappears into the silhouette. We will pull the wagon around to the main gate and go past the office and go left past the barracks to the tube. We will park the wagon by the tube and either go to our barracks or stand roll call while they strut before us deciding whether or not we live another day, and next to me the men will smell the sap. Rakowski, Rothberg, Schluman, Schrhafta —

here — Soloweicz, and the pine-scented hand will rise, black-patched and fragrant.

Inside the gate. It is quiet now, all the dead are laid out in the pits and fresh air wafts through the chambers, and the engine sleeps. It has been a hot day, so everyone will be inside drinking, and the corpses will settle on each other, disturbed only by boring maggots.

We will park the wagon by the fuel shed. In the darkness I see two men, Germans. Out for sport. Some of us will die. Why are they not inside drinking? My heart begins to slam in my chest. One of us, or two, will die now, because they have come out and are looking for sport — can you kill one of them by shooting him in the balls? Can one shoot down a throat so that the bullet comes out the asshole? If you shoot his nose off, will he lose his balance like a chicken whose beak is shot off? I have seen it. I have seen experimental murder. I have seen thoughtful tests of physics, chemistry, exploratory surgery.

But no, the men are looking for something. One of them is that man Weyrauch, who is so good to the workers. They are drunk. They are looking for something, one holding the other up. One of them seems to be weeping. I think he says, "It was here — I saw it here, a pen. I lost my pen somewhere here. I am sure of it," and then the sound of his strange weeping.

We park the wagon, and while the guards talk I reach into the pile of branches and feel along them for the half spheres of amber sap, which stick to my hands. Medicine against death.

OUTSIDE THE PERIMETER FENCE, TREBLINKA

AUGUST 2, 1943

Her dress is drenched with sweat, and the force of the cramps makes her stoop over as she walks through the pines, the brittle lower branches scraping her arms and face. She stops, listens for the sounds of those men, but hears nothing but the popping sounds of gunfire in the distance, less of it now. Through the canopy of pine branches the black smoke is still visible, not as dense now but spread out over the horizon.

She thinks that she should move around to the east, to get out of the way of those men, whom she now imagines are tiptoeing through the woods, their guns and knives out. In a space between cramps she looks into the woods to the east, the direction of the old 1939 frontier. When she was thirteen she and her brother and Michal Balicki hiked to it, to see Russians, Michal said. They never knew if they crossed the frontier, but they did see an abandoned church in a nearly empty village, and the church was full of dark green crates, and rolls of wire. And they saw a graveyard with all the crosses broken off the stones. Michal said that this meant they were in the Soviet Zone.

She continues toward home, still more than half a kilometer away. "I have made a mistake," she whispers. "Anatoly." She is sure the baby will be born before she gets there. Her legs are still wet, because more of that fluid has leaked out, and she thinks, you can use burdock leaves. Her mother snickered when she told Magda that. When you have your monthly you can use burdock leaves — they're so soft. But that was when her mother talked to her. Years ago. She doesn't any more, not only because of Anatoly but because of the others too, Michal and the other boys her own brother made her do it with. And then her father, knowing what she had done, made her do it with Anatoly for a little money. After all, you're experienced, he said.

She wants her mother. Emerging from the pines into lower brush she stops walking, and leans against a birch sapling, holding it with both hands. The heat is so intense that it makes her dizzy. She gasps for breath, her mouth dry, and waits for the next pain. Her mother doesn't want her, since long before the trains. When she found out that Magda's brother and his friends were using her as a whore she dragged Magda into the woods, made her take off all her clothes, and then backed away, fifteen or twenty meters, and yelled, How do you like that? How does that feel? And when Magda tried to move toward her, stunned with fright at standing there in the woods naked, she shouted, Don't you take one step! Stand there and feel what it is like! Then, weeping, she allowed Magda to dress and follow her back out of the woods.

Another cramp begins, pressing down from her chest in a slow, twisting undulation, radiating into her lower back and hips. She saw calves born, puppies. In the mothers' eyes there was always the strange, blank staring at some imaginary object in the middle distance. She grits her teeth and tries to tighten her body around the cramp, and when it begins to recede, her flesh is wet and trembling with chills even though the windless heat seems to groan out of the ground.

Her mother will not help her more than to let the midwife into the house. Then she will go to the Madonna image on the fireplace mantel and pray, probably more for herself than for Magda, who feels soiled beyond even God's help. Since long before the trains, if Magda had a question she would answer it as if Magda were a stranger. When she found out about Anatoly it became worse. Her mother does not know how frightened she was the first time her father arranged for her to be with Anatoly, how she thought that because he was a Ukrainian he would kill her when he was finished with her. That same day she stood in the kitchen wanting to speak of it while her mother carefully worked a large cabbage leaf into the bottom of a bread pan so that the baking bread would not stick, but the strange look of concentration on her mother's face meant that she wanted to hear none of it. She wanted to know nothing about it. She wanted to know nothing about the killing of the Jews or the money the farmers made by selling their daughters or what went on inside the camp.

She lets go of the birch sapling and walks again toward home, feeling heavy in the windless heat, as if she has suddenly grown old. She pulls up her skirt and feels her underwear, which is soaked and hot with the liquid.

Then she hears noise behind her. She stumbles toward a pine tree, but the tangle of lower branches prevents her from hiding at its base. Now she hears voices, men speaking in sharp whispers as their footsteps crunch through the dead leaves. She cannot move, and stands petrified, her breath held. The language they speak is not Polish — it sounds almost German.

Then she sees a man, and then another. "Don't hurt me," she whispers. "Please, don't."

The third man is hopping, one hand on the shoulder of the second. When he is in full view she sees his right leg, the bloody pant leg ripped halfway up and the part just below the calf dangling, the foot pointed the wrong way, behind him. He seems not to be in pain, his face a mask of wild exhilaration as if his mutilated leg is only a minor inconvenience.

Then all three see her. "Don't hurt me," she whispers. Beyond the men others sprint by, crashing through the brush. Another cramp begins, and she has nothing to hold on to, so she presses the sides of her belly with her hands. Her knees are shaking. The men whisper, then keep going, the man with the injured leg still appearing almost joyful as he hops away.

When the pain reaches its zenith, she wonders if she should lie down right where she stands. After the peak her flesh again feels the beginning of a chill, and sweat runs down her cheeks and neck. In the distance, toward the road, the dry grass recedes into a mirage that looks like a lake. The shapes of men move in it, going away from the smoke. The force of the heat presses on her like a powerful drug, and she cannot move.

There is a small stone arch with a wooden cross in it by the roadside between her house and Wolga-Oknaglik. If she should die, she should die there because no one wants her. Then during their weekly wagon ride to the village market her parents would see her body and say, very well, she is dead along with her bastard child, and we are rid of her.

She closes her eyes and rests, her fingers laced under her belly. She hears more of the swishing of movement in the brush, but does not open her eyes. Whoever it is passes, and she stands, eyes closed, concentrating on the center of her chest where the next pain will begin.

MALKINIA STATION, EASTERN POLAND

LATE AUGUST 1942

Irena Siedlecki pulls the children closer into the folds of her skirt and says, "It will not be long now, my little ones." Her feet flash pain up her legs, and her lower back aches. Zygmunt, the youngest, pulls his head away from her skirt and looks up at her, the blinking light coming in through the chinks of the boxcar's planking flickering across his dirty, anxious face.

"Grandma, I'm —"

"Remember, we weren't going to say that again, is that right?" She looks at Janusz, wedged into the corner with their shabby luggage. The oldest of the four of her grandchildren, he has recently been distant and surly, she thinks because of his beginning maturation. And of course there is the problem with his hearing, which she thinks is as much a strategy for him as it is a disability.

The railway car lurches violently, and the smaller children clutch at her dress. "Of course we are all thirsty."

"Of course," Janusz says. The fright on his face is tinged with a look of frustration and anger. She knows that at fourteen he will not accept her reassurances, and besides, she does not have the energy to shout at his surly, resistant face. That they are going to die is inevitable. She has heard the stories, that at Treblinka they murder everyone who comes on the trains. Irena Siedlecki looks at his face in the dim, shifting light of the railway car as it slowly increases speed. He has the beginning of a mustache, and pimples on his forehead and cheeks. In his square face she sees the features of her husband, his grandfather, who has been dead now — five years it is since the stroke that deadened and made drooling and slack the left side of his face.

Her heart begins to beat rapidly at the thought of how close they must be. That God has condemned them this way mystifies her. All that remains for her is to reassure the children so that their experience of it will be less painful. How can she tell them? No. She must accept His judgment. Her husband, in one of his more eccentric moods, would have granted it more devoutly: It is ours to pray that He multiply these travails a thousandfold.

"My hand!" Zygmunt says. For the past week he has had a sore in the palm of his left hand, and Irena Siedlecki has brooded and prayed over it, fearing that the infection might spread, and indeed, this morning she saw the redness around the sore beginning to leak up his wrist. He raises his hand, and the cut crowns a bright red lump, which has a kind of comet's tail, the beginning of the infection's spread.

"I hurt under my arm."

She sighs. That is surely a sign.

[44]

The railway car rocks with a mournful sluggishness, and she feels her heart fluttering, so that her throat constricts painfully. She feels soiled, hot, and smells the odor of her fear rising off her clothes. Soon even the embarrassment at her own bodily filth will be obliterated by death. The children clutch at her legs, burying their faces in her skirt. They will have to endure their thirst, endure their deaths, and she will have to hold on to her composure. Only Janusz will remain an impediment to her charade, and she is briefly angry with him. He does not pray or show any regard for the children. And that he would use a common if not easily treated problem with his hearing as a means of irritating her!

"Of course it may not be true," she says to him over the rumbling and creaking of the train.

"Don't do that," he snaps.

"Now there! You heard me, and I was not shouting," she says. "Besides, you could at least show some concern for —"

"Why?" he says. "They are going to kill us!"

The children's hands tighten on her legs. She leans over and says, "He's only frightened. Don't worry little ones. He's convinced by these rumors."

Now Janusz is crying, trying not to show it. "I am not the cause of this," she says. "Why are you so cruel to your grandmother?"

He gives her a stare brief and almost violent with contempt, and she closes her eyes. The train lurches, producing a collective gasp from the people crowding against them. They look around at the air with expressions of fatalistic acceptance, and she can hear their prayers rising above the sound of the train. In one of the other corners of the car a family of Hasidim are gathered, and from time to time, when the heads near her move to open the way to her vision, she can see their heads bobbing in prayer. Her husband was fascinated by their fanaticism, and was prone to wish for himself the capability of such selfless devotion. He had been for years muddled in his own

[45]

vision of God because his father had converted to Catholicism in order to escape the miseries suffered by so many Jews, especially in the east. Then, in a horrible rift in the family, their son, Janusz's father, went the other way. He married a Catholic, and tried to educate his children toward the way of Haskala, enlightened freethinking in the manner of the great Moses Mendelssohn. Our Socrates, he had called him, waving an old book in his father's face, and Irena Siedlecki is convinced that the stroke was caused by this rift. But with Janusz, much of his enlightened freethinking labor fell on deaf ears, because the boy apparently has no religion at all, fanatical or otherwise. And now Janusz's father and mother are gone, arrested and probably dead.

She puts her hands on the tops of two of the children's heads, the smaller of the tree. Oh little ones, she thinks. My only grandchildren. She remembers, more than a year ago, when there parents were taken away. No one in the village ever learned where they were taken, and she heard rumors that they were in forced labor, or had been shot and buried near the village. And now this. That all life of this family, however bitterly misdirected and squabbling it might have been generation by generation, has funneled itself down to this place and this day, and now the string will be cut off forever.

For a few minutes she nearly sleeps, letting her body bounce with the movement of the train. When she awakens, she does not know how much time has passed. There, off in the corner, she sees the heads bobbing.

The train slows, the car jerking back with its slowing motion, so that the floor shifts under her shoes. Another siding, or the place itself? Janusz is now looking around at the dusty air like a cornered animal. The crowd sways as one, and one man nearby is trying to peek out through the bright slice of light that comes in through the door edge and creates a glittering plane of swirling dust.

There is an odor penetrating the air. Carrion. She pulls the children closer. The train now inches, screeching and moaning with its movement. Then it slams to a stop, jostling the people violently.

The railway car door slides open, letting in light so harsh that it momentarily blinds her. She hears people screaming, and then the shouts of men. "We're getting off the train now," she says. "Remember, we don't say any more about water. They'll have water here." Jadwiga looks up, her face pale with a fatigue so deep that it overcomes her fear. "Jadwiga," she says, "keep the little ones together. Hold Zygmunt's right hand."

"I know what is happening," Jadwiga says.

"You cannot be sure, I told you."

"I know."

Space opens up, and Janusz shuffles toward the bright opening, sliding one large box behind him and carrying the old suitcase in his left hand. We are here then, she thinks. Father usher us to our death gently. Do not allow the children to know.

She has heard the stories from her brother-in-law Berek: They will be fooled into thinking that they are taking showers, and will be gassed then. If she can keep the little ones' spirits up until that moment, then it will remain only to breathe deeply the cloud of material that will kill them. She adjusts the strap of her heavy bag, which holds family photographs, papers, some money.

Moving toward the door, holding the little ones against her thighs, she smells the odor again, and sees those at the opening dropping into the violent light. She hears the sounds of people being struck, of moans and stifled shrieks of pain.

"*Alle heraus!*" a soldier yells. She is at the opening.

"Come, grandmother," a boy who seems to be a porter says to her. Janusz is already on the ground, struggling with the luggage. The crowd moves toward some buildings. "Come down, be careful." The boy, who is handsome, with beautiful eyes, helps each of the children down. "Pay no attention to those on the ground," he says. "They died in the trains."

"Yes," she says. She stoops, but her knees buckle, and the boy catches her under the arms and pulls her down to the ground. Her closeness to the boy embarrasses her, because of the odor of her clothes. Off to her left, along the cars, she sees bodies on the ground. Farther away — or do her eyes deceive her? — lies a nude body with a cloud of flies hovering over it. The smell is stronger now. Uniformed guards herd the people toward the buildings. The children clutch at one another, also understanding the source of the smell. Other tattered porters pull people off the car behind theirs, and those being pulled off appear either unconscious or dead. Yes, the cars behind their own were hitched on at the Malkinia siding. She and the children are pushed toward the crowd. The strap of her bag digs into her neck. "Grandmother," Jadwiga whispers. "There's a dead man —"

"Yes," she says. "He did not do what he was told. We must do what we are told and then we'll get water."

Janusz is ahead of her, looking around, his face ashen and stilled with awe. He understands. The more he looks around, the more bodies he sees. She steps toward the crowd. Feeling something sticky under her shoes, she looks down. It is partly dried blood, a dark brick color, almost black at the edges, thick as paste in the center. She shudders, feeling nauseated, as if she will heave her empty stomach out her mouth.

Protected inside the crowd, she and the children move with it, while at the edges, guards appear to be hitting people, mostly the men, with sticks and gun stocks. Janusz has made his way to the center of the moving crowd also, and keeps his head down. A porter has dragged the luggage off to the side and piled it on the blanket rolls, boxes, rope-tied suitcases belonging to the other people.

Ahead something is happening. It is the men. They move to the right, the women and children go straight, into a building.

Janusz moves away from her with the men. The children whimper and shuffle with her, staring at the ground under them. "Soon now," she whispers, patting Jadwiga's shoulder. She can no longer see Janusz.

Inside the building the women and children are undressing. She is suddenly hot with shame — that this sagging old body will now be visible to everyone. She is glad Janusz is not in the building with her. The guards posted around the undressing women and children stare above their heads, as if thinking of something other than what they are doing. Two guards toward the middle of the long room are laughing and pointing, apparently at a young woman. She looks around the shoulder of the woman in front of her and sees that they laugh because the woman is fat. One young Pole wearing a gray pajama-like smock walks along next to the undressing women, saying, "Please tie your shoes together, and bundle your clothes in one bundle. You'll get these things after your shower. Put your valuables in the box ahead."

When she has enough space, she begins to undress. The children do too, and when she removes her undershirt her hanging breasts are visible, and she sees them staring openmouthed. "Hurry now," she whispers. Her breath is high and shallow in her chest. Zygmunt struggles with his clothes, his hand out to his side. "Jadwiga," she says. Jadwiga helps Zygmunt with his clothes.

The children stand with their arms crossed over their little, round bellies, gazing up at her with awed, questioning eyes. "Well," she says. "This is not something we're used to." Jadwiga laughs ruefully and looks at the other two.

"My hand," Zygmunt says.

"It's always worse during the middle of the day," she says, picking up the bag of family things. It is true. Infections reach their zenith in the late afternoon.

"We'll get alcohol for it," she says. "Then you'll see a change." But it is clear to her that it may be beyond their control. The red patch at the base of the palm of his hand has now extended up the thin, delicate cords of his wrist. She could not see it before, on the train.

"I see Zygmunt's peepee," Krystyna says.

"Be quiet," Jadwiga says. "Maybe —"

The naked people move toward a door. Through it Irena Siedlecki sees one woman holding a towel and a bar of soap.

"There's a woman with soap," she says to Jadwiga.

That the woman would have soap strikes her as a sign, perhaps that after all death is not the business of this place. Why then would the woman have soap?

"We have no soap," Jadwiga says.

Something else is happening near the door. One man in a dirty, drab-looking outfit is ordering women to sit on a table. She leans up to see. He is looking between their legs.

She bristles with shame. What on earth would they be interested in? That they should be treated this way is bad enough, but to go poking around in women's private places this way? The guards look on with disinterested, almost bored gazes, and the women near the table stand with hunched shoulders in a kind of miserable submission.

"Children," she says. "Listen to me. They're doing a kind of private search." They look up at her. Zygmunt is wincing with pain. "I know," she says, patting him on the head. She looks at Jadwiga with her beautiful braid and her plump child's body, and thinks, no, they can't do that to her. "I will have to go and sit on that table over there. Just stay together." Zygmunt looks at her breasts again. "I am an old woman," she says. "It's nothing extraordinary."

"Grandmother," Jadwiga says. "Will it hurt?"

"Of course not!" she says, surprised at the high-pitched, almost strangulated artificiality of her voice.

"The bag, please," one of the workers says. She gives him the bag, and he walks off, bouncing it in his hands as if to test its weight. Now she is only two or three women away from the table. She is about to separate herself from the children when she sees the man in the dirty clothes fumble between the legs of a younger woman and come up with a small leather bag. The guards are suddenly interested, and the woman is crying. The man in the dirty clothes works at the bag and opens it, and the guards peer inside, one of them laughing and holding his nose between his thumb and forefinger. When the woman gets off the table that guard slaps her on the buttocks and laughs, and she runs through the doorway.

It is now her turn. She approaches the table, and the man in the dirty clothes gestures to her to sit and lean back. She does so, feeling the heat of the previous women in the wood of the table. "Oh get off!" the man snaps, and she struggles back down to the floor and rejoins the children.

Then they are walking along a strange, curved lane with pine boughs woven through wire so that the air has a fragrant, sappy odor. One of the guards standing along the way threatens them by stamping his foot as they pass, and ahead she sees another woman who has apparently soiled herself so that wet stains of feces show on the backs of her thighs. She is winded, and aware that women are running toward them from behind, and so she pulls the children to the side. The guards have apparently struck them as they passed. It occurs to her that such meanness could indicate that they never had any intention of killing them. Mistreatment makes little sense. But when she sees the low building with the little door, and the darkness inside, the low ceiling and back in the deeper recesses of the room the pale, ghostlike forms of other women and children, she knows that all that they had said is true. Her heart rises in her chest, high and ticklish and light, and she feels as if she has nothing inside her body, as if she will next be able to float, and the guards on either side of the doorway are two-dimensional and flat, like cardboard cutouts, and the hands of the children on her thighs and wrists feel like her own appendages, also hollow and floating. She knows that it is most important that they find a place in there where they can stay together.

Janusz Siedlecki is jostled out of the wide line of men and falls on something soft, the heels of his hands sliding out from under his weight. It is a corpse, and he scrambles away from it, hearing laughter through the hollow, muffled pounding in his head. He looks up at a tall guard who yells at him in some foreign language. Then a voice behind him says in Polish, "Take one of the arms! Take one of the arms!"

"Why?"

The man raises his hand as if to hit him. Janusz grabs the wrist of the corpse's left arm and pulls, feeling tendons popping in the shoulder. Then he feels a tearing, so that the skin of the hand begins to pull off, like a glove. He pulls the cuff of the man's coat sleeve down to cover the sticky, dark red opening. As soon as the corpse is moved, sliding on the yellow, sandy earth, the potent stench of putrefaction engulfs his face like a billow of heavy smoke. He sees that he is one of four carrying the corpse, and allows them to determine the direction.

The painful rush of the near-deafness makes him dizzy, and he stumbles at a half run, looking back over his shoulder at the spot from which he was pushed out of the line of men. He does not understand it — he should be with them. Then he sees the man who runs with him, holding the corpse's other arm. He is young, and his face is twisted with fatigue and a kind of grim fright. The corpse's head does not bob, but bounces stiffly on the neck. They pass a fence, then go around the corner of a building, and in the distance he sees more men pulling bodies into a long ditch.

His heartbeat bangs painfully in his ears, accompanied by a strange, distant roar. With this he pulls into himself, and looks down at his feet shooting out from under him one by one, until he feels the men slowing down. His hand is numb from gripping the dead man's wrist.

They let the body down at the edge of the ditch. Janusz looks at the face — the skin is blackish around the eyes, nose, and mouth, and part of the man's tongue peeks through swollen lips. One guard, a Ukrainian he thinks, pokes at the man's clothes with the barrel of his rifle. He says something to the man who had threatened to hit Janusz, and the man leans down and begins feeling the pockets of the corpse's clothing. He rises up with a little booklet, perhaps a passport, and a small wad of Polish currency. The guard takes the money, scales the passport into the hole, and shoos them away.

They run back to the train platform, yelled at by the same man. "Faster!" he yells. "If you slow down they'll kill you!"

Janusz's mouth is as dry as dust, and his throat burns. He hears a strange, flat crack ahead, and sees a man crumple like a dropped marionette on the parched earth. An SS officer holsters a pistol, and gestures at them to come over. As the four run toward the body, Janusz tries to understand what is happening. His grandmother and the children are somewhere beyond the low building to his left.

When he pulls up on the man's wrist he feels its warmth, and the body dangles loosely, the head hanging like a melon in a bag, dripping blood in a dotted line in the dirt. Again they are running toward the long ditch. As he runs he watches the man's head bobbing and snapping while feeling its weight pull in strong vibratory shocks.

"Why — why did they —" He draws breath. "Shoot him?"

"Shut up!"

After they drop the body off at the ditch they run back to the railroad siding, to a line of boxcars, not from the train he was brought in. The leader of their group gestures to him to pull one of the sliding doors open, but he does not know how to work the handle. The man pushes him out of the way and flips the handle up, then slides the door open, and jumps back. The bodies of three men topple out onto the platform, their heads bouncing on the concrete.

Inside no one is standing. The air wafting out the door is heavy with the odor of sweat, of human filth, excrement, vomit. Two more bodies at the edge roll out slowly and flop on the siding at their feet. At floor level are three faces, all with eyes and mouths open. One is a little girl with braids, pinned under the upper body of a man. As he is about to look away, he thinks he sees her blinking.

"Get inside!" the man yells. He climbs up onto the planking of the boxcar. The man below him says something he cannot hear, then looks with wary fright behind him. One of the SS officers is watching them. The man turns again to Janusz and gestures rapidly — bring them out, bring them out. His face is twisted with a combination of fright and irritation. Janusz pulls at the first body, whose legs are pinned under the body of an old woman who died clutching a package that looks like a present against her chest. Her mouth is open as if she is singing. A gold bracelet appears at the opening of her coat pocket, and he picks it up and slides it into his own.

"Idiot!" the man yells. "You do this right or you die, do you understand? We all die, do you understand me, idiot!"

"I'm not supposed to be here," Janusz says.

"Shut up!"

He leans down, and sees the chubby face of the little girl. She blinks again.

"This one is alive," he says. Then he becomes aware that he should not have put the bracelet in his pocket.

The three men appear furious with impatience.

Janusz tugs at the wrists of the closest man, and his legs

come out from under the old woman clutching the package, then drag over the braid of the little girl. Then he pulls the package out of the old woman's arms, and rolls her toward the opening.

After sundown they are lined up near the railway station and told to wait. The bracelet in his pocket feels somehow bigger, and he is now sure that he will be punished when they see the circular lump of fabric on his trousers. He tries to casually hang his hand there to conceal it. His head still pulses with his heartbeat, and the muffled rushing in his ears and the sweeping weight of fatigue make him feel as if this is all a dream. Dimly he realizes that he must find out where his grandmother and the children are. A prisoner appears carrying a bucket and ladle. Janusz is about twentieth in his line, and fears that the bucket may be empty when the man gets to him.

He looks again toward the line of railway cars they had worked at earlier. After removing a few of the bodies, the men were ordered to continue cleaning up the rotting bodies around the railway station, leaving that car as it was — the Ukrainian guard merely ordered the door closed, and they left the bodies as they were, including the little girl pinned under the others, blinking at the dirty floor of the car.

They are watched by two Ukrainian guards and one German officer, and the men do not show their desire for the water. Janusz understands that those who stand out in any way can be beaten or shot, and in his case, the bracelet would certainly get him killed. He hears the faint grating sound of the ladle against the side of the pail, and finds himself shaking, his knees weak. His turn — the man puts the ladle toward his lips, and he reaches out and holds it with both hands. When the water is to his mouth he drinks it down in two gulps, but too quickly, so that it catches in his throat and makes him cough. Some of the water is expelled painfully from his nose, and he can hear the men nearby laughing harshly — not the men in line, but the guards and the officer.

They are then marched around one building toward another that has a single door directly under the inverted V of the roof. He stumbles into a dark room. The men ahead of him move off into corners, to places where the raw wood walls meet the hardened dirt, and flop down. They curl up in sleeping positions. He has no idea what time it is, but imagines that it must be nine o'clock. In this sudden calm he pulls into himself, his mind focusing in on the muffled *whooshing* in his ears, which is intruded upon by a harsh voice from somewhere. He looks around for a spot to lie down, and feels a light poke on his shoulder, and turns.

"My name is Adam Szpilman."

It is the leader of their group of four.

"Janusz Siedlecki."

"Stop shouting — are you deaf?"

He can barely see the man's face in the darkness.

"Some of the time," he says. "Where are my grandmother and sisters and brother?"

"How can you be deaf some of the time?"

Adam Szpilman grabs him by the upper arm and draws him toward the wall, where there are small windows through which the reflection of guard-tower lights shine in yellow shafts.

"Listen to me," Szpilman says. "You are fairly strong for your age, which is?"

"Fourteen."

"You've got to hear me when I talk, do you understand? You worked all day today without dropping, which means I made it through the day also. But you've got to hear me."

"What is happening here?"

"This is a mess. The system has broken down, and that is why the corpses are everywhere. Normally —" Szpilman comes out with a derisive laugh. "Normally everything is quite smooth. Normally we get a little to eat at the end of the day."

Janusz remembers the bracelet and pulls it from his pocket. "I found this."

Adam Szpilman takes it and holds it up to the dim light. "You'd have been shot if they caught you."

"I didn't know."

"What do you want to do with it? Around here, people use things like this to buy water, food —"

"You can have it."

Szpilman looks at him. "I have no use for it now but I know of someone who does."

"All right."

"He — they have a use for everything — currency, jewelry, whatever. Some of us are trying to organize — well, some way of dealing with this."

"I need to find my grandmother and brother and sisters."

"You should forget about them," Szpilman says. "They're dead. I'm sorry." He pauses, then says, "That's how it is here."

Janusz imagines each of their faces, Grandmother, then Jadwiga, then the little ones, and sees them in a kind of rapid animation. But they are dead. He does not know what to think of that. Szpilman leaves him and lies down on the dirt floor of the barracks building, and Janusz does the same.

That they are all dead seems not to assert itself to him. He is aware that his hands still smell of rotting flesh. His stomach twists in painful cramps of hunger, and as he feels himself begin to drift, almost against his will, he pictures the face of the little girl in braids, who blinked at him as he pulled the few bodies off the top of the pile in the railway car. She is still there, pinned under a man, and her face remains superimposed on his imagination, her eyes blinking patiently as she waits to be pulled out of the car. He is aware of men talking somewhere on the other side of the room, but he remains encased inside his deafness, and it seems to him that it might be the deafness itself that prevents him from understanding that they are all dead, that the picture of the blinking girl remains somehow more important.

He awakens to the sound of yelling, and when he opens his eyes he sees a man hanging suspended from a belt, his tongue filling his mouth like food and his trousers wet from urine and feces. No one pays any attention to the man — they brush by him toward the barracks door, making him swing slightly, causing the roof of the barracks to creak in such a way that he can feel the sound in the ground under him and hear what sounds like a man groaning.

The men crowd at the door, then go outside to line up in front of the building. He looks for Adam Szpilman, but cannot see him. Outside, he sees that some of the men are using a small latrine building just across from the doorway. The rest are jostling around trying to form a line.

Adam Szpilman taps him on the shoulder, then says something he cannot hear. He shakes his head, and Adam repeats, "Stay with me."

They are given water, each a tin cupful. Janusz is more careful this time, and waits while he feels it working its way down his throat to his stomach — it is almost painful, and at first feels like he imagines acid might feel.

"When do we eat?" he asks.

"Not yet."

"What happened to the man in the barracks?"

"He was either an informer and got chummy with the Germans, or like many, he decided to take himself out of this."

When the men are finished drinking their water they are marched back to the railway station, to the same car they pulled bodies from the evening before. Janusz remembers the blinking girl, and as he walks, he recalls that his grandmother and sisters and brother are dead. As had happened the day before, he realizes that his perception of this fact is somehow short-circuited in his pounding head, that his attitude should be some kind of grief, but he does not feel grief. He feels hunger, and thirst, and his skin is irritated with dirt and sour body oil.

Adam Szpilman now has a look of a kind of terrified excitement on his face, and the two other men are aware of something by the railway cars. There stands a tall officer in black, who is jovially watching the activity, nodding and smiling and giving orders to Ukrainian guards and prisoners. Janusz understands that this man is important, and as his figure bobs in his vision his perception of the man clarifies — he is tall and handsome, the insignia on his cap and collar glinting in the sunlight. Adam passes near the man, who watches with a kind of thoughtful perplexity. His eyes are beautiful, and he has the face of a cinema actor.

He speaks to Adam, who turns and points at the door of the railway car. Janusz opens it, now knowing how the handle works, and peers inside. The girl is still there pinned under a man, and appears to be dead. In the darker corners of the car he sees the same corpses that he saw the previous evening. He climbs into the car, smelling a deadened version of yesterday's air, and starts by trying to work the body of the man off the little girl with the braids. One of the other workers pulls himself up into the car, one of the four from the previous day who has, so far, said nothing. Around him hovers the faint scent of pinesap.

When they drag the heavy corpse off the girl, Janusz hears a strange wailing sound that seems to come from somewhere outside the car, but sees that Adam and the other worker are looking at the little girl. Her face is contorted with pain. Janusz picks her up, and she reaches out to grab at his arms. He passes the girl to Adam, who lies her down on the siding. She continues to yell, and the handsome officer snaps at him with a look of distracted irritation on his face. Adam and the fourth worker pick her up and carry her toward the ditches, Adam holding both of her wrists in one hand, the other man holding both ankles. Her head bobs harshly, and Janusz can see her straining her neck to hold it still.

He sees her once again near nightfall, but seeing her brings out no more than a dull recognition that yes, this was the blinking girl with the braids. She lies in the long ditch pinned under the bloated, blackened corpse of a woman, so that only her braid is visible.

He turns with the other three workers and walks around a building to a place they call the Sorting Square. In the center of the square there is a colorful mountain of clothing with an officer sitting on top. The mountain of clothes looms over a pile of decomposing corpses. "Ten thousand," Adam Szpilman says. "And for days." He explains to Janusz that only a week ago things ran smoothly, but more and more the railway cars delivered to them whole villages of dead people, because of the suffocation. Janusz tries to process this information, but is distracted because his hands are hopelessly fouled with the odor of decomposition, so that he no longer puts them near his face. His hands are now like tools although they appear reasonably clean. The worker who smells like pinesap has hands that are blackened in places, yet Janusz sees that he frequently puts them on his face, as if the filth of death is an aroma he must reconfirm to himself whenever he has the chance.

They begin work, and he distracts himself by looking for things to steal — here a ring, there a watch, in this pocket, money. Polish, English, American. It all goes into his pockets and is visible, he knows, and he waits for them to catch him, to shoot him, and it is as if he does not care. When he finds something to steal, he puts it in his pocket giggling with a sensation of weak-kneed, demented mischief. It doesn't matter — the increasing pressure in his head and the pounding roar in his ears have reduced him to an automaton, and he exists inside that roar, calmly and objectively processing information: There are ten thousand bodies in that pile. Ten thousand? Yes. He comes from a town of three or four thousand people, so he labors over the mathematical logic of this information: This would be, then, perhaps two and a half times the population of his town. He does not even know one-tenth of the people in his town, having lived in its Jewish quarter.

And the corpses: How long have they been lying there in what they call the Sorting Square? Perhaps three or four days, because in the folds of skin, the mouths, sometimes around the groin areas there is the subtle, glistening movement of worms.

Sometimes when he picks up on a man's arm — always the same arm because Adam does not want any variation in the technique of their body-carrying — the arm simply pulls off, sometimes at the elbow, sometimes at the shoulder. Janusz has noted with a kind of scientific objectivity that children pull apart more readily than adults, perhaps because of the softness of their flesh. They have decided that when these arms come off, they shall be piled just so, ready for that one trip to the ditch when Adam orders each man to carry four adult limbs, or six child limbs. And always it is the same number, because Adam does not want any variation in the technique of their body-carrying. One of the guards, attracted by any irregularity, may walk up to one of them and shoot him carefully high in the back of the neck, just under what Janusz remembers is called the occipital point of the skull, shown skinless in an illustration in the encyclopedia as a protrusion flanked by red muscles that run down the neck. And why there? He recalls that under the occipital point of the skull there is the root of the brain, referred to as the medulla, and the bullet, passing through the medulla, shuts off all information transferred from the brain to the body, in effect turning the human being off like a lamp.

But for the moment, he realizes, his brain is still safely connected to his spinal cord, and so he is able to carry bodies and process information. From time to time they find food inside bags, boxes, in pockets, and they find money and jewelry, some of which he puts in his pocket. Adam has told him that this is unusual, because normally, when things run smoothly, those coming in, perhaps ten thousand a day, are gassed naked, and he pointed, over there, in Camp Number Two, the Death Camp. But these bodies are rotting so fast that there is not time to bother taking off their clothes. Those who run the camp do not like to eat their dinner with that smell hanging in the air. Eat while you can, he told Janusz, and as for stealing, you are risking what little chance you have at life. Be careful. Eating proved easier said than done — Janusz ran across a flattened box in a man's pocket, and inside the box were the melted remains of chocolate-covered cherries, and he stuffed a wad of this material into his mouth. He chewed, and it burst with a sticky, almost unbearable sweetness, and his jaws were stung with the sensation of a painful astringency, but the saliva he expected did not materialize, and he has spent this day with the sensation of the cherry skins stuck in his throat, which is so dry that he cannot swallow them.

This evening they are given cups of cold potato soup before being marched off to the barracks. Janusz is aware that the three other men in his group are excited about something, that in their surreptitious smiles and knowing glances they have found something. It is alcohol. When the door is closed on them and the majority of the fatigued workers flop down on the hard dirt, the rest seem too wide awake. Adam reaches into the front of his trousers and pulls out a bottle of clear liquid, and holds it up to the pale moonlight coming in through one of the little windows. Vodka. Other men have also waited until now to reveal flasks, bottles of wine, bags of candy, cigarettes.

"The four of us can get drunk," Adam says.

One of the others, who is called Marek, frowns and shakes his head. "And how well do you think you'll work tomorrow? Do you think we'll survive tomorrow?"

"I don't care," Adam says.

"I do."

The fourth worker with the dirty hands looks on with amiable indifference.

Janusz sits down on the hard dirt, fatigued at the effort of trying to hear what they are saying. Above him he hears another older man who is an acquaintance of Adam Szpilman's ask if that is the deaf one, to which Adam, taking a sip of the vodka, says yes. But Janusz feels himself receding from them, pulling into the rushing in his head, vaguely thinking, my grandmother is dead, my sisters and brother are dead. There are ten thousand people in that pile. There is no qualitative difference to these observations. It might just as well be a list of odd facts of the sort that you could find in a science book: There is a theory that birds are distant relatives of dinosaurs; the most interesting property of mercury is what gives it its common name — quick-silver; ducks mate for life; a pane of glass is a sheet of slowly flowing liquid.

He is being pulled to his feet, and does not protest. Adam is speaking to the older man, who holds up and then lights a candle stump, and grabs Janusz's right ear between his thumb and fore-finger, and pulls it up. When Janusz moves as if to prevent the man from looking in his ear Adam shakes his head and looks threateningly at him — could it be that Adam could have him shot? He does not know, and so decides to submit to the examina-tion. A hand rests on his shoulder, and he flinches — it is the strange one. As he is about to pull away, he smells pinesap, and looks at the man, who nods once with a kind of grave reassurance.

The older man walks off a short distance and begins to rum-mage in a small bag. "He's a doctor," Adam shouts. "His name is Herzenberg. He found that bag in a transport and they let him keep it." The older man rises, holding a black tube, which sweeps to a point on one end and has three silver rings on the other. Adam and the older man laugh about something, and Janusz feels his head reel in a nightmarish swoon. The older man unscrews the point of the tube, and Adam pours vodka into it. Janusz feels his knees jerk, and has the powerful im-pulse to run, but he remains rooted to the spot because the rushing in his head has neutralized even his physical will, and that sap-smelling hand is still there on his shoulder.

The older man's hand, which smells of carrion, grips the top of Janusz's head and tips it, and as Adam looks on with an en-couraging expression, Janusz feels the thin end of the device moving into his ear, sliding along the top of the canal. Suddenly there is a loud rush of sound, like a roaring waterfall, bitingly cold inside his ear, and the pain increases sharply, pressing in-ward, until there is what feels like an explosion, and the older man looks down at the dirt between them. He stoops, holding the candle. On the dirt the long wax plug looks like a fat worm, a rich brown blending to dark amber at the ends. His head is gripped once more, and once more the thin end of the device is slid into his other ear, and as this is happening, Janusz feels the stinging in the other ear along with something else: a lucidity of sound that mesmerizes him to the point of his being nearly unaware of the waterfall rush in the other ear, the increasing pressure that seems ready to burst his ear, and then the peculiar explosion.

The hand lifts from his shoulder.

"So how does that feel?" Adam asks.

Janusz can only stare at him, then at the strange one. He feels the cold moistness tunneling into his head from both sides, a powerful frigidity that chills his whole body. His hearing is so intense that he blocks out the recognition of what he sees, and absorbs the strange ticking sounds, the humming, the vibration of the building they stand in, the buzzing sounds emanating from each human being near him, and in the distance, the sounds made by trees, by dew falling, and yes, over there, the mumbling of praying men, far beyond that someone screaming. A number of people screaming — perhaps in one of the railway cars. He can hear each screaming voice as clearly as if they were just there on the other side of the wall.

"Now when I whisper to you, you won't call attention to yourself by saying, 'What?'"

"Do I say that?"

Adam laughs. The older man puts the black device back into his valise. The strange one moves around to face Janusz, and whispers, "David."

"He's a woodcutter," Adam says. "From the *Tarnungskommando*. Normally he would be cutting wood in the afternoons, but for this breakdown of the system."

"I cut wood," Janusz says. "Maybe —"

"Their system of selection of workers is random," Adam says. "Logic is last on the list."

"My ears sting."

"That's the vodka. It'll go away. I can't imagine that alcohol would hurt you."

"Who is screaming?"

Adam squints at him, looks questioningly at David, and then listens. "Oh, yes — that is most likely a few boxcar loads of people they stuffed into the gas chambers and forgot. They'll suffocate by morning."

Adam squats down and begins digging in the dirt with his fingers, and David moves off into the darkness. Then Adam sits down and gouges a little trench out with the heel of his shoe, and places the half-empty bottle of vodka in the hole. Janusz listens to every sound, the scraping of the shoe, the soft clinking sound of the bottle being laid in the trench, then the sound of bottle squeaking on the sandy earth as Adam covers it up. Then Adam curls up around the buried bottle and prepares to sleep.

"Listen to me," he says. "Now that you can hear, remember this: Don't call any attention to yourself. If you do they'll hit your face, I mean so that they will leave a mark. If they do that, then they'll take you to the Hospital tomorrow and shoot you. The Hospital, by the way, is a hole in the ground with a fire going all the time. In any case, if they ask you about your face and you lie, then they'll kill you with shovels, hack your arms off."

"How do you know they are dead?"

"I know."

"Why shovels?"

Adam laughs. "That was all most people carried at the beginning. They discovered that they work well as a kind of ax. You know, hitting with the edge. I imagine that it felt somehow familiar to them. So they use them like axes."

"I have two sisters, a brother, and grandmother."

"Please," Adam says. "We'll talk tomorrow."

"Who is the officer everyone is afraid of?"

"*Untersturmfuhrer* Franz? He will smile at you and give you candy, or he will smile at you and shoot you in the face. Some of us call him 'The Doll' because he is so handsome."

The doctor moves toward him. "How do you feel?"

"Good."

"You are the one who gave Adam the bracelet."

"Yes," Janusz says, then remembers. He digs into his pocket and pulls out a handful of bills and coins, a ring and a watch. "Here, he said that you have a use for it."

"Not so loud," Adam whispers. "Let's keep it to ourselves."

Dr. Herzenberg takes the money, ring, and watch. "Listen to me — some of us use this to buy food and sometimes weapons. The problem is that those of us who — The people trying to plan something —" He pauses. "No one really seems to live long enough, because we are frequently replaced. In your case — I saw you with that bulge in your pocket. That you are alive amazes me."

"You must not be caught," Adam says. "That is, if you tell them who you give the money to, well —"

"If they catch you and suspect anything," Dr. Herzenberg says, "they'll torture you until you tell them. They'll hold your hand in a pot of boiling water until it's overcooked, they'll blind you." He pauses, thinking, and then moves closer to Janusz. "Why did you give Adam the bracelet?"

"I don't know. He was friendly to me."

"Why do you give me money?"

"You cleaned my ears."

"You'll probably live around two weeks to a month, like the rest of us. How does that make you feel?"

He tries to think of an answer. "I don't know. I guess it doesn't matter."

"A philosopher," Adam says.

Dr. Herzenberg looks at him, then at the money in his hand. "You must be careful," he says. "I will pass on what you give me to others, but you won't know who they are. I can give you little in return."

"That's all right."

Dr. Herzenberg places his hand on Janusz's shoulder and then turns to find a place to sleep. Adam seems to have dropped off also.

Within a minute Janusz is lying on the dirt staring into the blackness, and as he prepares to sleep, he is aware of something ticking in the air around him that makes his heart beat too fast, that makes his breath begin to catch in his throat. It is not the certainty of his death or his fear of it. For some reason he cannot relax inside so complicated a collection of sounds, moans, snufflings, snoring, clearings of the throat, and off in the distance under the sound of tree leaves scraping one another, the softer wailing of those suffocating in the gas chamber. Then he understands that it is not sound itself — there is something else that makes his breathing irregular, makes it now halt and produce truncated sobs, and whatever it is invades his flesh as surely as a virus moving at the speed of light. He gets to his feet and makes his way toward the door, but his foot runs into a man's leg, and the man grunts and moves on the dirt.

Janusz is now trembling, his body threatening to crumple to the ground. Then he understands what it is: The children are dead, the little babies are dead, and Grandmother — she is dead, and he did not say good-bye to her. In fact he behaved badly to her, and now she and the children are dead. He is alone, tiny and soiled and locked inside this room, only a day or so away from his own death. His awareness has achieved so horrible a lucidity that he thinks he may vomit his insides out at his feet. The children are dead, and he behaved so badly, and now he can never put it right.

NEAR WOLGA-OKNAGLIK, POLAND

AUGUST 2, 1943

As she approaches the narrow dirt road that leads to Wolga-Oknaglik, she begins to think she may get home before the heat kills her. Although it must be after three-thirty, the boiling air makes her weak and shaky, and the cramps attack with such force that she must be near something to hold on to in order to keep from dropping into the brittle grass. She needs only to cross the road and go through a patch of woods and one large rye field, the same one she ran across every day to go to Anatoly, a locket he had given her bouncing on her chest. Her father allowed her to keep only that, and looked with bitter skepticism at everything else — why does he give you shit like this? But Father, you said the things he gave you were valuable. They were trash, he said. That lorgnette was plate and the diamonds were fake.

Next time tell him you want money. Thousands. They gas thousands every day and this is all he gets? He's an idiot.

"He is not," she whispers.

She is no longer sweating because she has no more water in her, and her mouth is dry and sticky. Each step on her swollen feet feels as if the skin down there will rip open, stretched so tight as it is. Her belly too — it will surely explode.

She is near the road. From here she can see to the horizon, pine and birch trees, vague rises in the land, all still and baking in a hot, bluish haze, with the boiling silver lake under it. Out of the intermittent shade of the trees, the full blazing weight of the sun hits her, and she becomes dizzy and feels sick to her stomach. When another pain opens its fingers and begins to squeeze, she stumbles to a bush and tries to sit down in the little patch of shade, but her hands and arms are so weak that they buckle under her weight, and she falls on her side, the shock sending a searing pain through her trunk, high up where her bruised organs ride. The pain mixes with the cramp, and she draws her knees up and holds them and then rocks, moaning with each breath.

The baby will die of the heat before it is born. Anatoly told her that babies die in the camp every day. Her eyes closed, she feels the pain recede, and then she sinks into a fatigued delirium in which everything Anatoly ever said to her comes as one long garbled speech in his West Ukrainian accent: I will leave that place and we will go to my country. No one will find us. They kill babies because the babies make too much noise. I hate them. The Germans shoot people for sport.

At first he could not do what he paid her to do. It was not until November that he could, and then going home she thought, at first I thought something was wrong with him but now I know there is not. And her father snapped at her, why does he give you shit like this? And she looked at him and thought, at first I thought something was wrong with him, but now I know there is not. She thought that the next day too, running through the rye field.

She hears something nearby, and opens her eyes. By the road. In the space between the pains she should be moving, so she rises from the ground, still dizzy, and looks toward the road, squinting in the bright light. There are two open-topped automobiles there, and men, and as they slowly come into focus she recognizes the black uniforms of German soldiers, and then two men dressed in civilian clothes. Anatoly is not with them. In the shimmering heat they seem like slow-moving dream figures, standing there chatting. Then one man walks to the edge of the road followed by one of the officers. The man turns his back to the officer and then the officer points, and the man flops on his face into the weeds by the side of the road. She hears the flat crack of a gunshot. The other civilian pulls something from his pocket and walks to the edge of the road, and the same officer then points at him, and he flops on his face, the sound of the shot delayed by half a second. She remains still, breath held. She cannot cross the road. The officer puts away his pistol and leans down to pick something up from the ground, and then topples forward as if he has lost his balance. He ends up sitting on the road, and then struggles to his feet, barely able to keep his balance, as if the crushing weight of the sun has drugged him.

She understands that the men have just been shot. In the hazy dreamlike stillness of the afternoon it seemed at first to be some strange gentlemen's game, but now she understands that the men have been shot. The officers climb into one of the automobiles and drive away, but the other automobile remains there. She looks around quickly, thinking that more officers may be here in the brush.

She turns and walks parallel to the road, thinking that she might cross it where there are more trees. She tries to fix in her mind what she has just seen, but it remains as fantastic as if she had awakened one morning to see an Arab float past her window on a carpet. Those men have just been shot. And the officer fell on the ground.

As she walks she remembers that she does not feel the pain, and thinks, the baby died. There is no pain because the heat has killed the baby, and she is next. And it is God's will that it should be so because Anatoly won't come to her. And when they pull out its remains, they will find that it is covered with scales, or bears the buds of horns, or the organs of both man and woman. And then she will be glad that it died.

She remains fatigued and dizzy, walking, and the heat radiates up from the ground, baking her flesh. Her walking becomes awkward and mindless, a drunken stagger, and the bluish haze lying like a heavy blanket over the fields stops sound, memory, even time. "My name is Magda," she whispers. "Magda. And the baby is dead."

She sees ahead of her a birch sapling with dusted leaves, and almost as if the presence of something to hold on to has caused it, another pain begins its slow, undulating constriction of her organs. She is almost too tired to stumble to the sapling. In the distance, by the road, she sees a group of farmers, or villagers, and one policeman in blue, and she studies them until she is sure that Anatoly is not there. He would be nearly a head taller than the others. The men carry axes, rakes, hunting rifles with long barrels. She remains still, because if they find her and one of them knows that she is carrying a Ukrainian's baby, then they will kill her with their rakes and axes. The forms of the men shimmer in the heat, and then become watery and indistinct as the cramp tightens, absorbing her senses into the hot well of pain.

ROLL CALL SQUARE, TREBLINKA
EARLY SEPTEMBER 1942

As the men gather in the Roll Call Square, Anatoly Yovenko takes his position near the gate to the railway station. Two officers look down at something on the ground, what appears to be a stain from someone being killed, which draws flies. *Untersturmfuhrer* Franz must tug on his dog's leash to keep the straining animal away from it. The Germans hate flies and have everything drenched with disinfectant and insecticide, and so they wait while a man runs off and comes back pumping the lever on a small tank with a sprayer on it.

Next is the roll call. First the Germans will strut in front of the hundreds of men and make speeches that Anatoly does not understand. After that is a drill using the caps that the men wear.

The sun is going down, reddish and sleepy, through the treetops in the distance. There remains for him only vodka and sleep. The fatigue he has felt for weeks now is because of all the death, and he knows that Magda may be growing tired of his doing nothing when he visits her. Gold jewelry and money go only so far with a woman, he thinks, and he blames his being a man in name only on all the death. He has become empty and dead because of it. Vlodya, too, is tiring of this business. Now Vlodya always wears an expression that says, I am through with all of this. But the Germans will never let them leave. They will kill them first. And that boy who wants a gun — he promised watches, rings, money, if Anatoly could find him a pistol. And he said to the boy, "I will get you rifles, bombs, if you promise to burn this place down," and the boy nodded. "A pistol will do for now," he said. In his hatred of the Germans Anatoly had felt a strange pleasure at the idea of helping the Jews with their foolish plot. They seem to him like pigs in a slaughterhouse yard, gazing at the fence and scheming while, one by one, they are butchered.

He stands guard while the speech goes on, given by the officer Max Bielas, and lapses in and out of attention, trying to remain awake. "*Mutzen ab!*" Max yells, and the men all slap their caps against their thighs. "*Mutzen auf!*" Their caps on once again, they wait until they must snatch them off.

In the warm summer twilight he feels himself dream, envisions the northwest Ukraine. In a country as flat as this, or his own, there is only one place to hide, and he has seen it, a maze of waterways, lakes, low brushy woodland, useless to the Germans except perhaps for fish, and probably dangerous for them because partisans hide there. Those marshes cannot be more than a couple days' travel. Somewhere in there, he and Magda would lie, perhaps half in and half out of the water like eels, like scaled creatures unaware of the world of humans. Standing at attention with his hand gripping the barrel of the rifle, he feels the sensation of being here but being not here, because in his mind he is on his way out.

As he stares across the line of men he sees Max turn, and then, as if in a dream, a man emerges in a single jump from the front line, his hand raised. Max falls, and above him stands the man, who is then approached by four guards who immediately hit him with the butts of their rifles. The man wilts to the earth while the guards continue hitting him, and Anatoly can see the power of their strikes as the prone man's head is flattened under the blows.

The workers begin running in different directions, and then there is gunfire, and the dog barking. Then the sounds of machine guns. Some of the men fall, and he sees them writhing on the ground while others jump over them trying to get out of the square. Those running in his direction stop as the gunfire explodes the earth in front of them. Anatoly raises his rifle and aims, and then, not knowing why, shoots into the air above the men's heads. His knees feel weak, and begin to tremble uncontrollably.

Then the gunfire stops. Another officer is yelling, trying to get the men back into their ranks. Anatoly is shaking so badly that he can barely hold the rifle. Other officers are now kneeling over Max. The workers who were not hit by the gunfire shuffle back into their ranks.

He stumbles out into the square. The officers walk around in rapid steps, their faces twisted with anger and a kind of vengeful assurance. More people will now die. Franz allows the dog to bite at one of the men cornered by the barracks wall.

"You!"

Anatoly steps forward, no longer nervous, as if he has awakened from a dream. Other guards are ordered to stand near Anatoly, and he wonders if they are to be punished for allowing this to happen. Vlodya is there, his face crossed with a look of excitement and shock. He is sweating.

"Take these to the Hospital!" an officer yells. He indicates a group of twenty-five or so of the men. All around the square there are wounded men moving in the dirt, and dead men lying in spreading pools of blood.

Anatoly walks behind the group of men while other guards flank and precede them. He can hear the men praying, muttering to themselves, cursing. The Hospital is in the far corner of the Sorting Square, a shack standing above a pit filled with a perpetually burning sulfur fire in which the remains of workers are gradually consumed, along with the remains of old women who could not walk to the gas chamber and babies no one wanted to carry there.

Anatoly stops at the shack, but Vlodya signals him to approach the pit. "Come on," he says in an intense whisper. "We all have to do this. It's our necks too."

By fives the workers are ordered to sit on a bench over the stinking pit. They do so with quiet, fatalistic acceptance. Vlodya points to the man at the far end, and trembling again, Anatoly positions himself behind the last man. As the other guards lift their rifles, he lifts his, and points the muzzle so that it hovers there a few centimeters from the top of the man's pockmarked neck, and he pulls the trigger. The rifle jumps in his hands as the man snaps forward, part of his forehead and some hair-covered scalp flying out in front of him. Disturbed by the men flopping into it, the fire splutters and belches smoke. The next worker to sit facing away from him is a boy, perhaps sixteen years old, with very fine black hair coming to a slightly curled point on the back of his neck.

When they are done with the executions Anatoly whispers to Vlodya, "I have to take a piss," and Vlodya nods. Anatoly walks around the little building to the back wall of the latrine, leans over, and vomits into the sandy earth. When he is finished he stands up straight, feeling a wetness in his eyes, from the force of his heaving, and bows once more, coughing up

[76]

what is left in his stomach. Then he returns to the Hospital, feeling his teeth grating against each other.

Workers are carrying wounded in their direction. It is dark enough now that they are black silhouettes running, the heads of the carried men bobbing low between the running men. Anatoly looks into the pit. The bodies of the dead men settle, tongues of greenish flame licking at their arms and legs.

Janusz Siedlecki stands wedged in a dark corner of the barracks building, shaking and unable to control his breathing. In the dead air smelling of the filth and sweat of the men, he hears the whispering of prayers. Some curse God, others beg Him to multiply this catastrophe many times over to bring man closer to the day of His appearance.

"Why didn't they shoot you?" Adam Szpilman asks.

Next to Adam stands a man named Waclaw Gitzer, who replaced poor old Marek after Marek was face-marked and killed, despite trying to cover the mark with some face powder he found in the Sorting Square litter. An officer saw the makeup, and ordered two guards to beat him to death with shovels.

"It is because he is nondescript," Waclaw Gitzer says. "He has a genius for being nondescript. He is the most nondescript person I have ever met, and here that is a special kind of genius."

"You're right," Adam says. In the voices of both men Janusz senses a nervous, almost vehement jocularity. That they are all to die is certain, when the sun comes up. The Germans will drink tonight and then plan the exact manner of their deaths. Shovels? No. Hanging upside down? Perhaps. Whatever strikes them at the moment to be the slowest and most painful.

"He just stood there at attention," Adam says, and laughs. "I believe he took his cap off, in honor of Max. Did you?"

[77]

"No."

"He did," Adam says. "And then he stood there while the bullets flew, and nothing happened. Even bullets ignore you."

"Yes," Waclaw says. "He has that unfinished look, as if the sculptor got distracted by something and left him that way."

"I have observed this," Adam says. "From the very first day, I saw that with his unfinished look, there was some peculiar genius hidden within, and you are right — it is that he is nondescript. He can steal gold and jewels while the Germans watch, and they just don't see him. Is it any wonder Dr. Herzenberg calls him 'the gold mine'?"

"He doesn't call me that."

"Then in my humble opinion he should."

"Where is he?" Janusz asks. "Was he hurt?"

"No, he's treating some men the Germans are chummy with."

"Berliner is the man's name," Waclaw says. "Meir Berliner, from South America I understand. He knifed poor Max. Since I came here I have seen suicides, but this is the best one."

"I talked to him," Adam says. "He came in with his family. I could see it in his eyes, that he wanted one of the officers."

"Max's last name is Bielas?" Janusz asks.

"Yes," Waclaw says.

"Why are they names that have the letters M and B?"

"I never thought of that," Adam says.

"Why would an MB kill another MB?" Janusz asks. Then he feels his eyes flood, and begins to giggle uncontrollably. "This place has a magic about it," he says, and his laughter grows in force, until Adam grabs his shoulders and shakes him.

"Stop it!" he whispers. "Please, stop!"

"I can't," he says. Then, as quickly as the laughter began, it now vanishes, leaving him feeling empty and without any substance whatever. Perhaps it is what death feels like. "There is a special magic," he says.

"I like you more when you are yourself," Adam says. "You have lived here for weeks, as I have. We have lived through the body pileup. We have seen hundreds of workers die. We are alive, perhaps, because of your nondescriptness."

Waclaw laughs ruefully. Then they listen to the sounds of the Kaddish, the entreaties to God, the weeping. It forms a single sound, something like a sustained groan.

"I wish I were deaf again," Janusz says.

"An undernourished body produces no wax," Waclaw says.

"What will they do with Max's little boys?" Adam asks. Janusz has seen them once, when he was ordered to take a package to the cottage in the patch of woods near the German barracks. He walked a little way in, and saw the boys wearing blue uniforms with silver buttons, and they were all pretty, more like girls than boys, and young, twelve or thirteen. He found out that Max was a homosexual who used the little boys as if they were women. He showered gifts on them, and fed them candy and sweets and all the best foods. It was his little harem. Janusz had wondered why it was that Max did not notice him.

"I was nondescript," he says.

"What?"

"Oh, I was thinking about why Max didn't dress me up in a uniform. I was probably too nondescript for him."

Adam laughs. Laughing along with him, Waclaw says, "You wouldn't want him buggering you in the night, I'll tell you. And now? I suppose it's the gas chamber for them."

"I was hit on the face," Adam whispers.

There is a silence. If the hit left a mark, then Adam is a dead man.

"I suppose it doesn't matter," he says. "They'll kill us all tomorrow."

"They need us," Waclaw says. "How many do you think died in the square? Fifty?"

"I was flat on my face," Adam says.

"Janusz was standing at attention," Waclaw says. "They missed him because they did not see him. But you did see how many died, didn't you?"

"No."

"Can you see anything?" Adam asks. Waclaw looks at his face. "The right side. I got a man's boot there hard."

"Nothing," Waclaw says. "You won't know until tomorrow."

"When they kill us," Janusz says. "Things were going normally until this happened."

"What is normal?" Waclaw asks.

"Listen," Janusz says, and then wonders if he should mention this in Waclaw's presence. But in the present circumstances it seems not to make any difference. "I have been giving Anatoly things, and asked him for a gun. He said he wants us to burn this place down, but you should know that he knows something. I mean, how can you buy a gun without letting them know —"

"Those are the risks we take," Adam says. "Just don't let on who runs things. Even if they threaten to shoot you."

"I won't. Besides, I don't know who runs anything."

"Like being nondescript, your other gift is ignorance," Adam says. "And that is not an insult. Anyway, you won't see much of Anatoly for a while. He's as worried as we are."

More men enter the barracks, and Janusz sees the slightly stooped form of Dr. Herzenberg, and then David Schrhafta.

"It's David," Janusz says.

"So," Adam says, "our walking sachet survived too." Waclaw looks questioningly at him.

"A *Tarnungskommando* fellow," Adam says. "He always smells like the woods, and when he is with us, brings a kind of — well, an aroma to our lives."

"He may be strange," Janusz says to Waclaw, "but he is aromatic."

Adam laughs, then stops laughing abruptly, and feels his face.

When the men fade away to find space on the sandy floor of the barracks, and there is more space tonight because of the number killed in the square, Janusz lies down, knowing that sleep will not come to him. On the other side of the barracks men are awake, whispering, trying to calculate their chances at survival past tomorrow.

Things were normal until now, he thinks. As a part of the Blue Kommando, who took people out of the railway cars and passed the baggage to the Sorting Square men and cleaned the cars out, he had settled into a routine in which the possibility of surviving seemed almost tangible, except for the risks he took stealing, and trying to bargain with Anatoly. Aside from that there was the habit the Germans had of selecting and then marching groups of men off to the Hospital, "retirees" they were called, workers who lacked the proper initiative, or who were worn down from the work and the lack of enough to eat. But now, with the murder of someone as important as Max, the certainty of death asserts itself with a force that makes him feel hollow and empty and already dead. He knows he must avoid any man whose initials match his, JS, for surely this event tonight was a sign. That two such men should end up this way, one driving a kitchen knife into the other, is not any great surprise, but that their initials are the same so violates the principles of probability that the event has to be a portent of his own doom.

He knows that Treblinka is a special, magical place. Once, when being ordered to deliver a heavy box to the men called the Jews of Gold, who were watchmakers and jewelers, he had to wait while one of them gave him something to deliver to an officer. He told Janusz that this was the most heavily populated quarter-square mile on earth, the only difference being that 95 percent of the people were spirits. Perhaps three hundred thousand. And then Janusz understood, with the force of a kind of mental thunderbolt, that he was a part of one of the

most significant enterprises in human history. That his grandmother and brother and sisters were already here verified the
truth of this. That some of the men, usually the newly arrived,
would hang themselves, also verified it. He could not attach
any judgment to this recognition, because it was somehow too
immense in scale to judge, and after all what is a pistol or a
grenade or a rifle in the face of all this? And the men who plot
the revolt — he thinks he knows who they are, an engineer
named Galewski and a Czechoslovakian soldier — if they are
aware of the truth, that all of them are no more than feeble
worker ants, how can they go on?

Then he remembers the boys. If Max is dead, then they will
gas the pretty boys. He envisions them being led in their blue
uniforms down the tube to the doorway of the gas chamber.
Where is Max? they ask. The tube officer Sepp says, inside,
boys, he is inside this little room. He wants you to come.

Janusz stands at attention in the Roll Call Square, his knees
shaking. No one has eaten since yesterday, when Max was
killed. In the barracks the workers have spent the night, and
then the day, waiting to die, and when they came to open
the barracks door everyone crowded against the far wall. *Untersturmfuhrer* Franz ordered them out, and they gave up and
went, their heads hanging.

Now Franz stands before them making a speech, which is
translated into Yiddish for them by the engineer Galewski, the
Lageralteste. Janusz understands half of what he hears — no,
you are not going to be killed. You are to be spared on certain
conditions. You will no longer be considered slaves. Rather you
are a well-trained workforce who will enjoy greater privileges
than before, better barracks, bunks with blankets, more and

better food, even entertainment. You must however agree to work and to —

As he goes on Janusz looks around at the men. They appear to be captivated by a growing astonishment, staring into the middle distance carefully going over what they are hearing. They are no longer to be considered a strange fuel whose purpose is to keep the Hospital fire going. They are no longer to be routinely liquidated, or beaten simply because someone needs exercise. In the line ahead stands Adam, who turns once to look at the man next to him. In his face Janusz sees the question, if we are now being "hired" by the Germans, then as a workforce are we now dedicated to obliterating ourselves, at least if we want to live? Adam's face shows the hint of a derisive sneer, as if the paradox mirrors exactly what Janusz told him, that Treblinka is special.

Janusz looks once more at *Untersturmfuhrer* Franz, who shakes his head sadly, it seems, at the very idea of the crudeness of Treblinka's beginnings. It is apparent that from here on the enterprise of this camp will be taken on with brotherly affection and mutual respect. He walks casually before the men, seeming to look thoughtfully at one, then another, then directly at Janusz, with those beautiful eyes that seem almost mesmerizing in their warmth.

Helmut Weyrauch and Joachim Voss stand in the large shack at the edge of the men's Undressing Square and watch the *Goldjuden* at their tables sorting deeds, certificates, money, and jewelry. Some with jewelers' magnifying glasses jammed in one eye are hunched over diamonds, wedding rings, watches. Their helper, a handsome boy of perhaps sixteen, looks from time to time at Voss with an expression that strikes him as flirtatious. Weyrauch's interest, he said, was really more scientific, but there were things here that would be of a practical interest to Voss. When Voss asked him what that was, he nodded with a kind of coy secrecy.

In the careful management of his alcohol Voss has found a balance, so that at least his stomach feels normal, and the problem of holding on to normalcy has been for the moment solved. Now, with schnapps still burning in his throat, he feels the gradual swoon of the alcohol's effect taking the edge off the morning. After the death of Bielas *Untersturmfuhrer* Franz took over, first reorganizing the workers in a sort of pact that gave them certain liberties and some security, but for Voss that meant reconsidering his own liberties, so that he was not sure how much in the way of valuables he could skim from the camp.

"So then it's Schiel you work for?" Weyrauch asks.

"Well, in a manner of speaking, since he oversees the recovery of valuables, yes."

He thinks, no, he must not name *Gruppenfuhrer* Kleist. He must not reveal the clients he represents, the collectors of Judaic artifacts, the people who never could shed their childish obsession for gold, whose faces lit up at the very mention of diamonds, platinum, fine watches. It would get to Franz, and he cannot allow the truth of their greed to be known.

"Secrecy in a place like this is appropriate," Weyrauch says. "I'll bet it's Globocnik and Operation Rinehard. It's the Reich Chancellery."

The handsome boy turns, apparently to a gesture made by a kapo, looks once more at Voss with an expression of feminine seductiveness, and walks away. "Now you'll see," Weyrauch says.

Voss studies the mountain of clothing in the Undressing Square, imagining the wealth that must be hidden in coat linings, shoes, hatbands. The handsome boy returns carrying a shallow wooden box, and Weyrauch steps in front of him.

"Show him," he says in Polish.

The boy holds the box up, and Voss sees two rings, what look like loose diamonds but for the sticky remnants of blood on them, and a small gold watch. He reaches out to pick up one of the rings, and then stops. "Wipe it off please," he says. Understanding, the boy carefully rubs it around on his shirt, which is new and looks expensive. Then he hands it to Voss.

"It's a marriage ring," he says.

The ornate gold filigree surrounds multicolored enameling of leaves against a rich blue background, with Hebrew writing in gold embossing so tiny that Voss cannot read it. An extraordinary piece. Italian, he believes. He puts it in the breast pocket of his tunic. Then he peers down at the other objects. It strikes him as disgusting. When Schneck had goaded him into inspecting the system, he had wandered over into the Death Camp and seen, from a distance, the dentists pulling gold teeth from yellow corpses — he could see a sheen of sticky residue on the closest dentist's hand, and watched as he worked the pliers back and forth in a quick pendulum motion, making the head of the dead man rotate in what struck Voss as a slow, emphatic expression of the word no. He went no closer.

"I assume these came out of mouths," he says. "What about the other places they hide things?"

Weyrauch laughs. "They check on the other side. The — process forces stuff out most of the time. On this side sometimes they check, you know, with a finger. But you can't catch everything. I imagine that over there in the pits there's a suspension of stuff that will consolidate in time, after all the bodies rot away. You know, bones and gold. Bones and gold."

Voss looks past the pile in the direction of Camp Number Two. Body cavities. Weyrauch is right — how much is lost in the pits? By the clothes pile a worker is being beaten by a Ukrainian guard, who carefully hammers the line of vertebrae bumps on the man's back with his dark gun stock. Voss clenches his teeth with each blow. The guard then walks around to face the man, and strikes him once with the forestock across the bridge of the nose. The worker is let go, and walks in the direction of the sorting shack stooped over and holding his face. Strange, he thinks. Tomorrow he will be dead.

Weyrauch steps over to the man, a sympathetic expression on his face. Then he speaks to him, pats him on the shoulder and returns, shaking his head sadly. "The poor devil," he says.

"You're very considerate."

"It's terrible," Weyrauch says. "Terrible."

Weyrauch's expression changes, and he crooks his finger at Voss, who steps over to him. He picks up and holds a satin jacket across Voss's chest, and says, "Oh! A perfect fit!" The boy watches, smiling. Voss pushes the jacket away, and sees beyond Weyrauch a smaller pile of clothing, apparently all baby clothes. Then with a sudden force the entire picture makes him swoon with nausea. What is he doing here? And this boy, with his seductive, flirtatious look, why is he here? His presence gives the scene a strange dreamlike quality, as if all this were invented by some perversion that Voss himself is also victim of, although he cannot identify it.

Then he understands: Weyrauch is a homosexual. That he is missing that one finger seems to Voss a symbol of some secret depravity. Indeed, there is a secret perversion in everyone in this place. Reeling with a strange dizziness, he thinks, and there was Bielas, a pederast, and he was deputy commandant. And now the place is run by one so handsome that they have begun to call him "The Doll." Voss's body begins to vibrate with a gruesome fright, as if some vast conspiracy has manipulated this situation so that he should end up here. That shit Weyrauch, who seems so like a friend, different from the barbaric children who argue over how many Jews can be killed with a single shot, has in fact been stalking Voss, waiting for the opportunity to seduce him, to —

"Don't let Franz see you staring like that," Weyrauch says. "You'll be labeled a person with a moral problem."

"Staring?"

"The baby clothes. You're looking at this judgmentally." Weyrauch laughs. "This is all Franz's fault. He got things going so well that the camp runs itself. It leaves us idle."

"I am here only to check on the possibility of a more complete recovery of valuables," Voss says stiffly.

"Yes, of course," Weyrauch says.

But the number of the dead and their possessions is such that he feels his heart sink — it seems to him impossible that there could be so many or so much. Then he recalls that, on their way to this part of the camp, Weyrauch pointed out a construction project — ten new gas chambers. Ten, he thinks. The mathematics of all this hover in the back of his mind, and he does not have the mental energy to make them conscious.

"This place makes me think about life," Weyrauch says.

"What?"

"Think of how elemental this is. Baby clothes."

"I think of the recovery of valuables."

Weyrauch is standing too close to him. The revelation of his clandestine perversion makes Voss's trunk warm with fright — that they could know something about Voss that would make assigning him here logical. He stands here looking at clothes. Next to a homosexual who is part of the conspiracy, a few feet away from a boy whose depravity signals an ugliness even deeper than this camp's enterprise.

But Treblinka makes sense as the logical extension of the *Einsatzgruppen*. Back then you went out with the men in their trucks, following men on motorcycles, you stood off to the side as the hundreds of Jews were called from their houses, and while some distance away the men went on about their business shooting the Jews, you went into the houses, into the stuffy, dank odors of cabbage and dirty clothes, and searched with that sensation of ticklish anticipation, a sort of neurotic desire, turning over dressers and wardrobes, pulling up loose floorboards. And there it would be — the black-painted metal box, or the wooden chest, or the leather bag, and inside that, old photographs, foreign money, and finally the small, sometimes extraordinary pieces of jewelry. Or there would be the watches, his favorite except for rare postage stamps — they would be gold and would feel oily in the palm of his hand. There would be the tiny stamped printing: Emile Garot, Faivre Perrin, Dietrich-Gruen. Now this new system is simply a matter of efficiency — bring yourselves and your valuables, deposit your valuables here and yourselves over there. "An hourglass," he says. "They are funneled here, and the narrow neck of glass is the chamber, and they come out to be buried over there."

"Come away," Weyrauch says. "You're becoming poetic."

They walk past the clothes pile and along the outer wall of the tube, or the "Road to Heaven" as they call it, and Voss shakes his head at the inanity of the name. Surely, sewn inside many of those coats, the valuables will be somehow lost. That the system is unable to filter this material out seems to him an outrage, a form of stupidity condoned by all of them, even the commandant, who is supposed to be an experienced police-man. But he's never around, polices nothing.

"Listen," Weyrauch says. They hear a train whistle. Its pitch is different from those of most of the transports.

"So?" Voss says.

"It's a passenger train from Vienna," Weyrauch says. "Be on your toes for this one. These are very wealthy people, doctors, financiers, so on. It's a luxury liner on wheels."

"Katerina," he says. "Do you want more champagne?"

She turns from the window, wishing it could be cleaner. The dreary little train station is now the tenth or eleventh they have seen in Poland, and her father has come apart. His in-decorous behavior is so unlike him! A man of such reputation, and so honored, and he acts like a child.

"You've only allowed me one glass all these years," she says to him. He nods and pours champagne into a crystal glass and hands it to Katerina's mother, who maintains a murderous silence. They could have gone to America months ago, but her father refused — his research was in Vienna. His colleagues were in Vienna. But her mother maintains her silence, staring out the window, the sunlight bathing her face and forearms, giving her finely wrinkled skin a pink translucence that Katerina always thought was so elegant.

Katerina's older brother, Julian, sleeps in the next seat beside his bags, which are packed with his clothes, books, and keepsakes. He doesn't seem to care about any of this — his attitude is a kind of poetic fatalism, and he seems more concerned about his girlfriends and his clothes than any of the rumored dangers of their situation.

The train lurches, and begins to move slowly out of the station. Katerina Sussmann again stares out the window and watches the brown fields and nearly denuded trees sweep by in vertical streaks, like a series of continuous lines issued from a watercolorist's brush.

But in minutes through which she is aware of the clinking of glass against glass near her, the brush and trees sweep by more slowly. She turns to the interior of the car, where the families recline in their bright blue velour seats. At the other end of the car is a famous surgeon whom her father had attempted to speak to, but because of the man's anxiety her father was rebuffed in a manner that embarrassed him, and he came back laughing and red-faced. The man had called him a blind clown. Her father had sat back down, poured more champagne, and said, "He is incapacitated by the virus rumormongeritus." Her mother stared blankly at him, and then at the veneer-paneled ceiling of the coach.

The train inches toward a gully with a stream running through it and then stops, and Katerina perceives the forms of people in the bushes and tall grass. It is a spread-out group of perhaps forty people, all dark-haired and wearing clothes that seem mismatched, too bright, the women in billowing skirts and tops and the children in rags. Beyond them is a line of strange, stout-looking wagons hung with pots and fowl cages. Just below her she sees a group of women, in the center of which is a girl changing her clothes. When she stands up straight Katerina sees that her skin is dark, her hair jet black, and naked, she exudes an absolute lack of self-consciousness about her nakedness. She has perfect breasts mounted high on her chest, and buttocks and thighs that look to have been chiseled by a sculptor, and in the front, a triangle of black pubic hair that strikes her as prehistoric. "Father, look!"

"Those are Gypsies," he says, "I think Lowara, or nomadic Gypsies." It is then apparent that he sees the girl, because he squints with sudden interest. "Yes," he says. "Redskins."

Katerina looks back down at the girl. Almost as if the girl sensed their eyes, she looks up suddenly, right at Katerina, and then in a single, dignified movement covers herself with a large red skirt, her breasts wiggling with a voluptuous abundance that makes Katerina momentarily breathless.

"They are a special people," her father says. "In ways there is a natural magnificence to them." Katerina's mother looks also, and then snorts with derision.

Katerina sees that the Gypsy group is not alone. German soldiers in gray uniforms are positioned around the camp's perimeter. There are also policemen in blue uniforms.

The girl now turns toward a bush, Katerina supposes to hide where she can dress without being seen, and she watches the unself-conscious movement of her body, her buttocks and back muscles rippling under the beautiful dusky skin. "Redskins," her father says. The train lurches forward.

And her mother says, "You can stop looking. She's gone."

Roman Merino sits on the ground near the little brook, thinking. In the narrowing circle of their freedom they have spent a difficult summer winding in and out of the border of the Soviet Union, staying near the lowland waterways, but as seemed to him inevitable, this freedom was interrupted by the Germans. As the *kumpania* moved, Merino noting the decreasing diameter of their circle of freedom, he read *vurmi* left by other tribes, written always in Romani, that confirmed the increasing difficulty of their situation. From where he sits now he sees most of his children, at least nine of the thirteen, some nearby, some the throw of a stone away playing in the water, and here and there the Germans with their rifles. His wife, Hela, helps Fiona dress over by the water. His son Vicente has been gone a week now, Merino assumes safe somewhere back near the border.

He sighs with a shaky exhalation of breath. When he was young, newly married, he had a vision, or perhaps a dream, he cannot recall, that told him one of his children would die. He perceived a child he knew to be his own bathed in a strange light, and knew that he was out of reach. The figure appeared profoundly exiled, wandering in a hazy, mythical landscape Merino assumed to be the vast geography of death. When his first child was born, and then the second, he could not bear the idea of seeing one of them die, as doomed to death one of them certainly was. So he had two more children, and discovered that by having more children he could dilute his tragedy. That only one of these four might die seemed less horrible, yet at the same time he could not accept it because he loved them all too much. Each time another was born, he waited for it to die of one of the conventional afflictions of early infancy, but indeed they were all too healthy, and grew beyond the time when he could have tolerated their deaths. Hela bore him more children, and she loved them too, to the point that the increasing number of their issue did not distress her.

During the normal travels of their life he began to forget that one of his children would die, but would recall at times, staring into the fire, that it would happen, and it would sadden him to think of the inevitability of it, that one of these eight beautiful children would die, then one of these eleven, finally one of these thirteen. By the time there were thirteen he would awaken in the middle of the night to air heavy with the scent of their bodies, and still, after all this, feel the grief he knew was inevitable to him.

Then there came the Germans. And with the decreasing circumference of their freedom and with the *vurmi* more and more threatening and the oppressive sensation like a cold vapor in the air, the peculiar pressure that spelled death, he began to develop a skepticism about the validity of his vision. One day he came upon three of his younger children finishing up their business in the camp latrine, a long hole in the ground with a plank suspended by two footstools above it. They were wiping themselves with pages of the *Krakauer Zeitung*, specifically with facial portraits of Hitler, Hoess, and other Nazi dignitaries, and they were laughing, each looking at how the brown swipes altered the pictures. They would look at what they had done to Hitler, and then covering their mouths, laugh themselves faint. He thought nothing of it until another day when he walked in a dark patch of woodland and came upon a clearing where German soldiers were shooting Jews into a ditch, by twos, in the backs of their heads. The activity was so mechanical, both by the victims and the killers, that he realized at once the horror of his error. One German lit a cigarette, ordered two women to go to the ditch. One woman clutching a baby refused, so, with the cigarette between the first two fingers of his left hand, he snatched the baby from the woman with his right, holding it by one foot, and dashed its head against a tree. That Roman Merino should see a child killed this way was no accident. They should have been in the south by then.

That night, staring into the fire, he told his oldest son to leave and hide near the border, staying always near waterways and rural villages, because farmers knew Gypsies and were, for *Gaje*, generally trustworthy. And he felt a strange, morbid satisfaction that, indeed, his son's face looked dreamlike in the copper firelight.

After his son left, Roman Merino found a place where nobody would see him, and wept. He had been tricked by his own vision: That one child would die was incorrect. In fact it was like a photographic negative — all of his children but one would die, and he and Hela with them. Unwittingly he had misread his vision, and his actions thereafter served only to magnify his tragedy rather than dilute it. He could not measure his self-contempt, and only days later he saw their trucks and open-topped cars approach. You will come with us. You are to be relocated. Roman Merino looked at the twin lightning bolts on the officer's collar, and at the little silver death's head mounted on his cap, and at the other soldiers positioned in a loose circle. Intrusions of this sort by *Gaje* were not unusual, so the situation was not necessarily menacing. But then he saw the officer's face in greater detail, its pink, soft skin, and the subtle hints behind the expression of businesslike nonchalance. In this facial treachery he read the certainty of his family's death.

Janusz Siedlecki lost sight of Adam Szpilman when the Gypsies came in through the main gate. *Untersturmfuhrer* Franz ordered him to do something, and now Janusz works feeling as if his subunit of the Blue Kommando is a body missing an important appendage. The picture that confronts them is so strange that even the SS officers look on with a kind of bemused awe. Before them sits a luxury train with large windows through which Janusz sees plush seats, tables that gleam with a dark brilliance, various crystal bottles and ashtrays, and, just visible through the open doorway, carpeting that looks as if it has come from a palace. There is little to do because there are so few people on the train, so they must act as if they are doing something to avoid being noticed by Franz, or Schneck, or any of the others who might find good reason to shoot them. Franz, "The Doll," is the worst. He moves about the camp with a large dog trained to bite men's genitals, but now Janusz sees that the dog is not with him. The Doll stands before the train with a strange smile on his face, as if the rustic condition of the camp is an embarrassment to him in the presence of these wealthy Viennese.

To Janusz's right there is a group of two or three dozen Gypsies carrying their pots, chickens, and odds and ends, the junk clanging with a distracting dissonance that makes the presence of the Viennese all the more absurd. Half of the Gypsies are children in colorful rags, walking barefoot, and the adults shepherd them, speaking in their strange language. When they begin to blend in with those stepping off the train, they who are so dark find themselves face to face with pale men wearing dark suits with high collars and expensive hats, with women and girls dressed as elegantly as film actresses.

Janusz turns to the doorway of his railway car, and there stands a man holding a glass of wine. "I believe we have arrived," he says in German, his face bright with curiosity. Behind him is a girl so beautiful that Janusz becomes embarrassed. She appears to be angry at the man in front of her. "Father!" she says. "The glass!"

"Oh," he says. He puts the glass down in the corner of the entryway to the car, and comes down the three steps onto the concrete platform. Then comes a young man who puts his hand on the girl's shoulder. He looks around at the camp, and then directly at Janusz, with an attitude of lofty contempt, as if there must obviously be some mistake.

As the Viennese step onto the platform and away from their cars, the Gypsies work their way through them, and they look at the Gypsies with a combination of distaste and amusement.

The Doll now speaks to some of the people from the train, holding his hands together in front of him with the ingratiating deference of a hotel manager. Behind him Janusz sees that two Ukrainian guards have noticed the girl, and are nodding to each other and whispering. It appears that she may take the long route to the burial pits. But through all of this the absence of Adam Szpilman frightens him. There is something nightmarish in the perverse contrast of things.

"Where's Adam?" Waclaw Gitzer whispers to him.

"I don't know."

"I don't like this."

"Let's get the luggage."

They go up the steps and into the car, their shoes sinking into the plush carpeting. Some of the chairs look like the kind you would find in a mansion drawing room. The luggage is piled behind some of the seats at the other end of the car, and they pass it out to other workers of the Blue Kommando.

Lucasz Gold, the fourth of their kommando, catches Janusz's attention, and indicates with his head the direction of the main gate. Peering out through the railway car window, Janusz sees Adam Szpilman walking across the railway station that is now emptying out, the Gypsies and Viennese having been herded toward the undressing areas. Adam is flanked by two Ukrainian guards, and he appears to have been beaten on the face.

His legs unsteady, Janusz walks to the doorway and steps down onto the platform. When Adam is only a few meters away, he steps toward him and says, "Wait, what did he do?"

Adam shakes his head rapidly, his face crossed with sudden anger. He jerks his head in the direction of the coach.

"What did he do?" Janusz asks.

"Janusz!" Waclaw hisses from behind him.

He steps closer, trying to catch the guards' attention. "What did he do?" They look blandly at him, then shove Adam along. Adam shakes his head once more, then points to his bruised face, first to his eye, then to his temple. Janusz feels Waclaw's hands grip his upper arms from behind. David Schrhafta steps in front of him and whispers, "No."

"But what did he do?" Janusz yells.

Schneck turns to him. "Get back to work, you shit!" he snaps, and then he is distracted by movement across the square. One of the Gypsy men is fighting with two of the guards, swinging at them with his fists as they jump away, watching him with wary surprise, as if he is some interesting animal who is behaving oddly. Schneck walks quickly across the station square, drawing his pistol. When he gets to the man he shoves one of the guards aside and shoots the Gypsy man in the head.

Waclaw pulls Janusz toward the car. "Let me go," he says.

"There is nothing we can do," David says. Then he grabs two suitcases and runs off toward the *Goldjuden*'s shack.

Janusz stumbles back into the railway car. Standing at the window, he watches as Adam is taken around toward the sorting barracks and out of his sight.

"You'd better pray Schneck doesn't remember this," Waclaw says. The station square is nearly empty now. Then he looks out through the window. "Look there," he says. "By the tube."

Three of the guards, who would normally be ushering people into the tube, have little to do because of the small population of this transport, so they have kept out that Viennese girl from Janusz's coach and are now taking her toward their barracks. Janusz looks away, back at the plush carpeting and the beautiful seats of the coach. "Why did Adam point to his eye and his temple like that?"

Waclaw shrugs. "He was trying to help you, you know. He wanted you to stay out of it."

At dusk Janusz learned what happened to Adam. He had been ordered to hold the leash of the dog belonging to The Doll, and when the Gypsies came in, the dog lunged at a girl, and Adam jerked hard on the leash, making the dog yelp. A guard observed this, and whispered to The Doll, pointing at Adam.

Janusz now stands at attention at roll call, listening to The Doll give a speech about how no worker in this camp shall ever hurt Barry. Adam Szpilman hangs upside down from a portable scaffold erected before the men who are arranged in a square. He is naked and his hands are tied behind his back, and he swings in a slow, slightly twisting arc, the veins in his neck and on his forehead bulging tightly. The Doll points out that this worker will be spared the pain of Barry's vengeance, that he will be allowed to die without having his manhood ripped off, because he was a good worker and will be hard to replace, but no one, no worker, guard, whatever, no one will abuse his dog. Anyone else caught abusing the dog will be set up in such a way as to have his face ripped off, and by whom? By the abused dog, of course.

Adam groans, then makes a sound as if he is trying to lift something. He jerks, then continues swinging. Blood now begins to run out of his nose and into the corners of his eyes and then over his forehead. He coughs blood, snorts it out his nose. The Doll then says, "Enough," and draws his pistol. He shoots Adam in the back of his head, making it snap harshly, after which the body swings in a wider arc than before.

Janusz feels soiled and empty, somehow without organs inside his body. He imagines that this sensation of being hollow and light is the feeling of death, and he needs only to have someone kill him to confirm it. It makes no difference — shovel, hanging, a bullet in the back of the neck. Any of these would make the hollow sensation permanent, and the only thing in the way is the fear of pain. He becomes aware of those around him: David Schrhafta standing in front of him; Izak Teichert, the fanatic, who whispers to anyone who will listen that their job is to help the Germans because this catastrophe is a veiled means of ensuring God's reappearance; Janka Wincenty to his left, an old man who complains daily that today is his last day because he is so tired, yet he has survived one month. Do any of them feel the emptiness?

Then he has a sudden, strange understanding: All of this should not be happening. It is the first time this understanding has worked its way into his perception. The simple fact is that what is happening here is wrong, and should be stopped. Of course he cannot stop it, no one can, but the understanding itself remains valid, in a way pure. He begins to feel his organs once more, resting inside the sleeve of his ribs, viscous, red objects the size of his fist moving against one another, squirting juices from one place to another, storing liquids and solids. There is, after all, no valid justification for one human being hurting another. There is no valid justification for executing Adam Szpilman simply because he jerked Barry's leash. Could it all reduce itself to something so stupidly simple? Yes, absolutely. And with this it occurs to him that revolt is valid. He had only thought of whether or not it was possible, but now he realizes that it is also valid.

Adam pointed to his eye and his temple because he was saying, perhaps ordering, Adam being their group leader in the Blue Kommando, that he, Janusz Siedlecki, should carry on, see, and remember, see and remember, see and remember. In this way Adam might barter for himself something better than the anonymity of mass death that the population of this tiny overpopulated kingdom must endure. All these people have been made to vanish from the earth, the reality of their existence wiped away, but for one thing: the presence of one person to see and remember. And in fact he was ordering Janusz to see Treblinka according to the long view. I order you to survive. I order you to see and remember, and then to survive.

When Joachim Voss went on leave, he carried a large leather suitcase filled with valuables and artifacts and three bottles of liquor, two expensive Czechoslovakian and French brandies and one bottle of schnapps. He was permitted to board a military freight train at Malkinia Station, and rode sitting on a bench staring at the backs of guards posted to keep an eye out for partisans. The train was delayed in part because of a transport bound for Treblinka, and in the cold November air he could hear the moans of the passengers. Although it was midmorning, his body already vibrated with tension, and every cell of his flesh seemed to scream with irritation.

He controlled the strange vibrations of his flesh with long pulls from the schnapps bottle, and then fell into speculating what it would be like with her. He imagined himself and his wife in bed and, superimposed on these images, there materialized images of Ukrainian guards and their brutal passion spent on thirteen- and fourteen-year-old girls. It was difficult to get all that out of his mind, as if the perversity of these images had become part of some involuntary sexual education.

The only thing he had to do before going to join his wife at their assigned place of rest in Poznan was to deliver a package of artifacts to an office in Berlin, which he managed to do in less than twenty-four hours. Then, fatigued with that sensation of seemingly perpetual drunkenness, the recollection of Berlin as dim as if it had been a visit a year ago, he got out of a staff car, pulling the bag out behind him.

The quarters were in a large country estate, a cluster of red-brick barns and a huge, elegant house surrounded by tall evergreens, which he and his wife would share with a high-ranking military officer and his wife. Reality did not have the intensity that it did at Treblinka, and struck him as normal, almost boring, as if he missed what he had come to hate.

Petra was not radiant, as he had hoped she would be. She looked tired, and in her face he read an expression of a kind of sustained fear, and he understood that it was because of the bombing, that the British had been pounding Bremen and Hamburg and the Ruhr. For this reason she had sent their son, Georg, to the High Sauerland to spend this week's leave with Petra's mother. She had heard things, she said. The war in Russia was going badly. This idiocy of squandering so many men to capture a pile of rubble called Stalingrad would cost the Reich. Whom had she heard that from? Well, friends, she said, and an old ghost came up: What man told her this? And what else happened between this man and Petra? But he shrugged it off and sat and listened to her, thinking back to the times when they would visit with friends at various drinking places on the Kurfurstendamm. She had been, at the time he met her, a formidable intellectual, and now he sensed that the liberal convictions of her past had been replaced by a more practical allegiance to the party, which, a few years ago, she would have thought of as preposterous. The same was true in his case — in the thirties the lure of the romantic idiocy of the movement was merely a diversion. But now the diversion had lasted eight years, and his own skepticism had become foggy and distant.

That first day they sat on a broad veranda, drinking coffee served by a Polish woman. The German owners of the estate had donated it for leave use, and it was just remote enough that few were interested in spending their time there. The officer they shared the house with stayed in the other wing of the estate. They met him once, the first day. He was tall, elegant, and had been wounded at the front. Voss was instantly jealous of him, and underwent a hot swoon of self-hatred at the simple truth that the officer was at the front and he was at Treblinka.

Voss understood that her fear of the outcome of the war had changed her, that she had lost some of her seductive Aryan aura. In fact, he looked forward to the coming night with mixed feelings, that, given all that he had seen recently, would so natural an act be possible, or pleasurable? He didn't know.

"You might have to give me a day or so," he told her. "Frankly, I'm exhausted."

"So am I," she said. Then she laughed, peeking at him over the rim of her coffee cup. "Look at us. We're acting like forty."

"Three years away," he said.

The first time they made love Joachim Voss found it easy to overcome his anxiety because he had consumed what he felt was exactly the right amount of alcohol. It worked out reasonably well, but as usual was a little mechanical. In that period of silence afterward, while she slept, he pulled on a pair of walking shorts and sat on the edge of the bed and drank more, and then slid the black leather valise into the light from the little lamp on the bedside table. Inside were a few things that he had kept out for her, an eighteen-karat-gold Agassiz watch with a diamond-studded band, a very old French pendant watch in a beautiful enameled case, and two diamond rings. He had a few other items that he planned to have her take with her and store in the basement of their house, in a well-concealed safe in the wall. There he had a number of other things he had gleaned from his work with the *Einsatzgruppen*.

Sitting there, he underwent another terrible swoon of nauseating heat throughout his body, and despite the cool air, found himself sweating. He sensed that he was at that point where alcohol would no longer help, that the raging irritation in his flesh was somehow chronic and that he had upset his own chemical balance so much that only a radical cure would work. Then he knew that he would tell her, tell everything that he had seen and done at Treblinka, and he knew that he would not be able to resist. He pulled the blanket back, and in the dim light of the table lamp looked down at her breasts, belly, and at the innocent repose of her sleep. Amid everything she remained clean, and he imagined the cleanliness and health of her flesh, of each individual organ and membrane, each fluid that ran through the various conduits of her body. To have sent himself into her seemed to him its own cleansing. She moved, then opened her eyes and smiled at him.

"Oh my," she said, "you want more."

He laughed. "But first I want to describe something."

"Well, go ahead." She sat up.

"This is technically treason," he said, "since we're sworn to the utmost secrecy, but I will tell you nevertheless."

She got a look on her face, a kind of knowing introspection. Of course she knew bits of what he had done before. Given her education, her former enlightened liberalism, he felt more or less like a thief telling his story to a priest.

Twice as he went through his description he paused to say that he was not deliberately trying to shock her. He told her about the gas chambers, about the transports and the railway cars full of people who died of thirst or asphyxiation, about the rapes of children, about Bielas and his little boys, about the deputy commandant and his dog trained to bite men's genitals, about executions of workers, about how yellow the bodies were, about the dentists and the gold sorters and the clothes sorters and the Ukrainian guards and about Weyrauch the homosexual and about the smell and all of it. He tried to be detailed, careful not to exaggerate or to understate, fair to all concerned, including himself, a man assigned only to oversee and check on the recovery of valuables, a man married and more fit for and interested in the front, a man secretly convinced that there were perverse forces at work responsible for his ending up there, forces he wished he had the time to investigate, because he did not belong standing next to a homosexual looking at mounds of baby clothes. After he was finished they sat in silence while she thought over what she had been told. Then he said, "There, you have it all, I believe."

"There have been rumors," she said.

There was another period of silence. He did not want to show her the baubles yet. It seemed to him crass.

"It is your job," she said. "Your — contribution?" Then she said, "Let me have a sip of that please." He handed her the little glass of French brandy. She took a sip, and said, "My, that is good."

"I got it at Treblinka."

"It is good nevertheless," she said. Then she sat up straighter, and pulled the blanket up around her shoulders.

He savored the sensation of what it meant to confess to someone so pure, so in possession of rationality, and sat there as if waiting to receive a welcome blow to the face.

"Why is it up to you to make any analysis of it anyway?"

"It is hard not to."

She shifted again, then turned to the small lamp on the night table next to her side of the bed. As she did so, he watched her back twist, so that the long muscles up along the spine bulged seductively, but then her nakedness reminded him of the women in the tube, or the Undressing Barracks.

"I saw you looking at that — that *Sturmbannfuhrer* so-and-so," she said. "You were jealous."

He flushed. "No, I —"

"Yes you were, because he was at the front. He's even wounded. That's so romantic." She paused, thinking, the blanket just up over her breasts. Then she said, "What is this 'front' anyway? I hear about it all the time. The front."

"It is the —"

"You are at the front," she said. She took on a haughty posture, as if talking down to him. "The front line of this is what you do. The rest is only a game. This is simply the elimination of a Judeo-Marxist plutocracy."

He felt himself swoon again, felt his body sinking with a sensation of a strange, melancholy gratitude, along with an understanding of just how absurd this conversation had become.

"It is what it means to think heroically," she said. She looked toward the floor on his side of the bed. "What did you bring me?"

The combination of statements turned his brain inside out. He nearly vomited there on the bed. *It is what it means to think heroically — what did you bring me?* He poured himself more brandy and drank it in one gulp. She giggled and said, "That's the way."

"Well, let me see," he said. He reached into the valise, felt the sack of gold coins, then a small box. He took the box out, and gave it to her.

Squinting in the dim, yellow light, she studied the watch. "It's beautiful," she whispered.

"I brought it for you. It's an Agassiz — eighteen jewels, eighteen-karat gold. The diamonds are, by the way, real."

"What is it worth?"

"In gold and diamonds, a good deal. As an object, more."

"What else do you have?"

The studious, objective assessment he made for each object, the two of them squinting in the dim light, made him think of that painting of the pawnbroker and his wife studying objects laid out on a medieval table. Heads together, they whispered values, countries of origin, quality. When he removed the last sack from the valise and handed it to her, she gasped at its weight, and then opened it.

"They're American twenty-dollar gold pieces," he said. "That is at least a kilogram or more." She held one to the light, and Voss found himself mesmerized by the rich depth of the color, the way it reflected orange light on her face, making her squint when it hit her eyes. "Those were designed by Augustus Saint-Gaudens. Note that the eagle has a — a voluptuous look, with its two curved wings arched over its body. They're considered among the most beautiful of coins, and, of course, are more valuable than their weight in gold."

She nodded slowly. "And this goes to the basement?" He nodded, and she said, "Good — so far as I am concerned you're entitled to it. How do we know what life would have been like for us were it not for them? You're entitled." She let the blanket fall and pulled him toward her. "Fuck me," she said. He proceeded with a kind of numb confusion — he pulled the cover back, removed the walking shorts, and positioned himself, not sure if he could do this. Then he recalled with a sudden uncomfortable wave of heat that each day he was here he was not at Treblinka, he was not watching as valuables were deposited by the people, not watching as, hidden in their bodies, the valuables were forever lost in the burial pits. But the warmth of Petra's body brought him out of his confusion, and he entered her. This time she clamped around him like a hot crab, and he found a strong, muscular rhythm that threw her further away from the almost sedate self-control that had at times irritated him. He watched, wide-eyed and amazed, as she surged and twisted and made noises that startled him. He was sure that in the moist silence of the cool Polish night the wounded *Sturmbannfuhrer* and his wife could easily hear them.

NEAR WOLGA-OKNAGLIK, POLAND
AUGUST 2, 1943

As she walks parallel to the dirt road, Magda
Nowak feels pains less intense than before, she thinks because
she has become used to them. It has now been nearly an hour
since she left the burning camp, and the smoke has dispersed
into the sky so that the entire southern horizon is made gray by
it. The sun has descended and become a hot orange color,
bleaching the blue haze into a whitish glare all along the treetops in the distance.

Her progress has been slow because she has had to stop to
fold herself around the pain, and walking, she has heard swish-
ings, strange sounds in the brush all around her, as if those making the noises have been moving with her like secret shadows.
And then, close by, there were the sudden multiple popping

sounds of gunfire, so close that she tensed, thinking the bullets were coming at her. The woods were crawling with escaped Jews who would kill her, she imagined, and now they were crawling with Germans and Ukrainians and Lithuanians chasing the Jews. When she became as fatigued with her fear as with the pain she stopped thinking about them, and walked, from time to time moving closer to the road to see if crossing it would be safe, but each time she saw either a car or a truck going past, raising thick clouds of swirling dust that then settled back on the road in the windless heat. And when the area around her was silent, there were the distant, dreamlike echoes of gunshots reaching her through the boiling haze.

Finally she senses that whatever energy she had left has been sapped out of her, and she fears most of all falling down in a faint, because she is sure she will not get up. If she is found by Germans or Jews she will be shot, even if she is having her baby. She walks, feeling empty of will, her limbs ticklish and weak, as if she has become a demented marionette.

She sits down to rest and wait for the next cramp. In the few moments of rest she closes her eyes and thinks that she dreams, floating in a blue nothingness, and then voices enter it, coming from farther in the brush. Polish voices, in fact sounding very much like village boys. Michal perhaps.

"Look in his shoes!" someone whispers harshly. She hears rustling in the weeds.

"Nothing. One's all bloody."

She stands up to look. It is Michal, and another boy from Wolga-Oknaglik, looking down, Michal wiping his hand on his pant leg. Michal was once, after all, her boyfriend, and she let him do what he wanted. But that was before Anatoly, and since then he has had nothing to say to her.

Michal sees her. "What are you doing here?"

"What about the Germans?" she says.

"They stay by the road. Where's your bull?"

She feels the beginning of another cramp, and tries to hide it. "I don't know."

"See what you get for bending over for him?" Michal says. His friend laughs, seeming embarrassed by Michal's crudeness. Michal raises his rifle and points it at her. "I should kill you now," he says, and then lowers it. "But then in a while we can get you another way — a bunch of us'll take turns and you'll forget your bull."

"I need help," she says. "I need to go home." She sees other men farther in the brush. "Who are they?"

"My father and a Navy Blue."

"A what?"

"Police," he says. "We're on a Jew hunt. If we do well they might hire us. Think of that. Maybe I'll get to work in the camp." He nudges his friend. "I'd be able to take what I want and kill for fun. Imagine." He looks at Magda, then down at her stomach. "If I get in there I'll have you brought in. We'll deal with your little Ukrainian."

The cramp builds, and she finds it difficult to conceal it. She can see in Michal's eyes that he understands. He laughs and turns to his friend.

"A bad case of gas," he says. His friend laughs and shakes his head, then shrugs amiably, looking at Magda.

"Can you help?"

Michal looks over his shoulder toward the other men. "No, get your dish-eared bull to help. We're on a hunt. As soon as we saw the smoke we figured it out, even before the Germans brought reinforcements from the penal camp down the road. They say hundreds of them escaped, all with their pockets full. My father got a gold watch and money." He looks down. "Nothing from this fellow, though." He looks at her once again. "Go home, have your Ukrainian ferret and don't bother us."

He and his friend walk into the brush. Once he is gone the distraction of all this talk is gone and the pain settles down over her, and she must bend over and hold her belly, until she feels the pain begin to recede, and the ticklish numbness leaks into her limbs. She must cross the road. She takes three steps and sees the dead man, the same man she saw before with the shattered leg. He lies faceup, flies hovering around the wound and around his face. Michal has set his shoes on his chest.

She turns and walks around him, toward the road. The orange sun begins to sink into the haze, and she shudders, thinking that being out here alone, in the darkness, would be more horrible than anything, even the pain, which has become so wearying and so familiar that she waits for it with no more than dull acceptance, as she imagines a cow might wait.

Then she gasps with a strange shock. That was a dead man — it was as if she had been dreaming. Even if she did get home what difference would it make? They would take her to the camp as Michal said. And Anatoly had told her about all that, the day he came out to stay, carrying a bag of clothes. He spoke in slow, awkward Polish. They brought the Jews of Warsaw in and took some of them around to a huge fire. They taunted them, called them cowards because they would not jump in. Schneck took a woman's baby and threw it into the fire and then invited her to jump in after. Then Anatoly opened the bag and showed her Ostrich-skin boots, and a velvet smoking jacket he said came from Bulgaria.

The next cramp begins, and she walks slowly to a birch sapling to hold on to, thinking, foolish little baby, if you only knew, you would stay in there. Michal will throw you in a fire. She giggles, thinking of Anatoly in his jacket. It was too small for him. As the cramp builds, the horror she felt moments ago begins to slide away, and she studies the gray and white bark of the sapling, the little horizontal dots and dashes against the pale background looking like some secret written language.

David Schrhafta makes his way through the darkness of the barracks toward the corner where Janusz Siedlecki sleeps, walking slowly so as not to disturb the other men. A number of them have come down with a disease, and they fear that it may be typhoid. A sick man finds it harder to keep a secret.

But now the men are sick for a second reason. Captain Bloch, the military expert in the planning group, has been sent to work in the Death Camp on the other side of the gas chambers, and they will not see him again. The officer Kuttner, second in command under Franz and nicknamed "Kiwe" by the workers, suspected something and used the excuse of some missing clothes to have him transferred beyond the wire, and now the revolt is a body without a heart, and a body without a heart dies. He saw the other planners after Bloch left — one of them, another Czech, was lying in his bunk crying. It is a blow, he thinks, but we must not show our pessimism — it is the doorway to death. Kuttner didn't simply shoot Bloch because, after Franz's pact with the workers, officers needed excuses to do what they pleased, and the best excuse these days is typhoid. Besides that, the men respect Bloch, and the Germans do not want revolt, they want order. It would be a blight on their reputation, just as Bielas's death was.

Some of the men are already stirring, waking themselves up, because lately there have been very few transports, and they fear what the Germans might be up to. The whisper of liquidation has floated through the air. Those who are sick must look healthy before morning roll call.

Janusz is sitting up, wrapped in a blanket. In the dim dawn light peeking through the high windows, David can see that the boy's face has the vacant stare of someone sick.

He catches Janusz's attention by hissing softly.

"I can't hear that well."

He moves closer. "Are you sick?"

"I don't know. I don't feel good."

The light coming in through the windows has become stronger, and now the sick begin to moan, to cough, to curse their conditions. Kuttner will show up sometime today to taunt them, and select a few to go get their "treatment" at the Hospital.

"Janusz, about your giving the money to Dr. Herzenberg," he says carefully, watching the boy's face to see if he hears, "it is more important that you keep it a secret. There're always new men, and they're always tempted —"

"I know one of them. I saw him come in. In fact he's right over there with Dr. Herzenberg." They see him leaning toward Herzenberg, speaking earnestly, gesturing with his hands. His name is Julian Sussmann, and he is from Austria.

"If he squeals, we don't want much to squeal about."

[116]

Then Dr. Herzenberg approaches. "I already explained it," David says to him.

Dr. Herzenberg bends closer to Janusz. "How do you feel?" he asks. Julian Sussmann joins them. David studies his handsome profile, trying to assess the look of concern on his face.

"I can't hear," Janusz says. "I feel weak. I think it is typhoid."

"I don't have any instruments," Dr. Herzenberg says. "I want you to eat as much as you can, and try to outlast this."

"What about Kuttner?" Janusz asks. "Kiwe."

"Kiwe is chance," David says. "Kiwe is the flip of the coin. Either he gets you or he doesn't."

"If I get you that medicine," Julian says to Dr. Herzenberg, "should I leave it somewhere, or just give it to you?"

"Slide it under my bunk mattress."

"Galewski is sick," Julian says.

"I know." Julian nods, and goes away.

"He knows a lot," David says. "Why is that? Do you see him with Chaskel and Blau and the other kitchen workers? They're Austrians too, like The Doll. It's strange how he has access to things — medicine, food." He watches Julian leave the barracks. "He found everything out right away."

"He is anxious," Dr. Herzenberg says, "as we all are. No one wants to die before the revolt. Besides, he can be useful to us." Dr. Herzenberg thinks a moment, then says, "In December the Russians captured fifty thousand Germans near Stalingrad. Things are going badly for them. It affects us." He squints at the dim windows. "More than ever now we've got to hold on and help each other. With Bloch gone down there," and he looks in the direction of the Death Camp, "we're all made weak." Then he says, "Janusz, I want you to visualize something — imagine that you are healthy. When you walk, imagine that you are strong and that your stomach is full."

"All right."

"Are you hungry?"

Janusz thinks a moment, and smiles. "Not at all," he says. "How do you feel?"

"I feel — whole. That is how I feel. Full and whole."

Dr. Herzenberg nods, and then walks away. As he watches Janusz pull his boots on, David recalls wondering at first, back in July when he had finally absorbed the shock of Treblinka, if allying himself with the camp staff might be the only way to survive here, because the kapos and more fortunate inmates had access to personal effects, and in the strange supply-and-demand economy of Treblinka, they wielded power nearly equal to the guards, who would do almost anything for money. But he sided with the forked sticks and the hopeless revolt. Back then it was hands covered with pinesap and water prayed for a whole day. Now it is the clean metallic smell of snow and the biting cold of it on his hands, and he wonders, even now, why he is still alive.

Janusz Siedlecki folds his blanket and stuffs it under the thin mattress made of clothes, and rises from his low, creaky bunk. He hears muffled sounds, sees the light coming flat and cold through the small windows. It is to be another day of cold weather, with the thin swirls of snow falling and moving in the breeze on the railway siding like wisps of steam. The pounding rush in his head is paced by a pulse, so that he feels his flesh flex with powerful, quick engorgements of pressure. Every joint in his body feels bruised, and he must practice normal movement for the moment the bullnecked figure of Kiwe comes in to select prisoners to be shot at the Hospital. *Full and whole.* Yesterday Kiwe took old Wincenty Turkow away, because besides being old and tired, Janka had become sick. He smiled with wan indifference as Kiwe led him away.

Some of the men stamp their feet into their boots and raise puffs of heavy dust that turn up into the light. Waclaw Gitzer sits up quickly, and looks around, seemingly dazed. Janusz worms his hand under his mattress and feels candy pieces that he has hidden there, each wrapped in a small square of oily paper, and draws out a small handful. Then he moves to Waclaw and touches him on the shoulder. "Here," he says, "take some of these."

"What about you?"

"I feel fine," he says. "You need it. You need to move around, straighten yourself up. I mean your clothes."

"Yes," Waclaw says, and then squints at Janusz. "You have some whiskers on your chin. Do you want to borrow my razor? It's American."

"Maybe next year."

Janusz then looks past Waclaw Gitzer's bunk at David Schrhafta's form hunched over the struggling with his boots. He puts one of the pieces of candy in his mouth. The sudden powerful sweetness sends a sustained shock of luscious pain throughout his jaw. He counts out five pieces of the candy, and makes his way to David's bunk. "Here," he says.

"I'm fine," David says. "You should keep that."

"Are you sure?"

"Janusz," he says, "do you see anyone throwing food around the way you do? One man is one man, but we would prefer not to lose you. Didn't Dr. Herzenberg just tell you to eat?"

Janusz looks down at the candy in his hand. "Well, here, take two," he says, and drops the candy pieces on the bunk. Then he returns to his own, and puts the remaining candy away.

Since the arrival of Julian Sussmann he knew that his time alive was limited and growing shorter, but he tried to ignore it, and like the rest of the men, he stood before the boxcar doors day after day as the weather grew colder, and pulled the suit-cases and bundles and boxes to the side while wide-eyed and fearful, or composed and almost condescending — You! Be careful! That microscope is an expensive piece of machinery — they came down to the platform. He stole, and gave the loot to Dr. Herzenberg. Janusz's attitude was influenced by his gradual recession into deafness, into that muffled roaring that insulated him from most sound. If he was to die there was nothing he could do. If Julian Sussmann would somehow be responsible for his death then so be it — it rested in his mind like the apprehension he would feel having to go to visit a doctor. For the moment he is safe because Julian Sussmann works in the tailor shop. He told Waclaw about it: "We have the same initials, don't you see?" and Waclaw said, "That is nonsense. Pick something more tangible to be afraid of."

The advice didn't help. There was no longer any Adam Szpilman to tell him what to do, or what to think. There was Dr. Herzenberg, but most of the time he was assigned elsewhere in the camp. Waclaw Gitzer and David Schrhafta were like brothers to him, and at times Janusz felt that it was his responsibility to make sure that they got enough to eat. The fatigue and cold and hunger had beaten them down. At times he would forget why they were important to him, and then think, so I will not be alone. You must not be alone here. His own superstitions, however sure of them he was, were trivial.

He does not know how many, or if there will be transports today, but feels the bitter cold, so cold that those who step off the trains will steam, having been jammed so closely together that they have been sweating. The cold seeps into his clothes, and he must spend the day resisting it, so that by sundown his muscles will ache from being tensed all day. The situation remains tolerable as long as there is food to be grabbed during the unloading and cleaning, and he is not ordered to do anything but his job.

Only occasionally he blunders into seeing beyond his railway cars and his friends David and Waclaw. A few days ago he was ordered by Kapo Galewski to run to the tube to pick up two suitcases that were waiting, and he walked in upon a picture he had heard about but never seen — naked women and children crowded in the evergreen lane. The guards were beating them because they cried. They cried because it was so cold. One boy shrieked like a siren in a nightmare. His feet had fused to the ice in the tube, and when he tried to walk he tore a thick layer of skin off one foot and pulled up a crusty slab of ice with the other. Irritated by his screaming, the officer they call Sepp shattered his skull with an iron rod. Confused inside the roaring in his ears, and convinced for a brief moment that the boy was his brother, Janusz yelled "Zygmunt!" and heard his own voice as a call from somewhere on the other side of the evergreen wall. But Zygmunt had been dead a long time. It took him three or four seconds to fix that in his mind. The boy's misshapen head steamed in the cold air, and the lower part of his body twitched. Janusz was so shaken carrying the suitcases back to the Sorting Square that he had no breath, and he realized as he walked that an officer was watching him with a skeptical smirk, as if perhaps this weakling needed a bullet in the back of the neck.

The transport is from the east. The workers have on their faces the expressions of blank disappointment, because those from the east come in rags and carry little or no food. They come with their heads bowed in seedy fatalism, some with long beards and sidelocks, bobbing, repeating the Mourner's Kaddish in anticipation of their own deaths. They accept their deaths, so there is no need for subterfuge. The shabbiness of the people's clothes signals vermin, and Janusz pulls into himself, feeling a shaky revulsion at the thought of having to go inside the boxcars and clean their filth and remove their dead.

Now the officers named Voss and Schneck stand before the line of cars, watching the people getting out. Waclaw and David approach the boxcar, and Janusz follows them, the frigid air making him tense and wooden in his movement.

One older man wearing a black overcoat and carrying two strange-looking valises moves along the cars. Jacob Mandel, a Blue Kommando worker Janusz knows, walks up behind the man and grabs one of the valises, but the man spins around, and then pulls back at the valise's handle, so that the flat, box-like case loses its shape. From the partly open crack there appears a colorful shower of confetti, which swirls, and then settles on the thin layer of snow on the station platform. As the two struggle, more of the confetti comes out, and moves slowly in the icy breeze, so that the man and Jacob Mandel step on the pieces of paper, gluing them to their shoes.

Then Voss leans down, looks at the confetti, and throws his hands to the sides of his head, making Schneck tip his head in curiosity. The confetti is now spreading out, dancing on the snow. One piece lands near Janusz's feet, a blue postage stamp, the profile of an English queen, he believes.

Red-faced and grunting, Voss struggles at the belt of his tunic. He brings out a small automatic pistol, fumbles with it, and then drops it on the concrete, then steps with a kind of jerky indecision toward the man carrying the valises. The man continues walking away, his face ashen, the vapor of his breath coming in short bursts. Voss then turns, apparently confused, and picks up the pistol and looks at it, then at all the postage stamps. He holsters the pistol and looks back toward Schneck, who watches with a bland expression on his face. Behind him stands The Doll, his face crossed with an inquisitive perplexity.

The man with valises pauses, unable to decide what to do next. The damaged valise flops open, sending booklets, envelopes, and more of the stamps into the gentle, icy breeze.

"Halt!" Voss yells. "Halt!" The man stands absolutely still. "You!" Voss says to Janusz. "Don't move!"

The Doll has now walked off toward the people crowding into the Undressing Barracks, all of them hunched from the cold. Voss tiptoes toward the man, avoiding the stamps. The man with the valises gazes off at the two silver lines of railroad tracks, the open valise by his side still producing pieces of paper, whole pages of stamps, little black books, a magnifying glass.

The wind has died down, and Voss appears calm, holds both hands up to Janusz as if to say, stay where you are. Then he continues to tiptoe toward the man with the valises. Schneck walks around the area where the stamps lie on the snow, careful not to step on any of them.

The man puts down the two valises and turns to Voss and Schneck, who continue their careful walk toward him. When they reach the man, Schneck draws a pistol, and smiling amiably he shoots the man in the face, making Voss flinch and stumble back. The man falls backward standing straight, so that his head hits the platform with a pop that Janusz feels through the soles of his boots.

Janusz has become stupid with the cold — having to stand still for three or four minutes now, his body has gone numb, and his perception has pulled into itself, so that everything seems like some bright dream. But Schneck frightens him, because during the shooting of the man, he showed no anticipation, no tensing of his face, as if he were pausing with no more thought than that required for shaking a little salt on a boiled egg before eating it.

Voss signals Janusz to come, and then points to the lip of concrete next to the railway car. Janusz tiptoes along the lip, careful of the stamps that lie near it. He passes Jacob Mandel, who stands at attention, watching. When he gets to the two officers, Voss holds something out to him. Tweezers. Janusz stares down at them, dizzy with confusion.

"Pick them up," Voss says in German, carefully pronouncing each word. "Each one, by the side, carefully, and put them in this." He holds the top of a flat box out to him. Janusz takes the box, and then stoops down to pick up the first stamp. When he tries to pick it up, his hands tremble badly. He becomes aware of Schneck's boots right there in front of him.

He concentrates on the stamp, this one a dull picture of a ship with tiny printing around the margins, and moves the tweezers toward it. Then his dizziness increases so that he feels a sweeping sensation as his body topples forward.

He feels himself being lifted, and the roaring in his head blocks out all other sound. When he is standing, he stares at Schneck, waiting to be shot. But Schneck looks at him with a vague sympathy, and turns back to Voss.

Voss holds another pair of tweezers out to Waclaw, who begins picking stamps up, working his way toward Janusz. When he is close, he whispers, "How do you feel?"

"Fine. I thought he was going to kill me."

"He helped you up."

"But he saw me. For him I am no longer nondescript."

Voss searches the dead man's clothes, and then calls Anatoly over to help. Janusz and Waclaw begin picking up stamps by the railway car, working their way along the concrete lip of the siding.

"What is Schneck's first name?" Janusz asks.

"I don't know."

"It begins with a J," Janusz whispers.

The collector had torn out sections of a catalogue written in English. Joachim Voss knows little English, but enough to trace the stamps in terms of their number, color, size, perforation count, and therefore value in American dollars. The collection is an extraordinary find, he estimates worth enough to let him live comfortably for the rest of his life.

He has requested from the commandant the use of the guest room, and sits in a pool of yellow light at a small desk squinting at the stamps until his eyes and head constrict with a kind of agonizing protest. It is after midnight, and the air is dry and chilly. Each time he is ready to rest, he finds another: number A16, black, portrait of Washington, unused block of four, nine-hundred dollars. How can it be that a tiny piece of paper, with "twelve cents" engraved under the stern portrait, is worth that much? Gold of that value would be indeed difficult to carry. But stamps can be easily hidden, and fortunately, none of the idiots here seem to know or care about what a find this collection is. Then the mortification at the idea that he had made a fool of himself in front of The Doll, Schneck, even the prisoners, washes over him like a fever. He dropped his gun. He could not even blame it on being drunk. He chuckles in miserable embarrassment. This can never be lived down, and nothing compares with the shame of having shown himself unable to properly operate a pistol or control his hysteria. His hysteria was prissy and childish, and they all saw it.

He gets up and goes to the night table by the bunk, where he has placed the schnapps bottle, away from the stamps so that spilling on them would be impossible. He takes a small gulp from the bottle, and looks out the window at the ash-gray space between the barracks and the railroad tracks.

After the fiasco was over he more or less apologized to Schneck: "Now that was a bit of an error on my part. I just got too excited and —" By that time the workers had picked up the last stamps, and that idiot Anatoly, having been ordered by Voss to help, had handed him a fistful of stamps glued together from the heat of his hand. But he supposed that someone from the Ukraine with the blank, flat look of an imbecile and those absolutely comical ears could not be expected to know anything about stamps, or be able to properly execute an order. As for the apology, Schneck simply smiled at him as if to say, why would you even mention it?

But then he wondered about the man to whom he was apologizing. Voss had never been that close to a shooting before, and he had seen Schneck's face just as he raised the pistol and then watched the man fall backward, the head having snapped from the impact of the bullet. Voss himself felt a sudden shock, and stumbled back a little, and at the same time saw Schneck's face, its absolute, amiable composure. He found himself thinking: What kind of a man can do that without even tensing his jaw?

In his work with the *Einsatzgruppen* he had observed shootings, but from a distance, and found himself tensing and then feeling a kind of rubber-legged weakness as the bodies flopped into ditches, a kind of neutralizing feeling. He saw it in the faces of the soldiers who did the shooting — they would be shaky and washed out, and in the lull after it was over they would smile at each other with a strange, wistful fatigue. Schneck, on the other hand, had apparently bypassed all that. The composure on his face was both horrible and fascinating.

Sitting at the table, Voss places the next stamp in the pool of light, lining it up with others of a set. Then he reaches for his pistol, which is cold, and places it on the table. It sits above a portrait of an old American president. The contrast is strange — paper and steel. He experiences a little stab of nervous satisfaction at the sight of the stamps arranged in a block.

The snow crunches under his boots with a glassy squeaking sound, and the workers of the *Tarnungskommando* stumble along in front of him, pulling a wood cart. The two wheels of the cart crunch in the snow, which becomes thinner on the ground when they reach the first pine trees. Anatoly Yovenko is afraid he will not be able to find the spot where he buried the other things, a rotted stump of a birch tree under which he burrowed a little cave. Snow alters the shape of things, and he is afraid that it might mysteriously alter whatever there is about the area that makes it recognizable to him. In his back pocket he carries a little wad of those stamps Voss made him pick up. Without wondering at all about value, he slid some with pictures of ships, groups of men, the larger ones with the higher numbers, into his pocket while Voss was distracted, and now he had carried them for two days because he has had no opportunity to go to the birch stump. He also carries a small automatic pistol and a box of cartridges, for Janusz, his main source of loot. He was afraid that the source would dry up if he did not give him something.

But there are no more transports, and he has little to give her. She will be waiting, hunched inside a heavy shawl, just beyond the area where they will gather wood. They will go to the little cattle shelter and he will give her a tiny wristwatch Janusz gave him days ago, for nothing particular, he said, but perhaps they could talk about other deals later. The transports from the east brought almost nothing, and the last transport was three days ago. And now that the men are sick, he begins to fear that one of them, Janusz perhaps, will squeal on him.

Vlodya pauses while the forked sticks march toward the work area, and makes his way back toward Anatoly. "Going to see your girl?" he asks. "You're crazy."

"You have no girls," Anatoly says. "I have one still."

"Well, I can get a village girl," Vlodya says. "Maybe I'll get yours."

"No."

Vlodya laughs, and turns back toward the work area.

Anatoly walks over the untouched snow in the direction of the shelter. The snow has a dry, metallic smell, and is perfect and clean, almost bluish in its purity.

When he reaches the shelter he knows before entering it that she is not there. The snow around it is unbroken. He looks inside, and smells the cold, dusty air. Perhaps she is no longer patient enough, that the one time they were able to do it he lasted only a few seconds and then tried to apologize to her. She shook her head — her expression told him that it was all right, that she didn't care. But she is not here. He turns and walks back toward the work area, thinking again of the birch stump and the loot he has stored there. He has made sure that the work area is far away from it, and decides not to make his way to the stump because he will leave tracks that would draw anyone, even the peasants, to the stump. If she will no longer come to see him, he wonders what the use is to have the watches and jewelry and coins. And now these stamps — what does he do with those? He stops, looking down at the snow, and has a strange impulse to stay where he is, that the bluish purity of the snow is something he might be able to somehow melt into, locking him into some eternal sleep. The strange, empty feeling is almost pleasant, as if the death they all fear is not a thing with pain, or with a tone, or a meaning — it is no more than an eternal nothing, no more than a welcome relief from a lifetime of sweeping fatigue, a sweet, bluish twilight.

OUTSIDE THE PERIMETER FENCE, TREBLINKA

FEBRUARY 1943

Anatoly has gone away again, and Vlodya sits on a stump watching them, from time to time taking sips of vodka from a flask he carries in his trousers pocket. Janusz Siedlecki carries large pieces of wood from the work area to the sled, fighting his way through the snow that has a crust on top. When he walks to the wood, blowing warm breath into his feeble, almost useless woolen gloves, he walks on the crust, but when he walks back carrying wood, he breaks through it with each step. The high-necked sweater he wears has a frozen block of spittle and condensed breath vapor surrounded by a smelly wet patch that bobs there against the top of his chest with the rhythm of his walking. He remains warm as long as he works, but he has eaten only a bowl of cold potato soup and a piece of bread, and his stomach cramps around a foul, gaseous vacuum.

With each trip to the sled he passes the remains of a stone fence in which he stored the pistol and cartridges Anatoly gave him weeks ago. Because they worked with another crew he could not take it back into the camp. Today he works with David Schrhafta, and will take the gun in, and every time he thinks of it his heart thumps with a morbid fright.

Through the bright slits of his vision he sees David struggling through the snow with a piece of rotted log on his shoulder. When they unload their wood they will talk. Janusz's hearing has solidified, almost as if the weather has frozen it, so that he hears speech, gunshots, the chopping sounds of the men of the other crew working in the deeper woods, as if he is inside a wooden box. The voices come through to him flat and distant and pitched wrong. His own voice is deep and resonant, and vibrates every bone in his skull, making the insides of his ears tickle.

When he and David talk, they speculate about new, strange things going on in the camp, and about what became of Waclaw Gitzer. After roll call one morning he simply disappeared, and Janusz waited for the flat, distant sound of a shot, but there was no shot. Kiwe was not around, was probably in the barracks drunk and keeping warm with the rest of them, all of whom seemed to keep their distance from the workers for fear of catching whatever they had, whatever was killing three or four men a day. Janusz slept like the dead and then just at dawn had strange dreams, where spiders rolled people up into cocoons, where the Germans were teachers and the workers were the pupils in a friendly, jovial Latin class that would break into song every few minutes, where corpses were thrown into the back doors of the gas chambers and came filing out, smiling and chatting, into the pine-bough-lined tube. The illness reduced the workers to stumbling zombies during the day, but in the clean, sweet-smelling woods, they could continue to stumble because the Ukrainians were not interested in hurting them. Like Anatoly, who left them to themselves every day, they wanted to drink or to barter with the peasants for vodka or *slivovitz* or girls. So they stumbled, carrying their wood, and Janusz worried about what became of Waclaw. He felt that Waclaw was still alive because he thought that with his deafness he could feel his presence, either a smell or a sensation or a tiny radio wave coming from somewhere. One day they saw a group of men, black forms against the snow, struggling along with a railroad track on their shoulders, and Janusz said to David, "One of them is Waclaw. It's the third one back. Look."

"How can you tell from here?" David asked. "They're nothing but specks."

"He is the third one." He was sure of it, could see the legs struggling under the body, snow exploding off the boots.

"He's in the Hospital pit," David said. "They shot him."

"No."

"You gave him your food and made yourself sick, and now he's dead. I admire what you do, but it makes no sense."

"I'm better now."

Janusz breaks through the crust on the snow, jerks his boot out, breaks the crust of the snow, his hands inside his threadbare woolen gloves becoming numb clutching the long piece of wood. They cannot move the sled closer to the wood because the rails will break through the crust. When he reaches the stone fence, he looks around once, and then pulls the cold rocks aside to reveal the pistol and the box of cartridges. He puts them in his coat pocket, thinking that they will be warmed up when it comes time to put them in his underpants.

When he reaches the sled he throws the wood on the pile, and blows into the fabric of his gloves. Because Vlodya is facing in the other direction, they can rest.

"What do the rails mean?" David asks.

"I haven't seen any in the camp. It means they are for the Death Camp. Listen, I am taking the gun in today."

"What would they want with rails?"

"Maybe that's where Waclaw is, the Death Camp."

"No one leaves the Death Camp," David says, looking at his jacket. "I can see the lumps. You'll be caught."

"But then, why would they put him in the Death Camp when there are no transports? Are they going to kill us all because there are no transports?"

"That could be it," David says. "A few at a time." He looks at Vlodya, who is eating bread. He pauses and looks at them, and they begin walking back toward the wood. Vlodya whistles at them to stop. Then he stands up from his stump and slides his rifle off his shoulder, and puts his cheek against the stock, and aims. Janusz holds his breath and faces Vlodya, as if to present a better target. David stumbles toward the sled, then stands at a sort of trembling attention. Vlodya aims, says, *"Pfuh! Pfuh!"* and then laughs.

He motions them over to him. When they reach him, he tosses his chunk of bread to David, who catches it and then holds it in his dirty glove, staring at it with his mouth open. Vlodya reaches into his coat pocket and pulls out another piece of bread and gives it to Janusz, who whispers, "Thank you."

"Rest," Vlodya says. Then he puts his finger to his lips and says, "Tcht, tcht, tcht," and motions them back to the sled.

Working his way back to the sled, Janusz bites into the chunk of bread and feels the beautiful pain sting his jaws.

"Why did he do that?" David asks.

"He doesn't hate us," Janusz says. "He's miserable because there are no girls to rape. It has made him generous."

"How will you get the gun in?"

"In my undershorts."

David laughs, and then chews thoughtfully. Then he says, "And what is the clanking sound we hear?"

It is a constant banging and then growling Janusz feels in the ground. Apparently they are building something in the Death Camp. "Since there are no transports, they are building something up there. Maybe they're making more pits."

"Since there are no transports, they do improvements."

"Like all the painting and prettying up around the station square." It is true — The Doll has set men to work doing all sorts of harmless-looking projects, as if he is trying to make Treblinka into a pretty little village of some sort, with buildings that have their trimming painted, gravel in the walkways, rocks arranged so that the place is beginning to take on the appearance of a spa. "Like the Shit Master."

"Yes," David says. The Doll had posted a guard at the latrine, an older man who stands at the doorway with an alarm clock hanging from his neck. The Shit Master's function is to time those who use the latrines. The officers continually harass him with jovial insults: "Honorable Shit Master, how goes your shit today?" "This place would fall apart, sir, if we did not have someone to watch over the shit."

Janusz stands behind the sled, and then pulls the gun from his pocket and slides it in the front of his pants, gasping from the cold steel on his skin. When it is nestled down next to his genitals, he waits, his fists clenched, until it warms up a little. Then he puts the box in, and settles it next to the gun, so that it bangs there. He tries taking a step, and the gun and box pinch his scrotum. He looks down at himself. He appears so overly endowed that he might be a cartoon. His coat does not cover it.

"Anyone can see it," David says. "Any fool can tell."

"I am nondescript."

"Not any more," David says. "Leave it here until you get another coat. Or let me carry it."

"I'll be all right. But it's a load. I got pinched."

"Leave it here."

"I'll be all right, as long as it doesn't go off."

"Put it in your pocket."

"They search pockets," Janusz says. "When was the last time you saw them grab a man's crotch?"

"When Max was alive."

In the distance Janusz sees the tall form of Anatoly coming through the pines.

"Anatoly's girl is pretty," David says.

"I dream all the time," Janusz says, "and I dreamed that Waclaw was alive. A huge spider rolled me up in a kind of cocoon and then stung me in the side, and while he was carrying me to a pile of other cocoons, I saw him sitting on a chair looking up through a telescope."

"Janusz, your fever makes you insane."

"I know he's alive. I know it," he says. "I don't feel the lack of him yet."

"It's time to go," David says, looking once again at the huge lump made by the gun and the cartridge box.

"It's a seven-millimeter," Dr. Herzenberg says, studying the pistol in the dim light of the barracks. "A ladies' automatic. I almost fainted when I saw you come in."

Janusz sits, his hands cupped over his groin, rocking slowly. "I have a blood blister on my —"

"We're lucky they let us in here to warm up before roll call," David says. "They'd surely have seen it then. It looked like a huge right-angle erection. And a cubed testicle."

"I got mashed up," Janusz says.

The chafing got so bad that the top inside of his thigh began to bleed. Janusz slides his hand down inside his pants and feels his leg. The wound has begun to scab over.

"So how many guns do we have now?" David whispers.

Dr. Herzenberg stares at the little automatic in his hand. Then he shakes his head and laughs softly. "Here is our arsenal," he says, holding the pistol up to the light.

SS BARRACKS, TREBLINKA

LATE FEBRUARY 1943

Joachim Voss sits at one of the smaller tables in the mess hall with Helmut Weyrauch and Josef Schneck, and the three of them try to carry on their conversation over the sound of raised voices from the big table, at which sit Franz, Miete, Kuttner, Liebner, and a couple of the younger fellows. The other tables are empty, having been vacated by officers too drunk to stay up. From time to time the cook Blau comes in smiling, carrying trays of food, wicker baskets of French bread, different vintage wines. His helper is a handsome Viennese named Sussmann, who has temporarily replaced a sick kitchen worker. The commandant has retired to his room, having said nothing to the men on his way out after eating his dinner. At Voss's table there are three glasses and one bottle of schnapps, a block of cheese, and a box of Viennese crackers.

Voss has participated in the conversation for half an hour now, exchanging information about places of origin, favorite cities, sports. Schneck asked Weyrauch about the missing finger, and Voss sat back and listened while Weyrauch went on about how he lost it. Voss tried to see if the man's homosexuality would reveal itself to Schneck, and if Schneck would be tempted. But he remained impassive, and Voss could see in Weyrauch's loose-lipped expression, surely a sign of his orientation, the careful pressing of his plan.

But this is only surface perception. What bothers Voss, in fact has reached the point of obsessing him, is something he has discovered about the collection of stamps. The job of evaluating them has taken more than a week, more or less like assembling a large puzzle, and he has found pieces missing.

"You're an extraordinary fellow," Weyrauch says, slapping Schneck lightly on the knee. Voss sighs and looks at the raw wood ceiling of the mess hall, then at those at the other table, who are watching an arm-wrestling match between two of the younger men. The table is crowded with beer glasses and dirty plates pushed aside to make room for the match.

"In any case," Schneck says, "in China in 1850 or something like that there was a little war and twenty-five million people died. How many of us remember that?"

"Twenty-five?" Weyrauch says. "My God, that is astounding."

Voss is irritated with the happy obsequiousness of Weyrauch's bearing, as if he cannot hide his perverse desire. The underhanded poof has selected his quarry.

"Less than a hundred years ago," Schneck says. "Predation in nature is the rule. And this here —" He gestures in the direction of the middle of the camp. "Who will remember it? I know I will — it's a sadist's dream, one of the few places I know of where you can exercise absolute freedom."

Weyrauch laughs, and as they continue talking, Voss sinks once again into thinking about the stamps. Obviously someone stuck a handful of around seventy or eighty of them into his pocket while they were picking them up. Day by day Voss saw that little pile of stamps expand in his mind, to the point that each night he would wake up thinking about it, at two or three in the morning. And of course the ones that were missing were the higher denominations. The thief was no fool.

One night he woke up sweating, despite the cold air, and studied the torn-out section of the catalogue using a pen-sized battery lamp he always carried with him. One of the sets, he believed the first to use pictures, or something other than portraits of men, was missing denominations of fifteen cents, twenty-four cents, thirty cents, and ninety cents, and may have included one or two with inverted centers, making that set alone extremely valuable. That freak Anatoly may have taken them, or perhaps that dull-witted boy or his friends from the Blue Kommando or someone who passed by later and discovered the pile of stamps hidden under a thin covering of snow. In any case Voss became determined to do something about it, because he could not stand the incompleteness of things. He tried searching the railroad tracks once, during the day, but the blinding brightness of the sun made him feel dizzy and sick.

The party at the big table is breaking up, because it is late, and a chill is descending over the room. Tomorrow, he thinks, I will question that idiot Anatoly, and that boy.

He leans up in his chair, and then becomes aware of an odor wafting into the room, of old putrefaction, a soily carrion smell. Weyrauch and Schneck do not show any awareness of it.

"So gentlemen," Schneck says.

Weyrauch nods, and the men move toward the other wing of the barracks. Sussmann comes in to clear the big table, and speaks briefly to Franz. Voss gets up and wanders to the barracks door. Outside, the moon bathes the lightly snow-covered buildings and grounds in a flat, silver glow. He steps outside and tests the chill in the air, and walks toward the station square. It has been so cold that if any of the stamps are still there, perhaps down in next to the railroad ties, they will be undamaged.

He walks along the main gate road, and once again that soily odor materializes in the air, and he stops, trying to determine which way the breeze is blowing. But it is so still that he can barely feel it.

When he reaches the station square he pulls the little battery lamp out of his tunic pocket, and goes to the platform edge. There he stoops down, and shines the lamp at the soot-dirtied snow sitting on the ties and collected over the crushed-rock bedding. Then he stands up, feeling the chill work its way through his tunic, and walks along the platform, running the weak cone of light over the thin covering of snow.

A bright shaft of light sweeps over his head, and he turns to its source, Schneck, it appears.

"Still the stamps?" he asks.

"Not really," Voss says, turning off his light and putting it back in his pocket. "I was just getting some air, and stopped to look. Besides, I found that they were worthless." He considers his lie, and decides that it was convincing.

Schneck runs the shaft of the light over the barracks buildings. The odor returns again. "What is that?" Voss asks.

"Well, you've been busy with your — work," Schneck says, switching off the light. "They're exhuming the corpses."

"My God, why?"

"They're experimenting with burning them."

Voss looks in the direction of the Death Camp.

"When we took Russia," Schneck says, "we found evidence of what the Soviets did to the Poles. There's a rumor of a number of discoveries of grave sites. Near Smolensk."

"It's inevitable," Voss says. "Stalin calls it liquidation. He's been doing it for years. It's normal for him."

"But this situation is not. This is unique, and evidence is, well, problematic. We'll have to stop fooling ourselves about who will be standing on this dirt a few years from now."

"Are they true, then, the stories about the front?"

"Yes. Last year's winter was a disaster, and this year's winter is worse. All along the front they're starving, freezing to death, surrendering." Schneck plays with the battery lamp, making a blindingly bright spot on the snow between their shoes.

"You know how reverse magnetism works," Voss says. "The closer you hold the magnets, the greater the resistance."

"I wish it were that simple," Schneck says. "We should have been satisfied with Byelorussia and the Ukraine. Stalin might have accepted that. Now we will have to begin making our individual preparations. Like you and your stamps."

"Excuse me?"

Schneck laughs. "Don't worry — I won't say anything about it. I make my own preparations too." He blows into his cupped hand. "It seems impossible, but I envision Germany being overrun."

Voss does not believe that, but knows that it is human to speculate on catastrophe. It induces an almost pleasant sensation.

Schneck shines the battery lamp into the sky. "And we lose our freedom," he says. "For me it goes all the way back to the first invasion, then Russia, you know, Vinnitsa, Dragobich, Lvov. I experimented with it during the killing. It's one of the sharpest pleasures, shooting someone in the neck. I've done it tens of thousands of times. I thought I would grow old doing it, but now —" He pauses, then says, "I used to do this when I was a child, you know, a beam of light going into infinity." Voss chuckles softly at this demonstration of innocence, considering that it comes from one who would be labeled by anyone a monster.

"What did you say you did before —" Voss pauses. "Before all this?"

"I was a medical student," Schneck says. "You know, when I first started killing, I was afraid, but then everything went opposite — I found that it was more satisfying to put a hole in a person than to sew it up, and since then I have become a master." He sweeps the battery-lamp beam around in the sky. "I hate the idea that we have started something we might not be able to finish."

In the night there was a flickering over the beams of the barracks ceiling. Janusz Siedlecki lay on his back, staring into the ashy half-darkness waiting to see the flashing again, and again there it was, as if somewhere outside there was the reflection of sheet lightning. His stomach yawned with that miserable vacuum that had kept him in pain all week. He ate snow to give himself the sensation of something going down, but that only made it worse, and his throat became sore from involuntary swallowing. Then once a day it was cold potato soup and that grainy black bread, and there was never enough of it.

And as the ashy light in the beams intensified, he became aware that it would be another day in the woods, always hearing somewhere in the back of his skull that banging sound, that thumping in the ground. He turned over on his side and put his cheek on the oily wad of clothing that served as a pillow and breathed in the smell of his own filth, and felt the cold, oily hardness of the fabric of his shirt encircling his neck and binding his armpits. The light meant something, and his heart started thumping in his neck and ears. Something secret was happening, and in his dreams he thought he saw death casting his gaze over the sleeping men, and then death looked at Janusz with an expression of perplexed sympathy, as if he had decided, after all this time, that this boy was finally sick enough now to take away from his pain. There would remain only the sudden, white-hot flash of the bullet blowing through his skull, perhaps a hundredth of a second of intense pain. In his dream death was a German officer with a warm, understanding face, who reassured those about to die that no, it would not hurt, and yes, you would sleep for eternity in comfort and warmth.

Staring into the gradually intensifying light in the barracks, Janusz realized that he had had the same dream in one form or another every night since he came to Treblinka, as if to practice expecting death so that when it came he would be ready and not afraid.

He stares at the door now, wondering if Kiwe will come in and decide who needs a visit to the Hospital. The weather has been so cold that Kiwe has not killed anyone in a week, and a kind of stability has settled over the barracks.

A few of the men are beginning to stir. Janusz sits up and swings his legs off the bunk. The thought of cold potato soup and bread makes his stomach cramp painfully, and his mouth begins to fill with saliva. The cramp sends a wave of trembling throughout his body, and his hands feel ticklish and nearly numb. He digs his fingertips through the fabric of his Scottish woolen socks and rubs between his toes, and then smells the odor of his feet rising around his face.

He puts on his shoes and his woolen jacket. From under his bunk he takes out his soup cup, a tin can with a paper label picturing sweetened pear halves. In the next bunk David Schrhafta stirs, looks groggily at him, and puts his coat on, and then his boots, and they make their way along with other men toward the doorway and the barracks yard, where the field kitchen will be set up for them.

Men talk around him, but Janusz does not hear. Now that he is awake, the pounding rush in his head has increased, and he is locked inside his partial deafness. He drums his knuckle on the bottom of the pear can, and feels the sound pulsing up from the hand that holds the can. He has forgotten his gloves, but does not want to go back for them now. Near the field kitchen he sees the cook, a kapo named Chaskel, and the Czechs from his barracks, Julian Sussmann who has been promoted to kitchen helper, and Schneck, who looks around at the workers, making Janusz suddenly wary.

The men pass by the field kitchen, and the soup steams as it pours into the cups. Today the soup is hot. Janusz feels his knees weaken, and he begins to tremble, because the anticipation of the food is almost too much for him to control. He fears that he will not be able to hold the cup steady when the kapo pours the soup.

Schneck is up to something. He has the look of selection in his eyes. The sick men in line stand up straighter, trying to look well. Janusz steps into the line, keeping his eyes on Schneck, and then turns to David and whispers, "Act normal."

Janusz's knees weaken. His head pounds and he can feel his heart *whoosh*ing in his ears. Schneck approaches the line and orders one man out, and the man speaks, his hand on his chest. Schneck makes a move to his holster, and the man puts both hands up and steps out of the line. Now Anatoly stands behind Schneck, but his rifle is still hanging by its strap on his shoulder. Schneck moves along the line, and his eyes rest on Janusz, and then he seems to recognize him, yes, the boy who fell on my boots. He smiles and says, "You, out."

Janusz looks once at David and nods, and then steps over to where the other selected man stands. He feels as if he is nearly blind, and in the snowy brightness the dark forms of the men seem two-dimensional, like animated cardboard dolls. He sees the other man's face, its look of nausea and a stunned fatalism. "It's time for our cure," he hears himself saying, his voice tinny and high-pitched.

Then a strange, almost pleasant sensation of lightness sweeps over him. His vision returns and he stops trembling. He feels all his organs rising, as if they are hollow and pumped with helium, and the rank smell of his own fear and bodily filth rises like steam from his shirt — soon all that will be over. With a single flash of a bullet all the fear and pain and hunger will vanish, and it seems to him now that these sensations have been with him so long that they have become crushingly boring, useless and tyrannical.

Janusz clearly sees David still in the soup line, and begins to giggle. When Schneck is close, Janusz says, "Are you going to use your pistol?" Schneck does not hear him. Janusz studies the dark handle of the pistol peeking out from the holster flap on Schneck's belt. Then he looks at Anatoly and studies the rifle, its barrel encased by the oily wood of the forestock. "Anatoly," he says. Anatoly looks at him blankly, and he can see the flat, harsh light making his ears glow red and translucent. "Are you going to do it with your rifle?"

"Shut up," one of the selected men whispers harshly.

Janusz laughs softly. The sensation of exhilaration he feels is the first truly enjoyable feeling he has had since he came to Treblinka, and he knows now that death is nothing to be afraid of. He feels as if he has lived almost too long, as if he has been alive for thousands of years and now it is time to die amiably and without any malice for those who will kill him. They are all pitiful, captured inside the rampage of killing. He can tell simply by looking at the expression of bland cruelty on Schneck's face, him in his black uniform clubbing children and whipping women and kicking old men — he hates Schneck but more than that he pities him. He laughs again, this time drawing his attention, and suddenly Schneck is in front of him, and lashes out with his booted foot.

Janusz tries to sit up, the heels of his hands bruised by the hardened snow. He feels his eyes go cold with tears, and tries to get his breath. When he does, rising to his knees, he nods at the dirty snow. "Right here," he says, pointing to the back of his neck. "This is the spot."

The other three workers have moved away from him, and dimly he is aware that Chaskel continues to ladle soup to the men. "Where is my can?" he asks, then sees it on the ground. Picking the can up, he stands unsteadily, and moves to rejoin the other selected workers. The force of the blow to his stomach, or the shock of sitting down, has loosened the wax in his right ear, so that he hears better, is aware of ticking, rustling sounds moving around him. By the field kitchen stands Julian Sussmann, his face held in a mask of vicarious fear, and Janusz smiles at him and then shrugs in amiable resignation.

Anatoly waves his hand in the direction of the gateway out of the Roll Call Square, and they march toward it, Janusz stumbling gingerly with what feels like the onset of great age, a kind of anticipatory decrepitude. They walk along a fence past the latrine, not toward the Hospital. "Are they going to gas us?" Janusz asks. When they get there, he sees that the old gas chamber doors are locked, with snow collected in the corners, and beyond that, the new gas chambers seem shut, and fringed with unbroken snow.

Janusz realizes that they are being led into the Death Camp. They approach a barbed wire gate at which stands a guard. But he understands also that they are not being shot, which makes him pull into himself. He is held in a strange sensation of pleasant shock — that his death is being put off is a tremendous relief, but at the same time it is a strange disappointment. The men ahead of him, walking with their heads jerking around quickly as they look at what they have never seen before, must also be wondering: No, this is not my death, this is something else. They must put aside the preparations for the bullet and hold them off for now. He imagines that now, discovering that they will live longer, their stomachs begin to complain, they feel the bitter cold, they become aware once again of their own filth and mortality.

As they walk through the fence gate Janusz sees Camp Number Two open up before him, to the right the high dirt bank that separates it from the Sorting Square, straight ahead a huge cranelike piece of equipment that a man is climbing into, off in the distance barracks buildings. From out of the barracks buildings he sees the forms of men walking, watched by guards and an officer. Beyond that there is a high guard tower.

Looking down at the can in his hand, Janusz remembers that they didn't eat. "Excuse me," he says to one of the workers, "but we didn't eat."

The worker stares at him with a frightened, distant expression, as if he has been hypnotized.

The huge machine, which looks like a boxcar with the crane device rising at an angle from one end, produces a grinding roar and belches gray smoke. The crane cables vibrate, and he hears the clanking sound that he has heard the past few weeks. The cables shake, and an excavating mechanism shaped like two hands cupped to each other, the steel teeth like fingers that intertwine, rises from the ground, swinging heavily.

The men from the barracks approach, breath vapor curling away from their heads. One of them is Waclaw Gitzer.

"Look!" Janusz says. "He is alive. I was right."

Schneck walks to the excavator and speaks to someone inside. Then he waves the men over to the excavator. Janusz puts his can down and shuffles behind the three other men, and a wave of hunger washes over him and changes into a fit of trembling that leaks outward into his limbs, so that his walking is jerky and uncoordinated. As is true a lot of the time he feels the ticklish urge to urinate, and remembers that he has not had to go to the latrine for three days now, because he has eaten so little food.

Anatoly has wandered back out of the Death Camp area, and the four of them are left standing there. More men emerge from the barracks buildings, and the excavating box hanging from the cables clanks, and then the oblong cab of the machine turns, with the box swinging under the steel hoist beams.

Two guards appear at the gate, and another officer comes in, a short, slightly pudgy man who seems distracted and nervous.

One of the workers runs in Janusz's direction. When he arrives, he says, "We are a labor detail. Follow me."

"What are we doing?" the man next to Janusz asks.

"Digging up and burning all the bodies."

Walking, Janusz sees Waclaw Gitzer standing by the excavator, shoulders hunched. He tries to catch his attention as they pass the excavator, but Waclaw seems not to recognize him, although he has glanced once in his direction.

The leader of their labor detail walks them to the edge of a frozen pit a few meters away from the huge-toothed excavating mechanism. Inside the pit Janusz sees, layered like a cutaway cliff of different rock formations, the edges of bodies, heads, one arm dangling downward, a black foot, long flattened thighs and torsos. The more recent bodies on the upper levels from November and December remain pale and whole, while the ones down deeper are blackened and rotted. The other men stare at each other with fright and wonder, and Janusz now understands the excavator's placement.

Other crews position themselves at different locations, and the busy-looking man snaps orders, points here, there, instructs kapos. Schneck is now joined by Kiwe, and The Doll, who stand back out of the way. The excavator box jerks with a loud grinding sound, followed by the sound of clanking. Then the huge arm swings the clawed box over the pit. The box divides like hands opening, and then falls, the teeth driving deeply into the layer of earth on top of the bodies. The box draws shut, gouging down into the layers of bodies. Janusz sees the legs and arms and torsos surge against each other, and a dangling arm falls off to the side. As the toothed box draws shut he feels the ground shudder. Then a slab of bodies fused to each other by ice rises out of the pit, those underneath having been severed in half by the jaws of the box. A mummified head falls from the box and lands on the lower layers of corpses. The mouth is open and full of dirt and there are blackened pits half-filled with ice where the eyes should be. When the bodies rise and the smell wafts across their faces Janusz coughs and covers his nose. It is different from the fresher smell of putrefaction he remembers from the first days. It is an older smell, sharper and he thinks more chemically seasoned, as if the months the bodies have had to decompose have created more toxic admixtures, which even frozen seem to him more acidic, blacker.

The box swings toward them, and the head worker waves them out of the way, and just as they step back the box hovers where they stood and opens, letting the slab of corpses fall to the ground. The bodies impaled by the teeth and crushed in the corners of the box stay there until the excavator operator jounces the box, making the cables snap and vibrate again. The remaining bodies drop stiffly onto the pile.

"Now!" the head worker yells over the sound of the excavator engine. "Listen to me!" Janusz cups his hands around his ears. "We are to sort the bodies as follows: fat women in one pile, thin women and children in one pile, men in one pile." He continues speaking, but his voice is drowned out by the engine as the toothed box slams down into the pit once again. The worker waits while the box grinds shut. The closing sides sever torsos, scissor limbs off, divides the corpse of a child, and drops other body parts back into the pit as the box rises up and swings toward them.

The worker waits until the box swings away once more, and goes on to explain that fat women burn best and are used to kindle thin women and children, who in turn ignite the men. The carriers must have them sorted just so, because they will be piled on the roast with the fat women on the bottom. Body parts will be sorted in the same manner — a fat leg goes with the bodies of the fat women, and so on.

One of the men leans over and vomits a string of dark fluid into the thin snow at his feet. "Yes," the leader says, and the box swings away to the burial pit. "This will take some adjustment. Do this right and you will live. Make a mistake and you go onto the roast." The next load swings in their direction and is dumped next to the others. "Now get to work."

Janusz looks at the man who vomited and says, "I did this once, a long time ago." He walks to the pile of bodies, thinking that if he has to do it, then he will do it without hesitation. He pulls a slab of frozen dirt from the side of the pile, uncovering a man's head, the ears plugged with dirt. He drives his fingertips into the snow caked on either side of his neck and pulls up, and the body separates from the rest like a heavy board. "A man," he says, and giggles. The leader nods quickly, and points to a spot on the ground. Nearby the open jaws of the excavator box slam down into the pit, and in a screeching shudder, close downward on more of the bodies. One of the other workers comes out of his stupor and grabs the frozen ankles of the man, and together they swing him away from the pile and launch him to the spot the leader indicated, and he lands on his hip and shoulder with a rigid crack, then flops over on his face. Janusz raises his hands and looks at them, the sensation of their having made contact with the frozen body still tingling in his fingertips. The worker who vomited pulls out a small leg, and trembling almost uncontrollably holds it before Janusz like a garden tool.

"A child," the leader says. "Yes. Over here."

Again they must move out of the way. The excavator box swings around and opens, and another slab of bodies drops, those from lower down in the pit, their torsos and limbs blackened by decomposition, their trunks split open with dark brown material crowding the openings. There is what looks like a black statue of a woman running. The powerful odor comes from these deeper bodies, and Janusz clamps his hand over his nose, and then realizes that the odor is on his hand. He grabs the hem of his coat and rubs it harshly across his mouth to get rid of whatever he left there. But it does no good.

As the box swings away, he sees that men are running their way carrying litters. The lead worker in their group becomes impatient and flaps his hands around. "Hurry!" he yells.

Janusz needs gloves. He turns to the lead worker to point this out, but the men with the litters have arrived and are loading them with the first bodies they pulled out. The excavator box, limbs and blackened tissue pinched in its steel teeth, swings again in their direction, simultaneously releasing another wad of corpses. A wet, blackened head of a child rolls down at his feet, and numb with shock, he leans down to pick it up. This time the powerful stench engulfs him like a cloud of heavy steam.

By late afternoon the stench has become a tattoo on his hands. But at least they were fed around noon, cups of cold soup that tasted like the odor coming off his hands. His shoes are sticky with fluid and scraps of rotted tissue. His legs feel rubbery, and his body hot from fatigue, but he is cold to the point of numbness in his feet and hands. At the "roast" he stands near the other men watching the new officer march around the piles of corpses, which are interspersed with long pieces of wood that hold them slightly apart in the manner one uses to make a campfire. At the base of the pile nearest him, Janusz sees railroad tracks suspended above concrete foundations, and then remembers Waclaw, and looks around for him. He had one chance to speak to him earlier, and saw that he had that hopeless, distant look in his eyes. He recognized Janusz, but before they could speak Waclaw was ordered away. Now he stands with a group of men who spent the day carrying litters.

Janusz moves closer to one of the men he worked with, who is vigorously washing his hands with dirty snow.

"Will they feed us again?" he asks. The man works at his hands, his face twisted with disgust, and then nods.

He speaks a short sentence, not looking at him.

"Excuse me, I can't hear well."

"If the fire goes well," he says, turning to him.

Janusz stoops down and gathers a wad of gritty snow off the ground, and rubs it between the palms of his hands. As it melts, it feels hot, and when he has rubbed his hands raw, he dries them on his coat and then puts them in his pockets. He holds them there in icy fists.

"That man over there," Janusz says, "the one by himself — he is my friend Waclaw Gitzer."

The man laughs, still working at his hands. "We call him 'The Failure,' because he tried to hang himself the other day. His belt broke, and when he fell he hurt his back."

Suicide? It does not seem logical for Waclaw.

"We have these titles," the man says. "That officer is called 'Tadellos,' because that is what he will say if the fire goes well. Then he'll give us something extra to eat. We wait for him to say, 'Tadellos.' It means 'perfect' in German."

Janusz has the odd feeling that things are less ordered and strict in this camp, because there is a lazy casualness in the bearing of the workers. At noon they ate casually, and the officers seemed less inclined to closely observe them. Of the many who worked in the various details, only one man was killed, the man in his detail who had vomited when the bodies first came out, and in his case the shooting was his own fault. Janusz learned from the very beginning that if you worked, if you drew no attention to yourself, then you might be left alone. But the man, his face gray with exhaustion after a couple hours of pulling the rotted bodies apart, simply sat down and refused to work. Kiwe, Schneck, and The Doll were off toward the gas chamber side of the camp, probably to be upwind of the smell, and did not see what was going on. The lead worker negotiated with the man, trying to cheer him up, but the man kept saying, Take me to the Hospital, take me to the Hospital. Finally Schneck came over and, understanding what was going on, ordered the man to stand, walked him to the pyramid-shaped piles of bodies that were being prepared, and then Janusz heard the flat report from Schneck's pistol. Now the man is in with the rest of the corpses, near the top, because fat women were on the bottom, children above them, and so on.

The new officer is now pointing at the first pile of corpses and giving orders. Workers climb carefully up the sides of the pyramid-shaped pile and pour liquid on the bodies and on the wood peeking out from under them. The man Janusz talked to turns and tips his head — follow me — and walks closer to the pile. The officer called Tadellos now walks quickly around, appearing agitated, but Janusz sees that his excitement is a kind of pleasant agitation, that this man seems to harbor no anger toward his men, only toward the situation in general. Then Tadellos slips on the snow and almost falls down, and rises with an embarrassed expression on his face, making the man near Janusz smile.

The workers start the first fire. The petrol ignites instantly, producing a blue-green flame that turns yellow as the wood begins to burn. Tadellos watches, staring with a kind of mesmerized expectation as the flames lick at the bodies. The worker near Janusz gestures for him to move a little closer, and when he does, he feels the reflected heat on his face. The other men are gathering closer too, and the flames increase, rising up the pyramid of corpses. In the increasing firelight the flat twilight recedes around them and the rich, orange globe around the fire illuminates the corpses, so that faces appear, shapes of torsos are clarified, and the heat on Janusz's face intensifies. He can now hear the crackling sound of the fire eating the wood, and stares at the fire wide-eyed, hypnotized by the heat and the rich, orange light.

As if in a dream he sees one face halfway up the pile, that of a child, begin to sweat, so that tiny beads materialize on his face, and then his mouth begins to move, almost as if the dead child is beginning to feel the heat and is starting to writhe in agony. His eyes open wider, and then the sweat begins to run in little bright rivulets down his cheeks, and drips downward, where the drops explode in little flashes of light. Tadellos moves his arms up and down as if to order the fire to intensify, and he then claps his hands together and speaks over his shoulder to the officers who have spent the day avoiding the smell from the pits. Janusz sees that they had set a table, and bottles of wine and whiskey glint from the movement of the flames.

"It worked!" the man next to Janusz says. "Yesterday we had a time of it, but tonight it works! You just watch — now we'll get sausages, bread!"

Other faces appear to Janusz, sweating and changing expression slowly as if their sensation of the pain of being burned comes to them with a kind of demented interruption. Mouths open and fluid spills out, creating plumes of steam below, and now body parts start to writhe, again in an agonized slow motion. The dead appear to be rising slowly to stumble out of the fire. Severed body parts appear to move in search of the rest of themselves, and the faces continue to open up in a slow, roaring scream of agony. Then Janusz is aware of another odor, the perverted aroma of cooking meat, something like pork roasting in an oven, mixed with the acrid, salty odor of decomposition.

On the side of the pile a woman's stomach has expanded, and then he is distracted by the man next to him, who is rapping him on the shoulder with his knuckle. "Candy," he says to Janusz, and one of the lead workers from the fire-starting group reaches into a tin bucket and draws out a handful of pieces of wrapped candy. His hands shaking, Janusz takes the candy and puts it into his pocket, and still looking at the woman, he counts them with his fingertips, ten pieces. He draws one out, unwraps it, and puts the paper in his other pocket. Hard candy. When he puts it into his mouth the powerful sting of a sugared fruit flavor rushes throughout his mouth. Tadellos has now settled at the table, whose white cloth and wine and whiskey bottles show brightly in the firelight. The other officers clap him on the back and pour wine. As Janusz looks up once more at the huge fire, which has become so hot that he and the others now have to move back from it, he sees the belly of the woman split open. A fetus rolls out of the opening, a tiny incandescent body, like a bright doll, and explodes in flames as it settles into the white-hot base of the fire. Chewing on the candy, Janusz sees that some of the men have turned around so that they can warm their backs.

NEAR WOLGA-OKNAGLIK, POLAND
AUGUST 2, 1943

Just off the dirt road ahead of her, in brushy woodland where she has always seen a lot of birds, there is continuous firing of guns, even a machine gun, and then yelling in different languages. Then two trucks appear trailing billows of dust, and pull to a stop only fifty meters from where she hides in a bush, rocking and moaning from the pain and the heat, which has muddled her so that she cannot think of what to do next. Perhaps she should lie back and have it here, then bury it and go home.

The gunfire has stopped, and to her right, after she hears the shrill shouting of orders in German, men emerge from the brush in a line, their hands on the tops of their heads. Then guards appear, and an officer. She counts. Seven men, three guards, none of them Anatoly. It doesn't matter.

The officer flanks the walking men, and then begins hitting them with a cane on their intertwined fingers on the tops of their heads. They walk, appearing unconcerned about being hit, as if they have no nerves, as if it doesn't matter.

Another truck comes down the road from the direction of Wolga-Oknaglik, and stops facing the two that arrived earlier. There are men sitting in the bed of the truck, their fingers laced on their heads. One of the seven men marching toward the trucks stops and sits down, and the officer draws a pistol and speaks to him, then hits him over the head with his cane. The man sitting does not cower. The officer points his pistol at the man's face, and the man simply looks at it as if it doesn't matter, and then the officer shoots him. The pop sound reaches her almost instantly because she is so close.

Then a figure appears walking out of the brush toward the road to the left, small and stooped and dressed in black. It appears to be an old grandmother. She uses a cane, and is bowlegged, and so small that she might be a deformed child. As she approaches the trucks, the officer, then two of the guards, and then some of the prisoners, stop and look at her, none of them moving. And as she sees that they block her way she walks around them, and their heads slowly turn, their eyes following her. She passes one truck, then the second, and then walks between the second and third into the brush, and disappears.

The officer turns to the six men with their fingers laced on their heads and continues hitting them with his cane, on their fingers, and they stand at attention as if this doesn't matter to them.

The world has gone insane, she thinks, feeling the sluggish signals of the next cramp. She will strain the baby out right here and bury it in the hot soil because the world has become a wonderland of nightmares.

OUTSIDE THE UKRAINIAN BARRACKS, CAMP NUMBER ONE, TREBLINKA

LATE MARCH 1943

Anatoly Yovenko stands guard at the site of a construction project directed by The Doll, thinking that when he goes out with the *Tarnungskommando*, it will be cold in the woods, and when she comes they will have to walk through the gray remains of the snow to the shelter. He has not been able to give her anything because there have been no transports for two months now, and Janusz, the best thief of them all, has been sent to the Death Camp. That officer Voss comes to the barracks yard and looks around, at The Doll and the workers hunched over their carpentry. Then his eyes rest with recognition on Anatoly, making him nervous. The look on Voss's face is a strange combination of dark-eyed hangover, along with a vengeful infuriation, as if someone has insulted him and he demands satisfaction.

"You," Voss says to him. "Come with me."

He follows Voss away from the barracks, becoming more nervous. Has someone squealed? Janusz, or perhaps that friend of his who saw them trading — David, who is now working on something right under The Doll's eyes. Voss marches quickly along the street past the Jewish barracks, and then, curving to the right, toward the Death Camp. Anatoly can hear the pounding of the excavating machine digging the bodies up.

Voss marches into the Death Camp and stops, watching the workers sorting the rotted bodies for the litter carriers. Under the rail grids the embers of yesterday's fires still push up a lazy, pale smoke. He is apparently trying to recognize someone, and then seems to, over by the excavator. They walk toward the machine, which raises its grab full of bodies and swings it around with a screeching shudder. Then the stench reaches them, and Voss coughs, then clears his throat.

"That one by the machine," Voss says.

"The boy?" Anatoly recognizes Janusz. That the little bag of bones is still alive is a surprise.

Voss nods, and Anatoly walks toward the excavator. When he is close enough to catch Janusz's attention, he waves him over. The boy puts his hands on his chest. Me? Anatoly nods, and the boy walks in Anatoly's direction. When Janusz reaches them, Anatoly notices the smell again, but now it comes off his clothes. His hands are dirty, and he holds them a little away from himself, with the fingers separated.

"Your Blue Kommando friend," Voss says to the boy in that careful pronunciation of German. "Where is he?"

Janusz points toward the fire pits.

Voss orders the boy to get his friend, and Anatoly begins to feel cornered. He has a strange impulse to aim and shoot Voss in the back. When Janusz comes back, Anatoly sees that something appears to be wrong with the other fellow.

Voss leads them away from the pits and excavator toward the gas chamber buildings, and when they reach there, Voss walks them around the new gas chambers to the earth bank separating the Death Camp from the Reception Camp. There, in a hollow between the dirt bank and the gas chamber building, Voss stops, and then turns to the two workers.

"I want to know where the —" Anatoly does not understand the rest. He looks at Voss, again aware of the expression on his face, the look of an anger about to erupt. *Briefmarken.* He does not know the word. Voss gestures as if to lick his thumb, and then drives it into the palm of his other hand.

The stamps. Anatoly feels his face go pale.

Janusz shakes his head and says that he gave them all to Voss. The sick-looking man now has that cornered look, but Anatoly wonders if it is because of something else. He appears to be insane. Voss's eyes rest on him, and he looks away as if he fears any eye contact with Voss. This appears to aggravate Voss, whose expression shows a vengeful anger and a kind of jerky tension in his limbs. He struggles at his belt for his pistol, and Janusz steps in front of the frightened one, as if to shield him. "He knows nothing," he says. "He's not right in the head, sir. He hasn't had enough to eat. But I know that he knows nothing."

"Stand away," Voss says to him. Janusz doesn't move.

Then he says, "He isn't right in the head. He's harmless, a good worker, but he knows nothing about stamps."

Voss becomes impatient with him and holds the pistol up as if to strike him. The boy hunches his shoulders and cowers, but remains placed before the other. "Tell him what you know," he says to the other. "Tell him you don't know anything."

The other still has that pulled-in, guilty look. Voss steps closer, and pushes Janusz out of the way, and then his expression changes from the fuming anger to a kind of inquisitive revulsion.

The smell. He looks at the hand that has pushed Janusz out of the way, realizing that he emits the smell.

Anatoly's nervousness has now settled into a kind of aggressive excitement. If he is ordered to kill them, then he will kill the witness to his treason. He pulls the rifle off his shoulder and steps forward. Voss steps back and nods. They all die anyway, Anatoly thinks. It is like a strange dream: He swings the rifle around and strikes the insane man across the head with the stock, and as he falls down, Voss steps up to him and asks him again where they are. The man shakes his head, and Janusz leans down to help him. Voss shoves him out of the way and turns again to Anatoly, who pokes the shoulder stock downward into the man's face. They all die anyway.

Voss puts the pistol in its holster and shakes his head. "Idiot," he says. He walks away toward the gate. Anatoly looks down at the man, who lies holding his face, which is bleeding. Janusz crouches by him, and does not look up.

"I had to," Anatoly says. "I hate them, but I had to. I'd like to see them all die. I would."

"I know," Janusz says. "We would never squeal, though. Is David still alive?"

"Yes. When the time comes, I will give him guns. I promise. Rifles, petrol, money."

"Thank you, Anatoly." He turns to the man. "Come, Waclaw, we have to roast more bodies."

"You have no nerves," the man says thickly. "You're too young. And now my face is marked."

"They don't mark faces any more. Come, Tadellos will give us candy if we roast more bodies than yesterday."

"Will he be all right?" Anatoly asks.

"Yes," Janusz says. "I'll watch him." The man laughs.

As he leaves, Anatoly thinks, I must go and get them and put them somewhere were Voss will find them. He will have to take the chance and walk through the patches of dirty snow to the dead birch trunk. Voss will keep at it until he gets his little pieces of paper, and Anatoly sees himself as an inevitable target, that, after all the other options are crossed off, Voss will come for him. It is something about the man's face. Underneath the pale, swollen-eyed mask of alcoholic poisoning there lies that combination of wrath and desire that is as involuntary as a disease. He will have to take the chance.

Joachim Voss sits down on his bunk and pours brandy into a coffee cup. He should have had more before he went out to interrogate the workers, because he shook so much, and wonders if it was visible to the guard. He is still shaking, as he shakes every morning, and quickly drinks the brandy, waiting while the hot liquid works its way down into his stomach. In a few moments he feels a swoon of relief, and pours another drink.

With the relief from the brandy comes the sensation of being settled, and then a calm, neutral aura of logic and clearheadedness. That imbecile Anatoly hit has no interest in stamps, nor does the boy. It is Anatoly. He was the only other person present when they picked the stamps up except for one man standing off to the side, and being Ukrainian, he would steal anything he thought was of any value whatsoever, whatever might buy him a whore or a bottle of vodka. But the Ukrainians are crafty, he knows, and must be outwitted. Anatoly takes *Tarnungskommando* details out to cut wood, and if he has saved anything, he will have it hidden out there somewhere. Watches can buy whores and alcohol, but stamps can't. He has to save those and then apply whatever small modicum of intelligence he has to selling them. A difficult goal to be sure, Voss thinks, chuckling, because like virtually everyone else here, including the officers, Anatoly has a brain more or less the size of a dried plum.

He takes one more drink, then rises and decides to go back outside, in case Anatoly goes to the woods. This has gone on long enough. But he realizes also that if Anatoly has no reason to go to his hiding place, then Voss might have to wait until the transports come again, if they will ever come again. Outside, he sees the officers gathered near the Ukrainian barracks watching The Doll's project. Voss has no idea what it is. Then the commandant himself comes out and talks to The Doll, and the two of them go toward the commandant's quarters. Weyrauch and Schneck stand near the work. He decides to join them. Lately he has felt as if no one here is worth associating with, and has felt himself pulling inward, as if he were forming a shell around his body. He does not like the feeling because he is ordinarily sociable.

"Doing some police work?" Schneck asks. "I saw you go over to the roasts."

"Someone stole something," Voss says. "I went to interrogate a couple of workers. I got nothing."

"Next time let me know," Schneck says. "I can make anyone talk." Then he smiles with a kind of wan jocularity, and Weyrauch, who sees the expression, bursts out laughing.

"To be sure," he says. "An extraordinary fellow."

"I will help you," Schneck says. "I promise that by sundown you'll have what you want."

David Schrhafta selects four sections of birch sapling pieces each around thirty centimeters long, preparing to split them using a small hatchet. The March sun warms his back, and he works the blade of the hatchet into the grain of the first birch piece, and then hammers the other end gently on the hard ground so that it will split evenly. Just a few meters away from him stand Schneck, Weyrauch, and Voss, beyond them a couple of younger SS. He works with extreme care because he is being watched. The leader of their *Baukommando* detail, a cabinetmaker from Warsaw, oversees the construction of a small zoo. The other workers use wood gathered from around the camp to make frames for the cages, and David nails the split birch lengths onto the frames in order to make the walls, with the white bark on the outside. Each line of eight or nine split birch chunks laid side by side forms a square, and these squares are to be nailed onto the large frame grid in alternate order, up and down against sideways, making a geometrical design. The Doll has watched the process carefully, because he wants his zoo to be constructed without any shabby cutting of corners.

What makes David wary is that something has happened, some order has come down, and he fears execution. Galewski and one of the newer men, a Czech named Masarek, have set the revolt in process again — they have a few weapons, petrol, and money hidden away, and word has it that they have acquired a number of grenades, stolen from the new arsenal building. But the officers have become strict because of the lack of transports, as if they fear losing their jobs and must impose absolute order so that there be no unseemly events to blight their reputations.

Earlier The Doll had gone back toward the camp office, apparently having been summoned by the commandant, whom David saw standing out on the street by the office, his white jacket like a lamp in the March sunlight. Aloof and distant, the commandant sometimes wanders around the camp carrying a riding crop. He has a sharp, hooked nose, and his hair is cropped close to his scalp, and in the white jacket he seems somehow separate from the camp, looking around with the bland curiosity of a tourist. Whatever news The Doll got from the commandant excited him, and he whispered it to the other officers, making the hair on the back of David's neck bristle. Liquidation would be a simple matter — merely a slaughter, or a mass gassing.

His hands begin to shake, and a powerful cramp washes throughout his trunk, making sweat form on his forehead. Because there have been no transports since January, their food rations have been cut, again and again, until they are reduced to eating cold potato soup and a little chunk of bread each day. He finds himself getting up each morning for one detail or another, *Tarnungskommando* or *Baukommando* or clothes sorting or clothes loading at the boxcars, with the desire for food torturing him so much that he cannot function, and he comes close to being shot more than once because of it.

He takes a deep breath, and trying to look nonchalant before the casual stares of the officers, makes a test arrangement of some of the birch lengths so as to appear busy. The typhoid has run its course, and he feels that he can confirm to himself that he has survived. Many did not. Kuttner marched nearly half of them off to the Hospital during the worst month, and those he did not select went on plotting their survival. Then there was another blow to the revolt — Dr. Herzenberg was transferred to the Death Camp. Contact with that camp-within-the-camp is nearly impossible, except for information about who is still alive, provided by guards who are sent down there for one reason or another. Anatoly told David that Captain Bloch was still alive.

And he thinks: What does it matter anyway? Kapos and cooks and forked sticks and even the *Lageralteste* are all Jews and destined for the gas chambers eventually.

A few meters away from him workers measure out lines on the ground, preparing to build a garden. Others are digging a small side road to the proposed zoo location that connects to the street that curves around to Camp Number Two. Treblinka is becoming pretty. Even their awareness of the function of the camp is becoming vague, as if the gravel paths and neatly trimmed buildings show some sort of a graduation from its awful origins.

The acrid stench of the burning corpses comes their way only occasionally, but the black smoke is always visible late in the day, and he can hear the pounding and clanking and screeching of excavators, beginning early in the morning and going on until late afternoon. But to the untrained eye all of this might mean nothing. No one could know that hundreds of thousands died here.

Now The Doll appears carrying a bottle of liquor. David continues carefully lining up the birch lengths, his heart pounding. When he sees the shiny black boots, he looks up. The Doll smiles and says, "Go get the *Lageralteste*. I have a gift for him." David stands, aware of The Doll's height, of the smooth, handsome face, the smell of polished leather.

"Yes sir," he says. He wonders how it is that a man who looks like this can be such a monster. Turning to go toward the Jewish barracks and the camp elder's room, he feels himself shaking, as much with fear as with hunger.

Because Kapo Galewski is sick, the current camp elder is Rakowski, a huge, burly farmer some consider a buffoon, because he talks revolt too, but in a manner that is so open that even the Germans hear of it, and therefore do not take him seriously. He is useful because his arrogance masks the subterranean reality of the true revolt. Rakowski is merely a puppet, but the Germans, particularly The Doll, are fascinated by his size, as if he is some magnificent zoo animal. Day after day Rakowski forces the inmates to exercise, and tells them that he is preparing them for their escape, and they all dutifully exercise no matter how hungry they are, because if The Doll sees that they show too much open discourtesy to this amazing creature, they can easily be shot.

David walks into the space between the barracks buildings to the doorway to the kapos' quarters. Next to the *Lageralteste* quarters is the Revier, a medical ward, and he sees men lying in bunks there. The *Hofjuden*, jewelers, the SS barbers and handymen. He snorts, thinking of Kiwe and his answer to typhoid — a bullet in the back of the neck at the other Hospital. So went Treblinka's class-oriented society.

One of the elite, Rakowski has his own room. David knocks, and Rakowski calls, "Come in!"

David steps into the room. Rakowski sits at a table eating, while his girlfriend, who is wearing a nightgown, sits on a bunk. She is beautiful, with dark blonde, almost red hair, and David is captivated momentarily by a white thigh that disappears under the filmy material. Then he looks at Rakowski, who is eating meat of some kind, and drinking champagne. The man is huge, with shoulders so broad that he appears to be some grand natural error. "The deputy commandant wants you, outside."

"Would you like a little bread and cheese?"

"Yes, thank you. He says he has a gift for you."

"Have the kitchen Austrians squealed on me? Blau and Chaskel, who put killing another Jew as such a high priority?"

David looks at the table, spread out with meat, cheese, bread, candy, cigarettes, alcohol.

"Oh, the cheese," Rakowski says. "Here." He sets a block of yellow cheese on a thick slice of French bread and hands it to David, who immediately bites into it. As he chews he finds that the cheese and bread are too dry, and Rakowski, anticipating this, hands him a bottle partly filled with champagne. As David drinks, the foam ballooning his cheeks out, he looks once more at the woman, who stares back impassively at him. He can almost see her through the filmy nightgown. She is well-endowed and pale, and the impassivity of her expression seems to him an attitude born of her situation, of everyone's situation, that they are a small population of people who have for the moment evaded death. What use is it after all to be modest in the presence of a stranger or to worry if he sees through the fabric of the nightgown probably taken from a woman who now lies under that yellow, sandy earth, if he sees the heavy, soft breasts or the subtle hint of pubic hair?

"How are you people in the barracks holding up?"

"Fine," he says through a mouthful of champagne-saturated bread. "Something seems to be up. They seem to be excited about something." David eats more cheese.

Rakowski rises from his chair.

"I'd better get back," David says, and backs out of the room nodding once to the woman. As he leaves, he realizes that he has taken too much time, and hurries back to the site of the zoo, feeling the effect of the champagne, or the food, he is not sure. Now the men working have a strange, two-dimensional look, and his hearing seems flat and hollow, as if the one long pull from the bottle were some powerful drug. When he gets back to his hatchet and birch lengths, he looks down at them with his vision swimming crazily, as if he has been transformed suddenly into an imbecile.

Later in the day he makes his way to the barracks, his stomach churning, as if the food he did not expect has awakened the sensation of hunger more than would the denial of food. And the champagne — if anything it has acted as a kind of poison in his system, leaving the sensation of a hot, nauseating percolation that drives its way into his throat each time he comes out with an involuntary belch.

When he enters the barracks he goes to Galewski, who is nearly recovered from his sickness. Galewski is talking with Julian Sussmann, and when David approaches, they both stop.

"Some order has come down," David says to Galewski.

The older man takes his glasses off and rubs the corners of his eyes. "If they were interested in liquidation, why not a month ago?"

"An order is an order," Julian says. "Suppose Himmler simply decided to close us down?"

"We can't be transferred," David says. "We know too much."

"If it is liquidation, then we should fight now," Julian says. "We're ready. We've been ready for months."

"You heard about the grenades," Galewski says.

"What about them?" David asks. "I thought we got them already. Didn't you say —"

"They don't have fuses."

David's scalp prickles. For weeks the story of the grenades has floated around the barracks. It made revolt tangible. He did not know who got them out of the camp's new arsenal or how because he was not supposed to know, but he has held the image of the grenades at the back of his mind for weeks, because grenades made revolt tangible.

"More delays," he says. He looks at Julian Sussmann, and can tell by the tense, anxious expression that his desire for revolt consumes him. After all he may be as trustworthy as any of them.

"I will work on the fuses," Julian says. David stares at the floor. Ridiculous. Survival is a habit, revolt is a fantasy. They might as well dream of being kings.

Galewski shrugs, shakes his head. "We must —"

The barracks door opens and The Doll walks in smiling. David stands, as does everyone else, and other workers nearby are suddenly wary and look at The Doll with obsequious smiles. David nonchalantly moves toward his bunk, to put distance between himself and Galewski as he had been ordered. His head reels with fright — a mass execution. The Doll is getting ready to herd them out to be shot, or stuffed into the gas chamber. A master of jovial treachery, he will invite them out for something, and they will not find out about how they will die until they are outside. He looks around, tall and handsome, wearing his long leather coat with the square silver buckle glinting in front, and peaked cap with a flying eagle above the silver death's head, and his arrogant assurance unmans every one of the inmates. David can see the barely controlled trembling, the nauseated, ingratiating smiles.

"Gentlemen," he says. "I have an announcement to make."

The men shuffle, but remain suspicious. An announcement?

"As of tomorrow transports will roll again."

There is a brief silence while the men process this information with slow-functioning minds. One looks at another, eyes wide in a blank astonishment. Then, as one, their voices rise in a deafening, exultant cheer. David looks around, still shaking with nervousness, and then, almost as if the act is involuntary, delivers his own voice into the collective expression of relief. The Doll stands at the doorway nodding brightly, his fists on his hips.

A little later, after The Doll leaves, David hears a man on a bunk near him weeping into the wad of dirty clothes that serves as a pillow. The others file out toward the field kitchen for their supper, and he sits thinking about what has just happened. It means life. New transports mean food, valuables, the chance to barter for more time. He does not know if the man weeps because of shame at the obvious absurdity of their situation or because of relief that he may live a little longer, even if it does mean the deaths of tens of thousands. The fact that he himself cheered along with the rest makes David sweat despite the coolness of the evening air, and he thinks, what have we become? But at the same time, he reasons, if transports are inevitable, and a natural result of their inevitability is his survival, then he will not think about it. He walks to the weeping man and says, "The field kitchen is here," and the man looks up at him and nods.

In a few minutes he finds himself standing outside in the fading light with the other men, holding in his hand a cup of lukewarm potato soup, on the top of which float perfect little disks of grease that show a tiny reflection of his own face and upper body repeated for each little circle. He drinks a sip, and bites off a piece of bread. He has just been told that the transports are coming from Bulgaria, and that these people will each be carrying fifty kilograms of personal effects. These are not the destitute, vermin-ridden people of the east. These are city people, laden with valuables and food.

Joachim Voss and Josef Schneck stand next to the Hospital shack waiting for Anatoly. Schneck has sent the kapo named Kurland away with orders for Anatoly to meet them here. Voss looks around at the small mounds of dirty snow that have remained in the shaded areas around the shack, and has looked once into the pit at the remains of typhoid victims still smoldering a dark, salty smoke. One blackened skull sits perched on a mound of ash with wisps of smoke curling lazily out of its eye sockets.

"All that yelling was Franz telling them that the transports are coming," Voss says. "And we've got the new gas chambers." It makes his heart race. Wealthy Bulgarians. "Listen," he says. "We don't have to do this."

"You want the stamps, don't you?"

Voss looks at what Schneck has brought with them: a noose made of stiff wire, another piece of wire, and a pair of hedge clippers. "I'm not used to this sort of business."

Schneck smiles at him. "You should have seen us in Russia."

Voss shudders, and feels shaky already. Schneck had explained to him that he got the idea by looking at Weyrauch's hand, with the missing finger. Ukrainians, he said, hate mutilation. Fire, he said, will derange a man and make him lose his sense of the logic of torture. Electricity too. You must use something elemental. Then he asked Voss, "D'you have hedge clippers? Not the kind with straight blades, but the ones with short blades that look like a parrot's beak?" He went on to explain that mutilation keeps the subject lucid, which in this case is most important, because Anatoly will hold out and try not to reveal the location of his loot.

Voss hears the slamming and screeching of the excavation machinery a hundred meters away at the burial pits. He wanted, originally, to oversee that process, because he imagined that gold and other valuables hidden in body cavities would eventually drop down into the ash pits, but when he saw it, he realized that it would be insane to go digging around down there.

Anatoly and Kapo Kurland approach the Hospital shack, and Schneck draws his pistol. As Anatoly rounds the corner of the shack Schneck points the pistol at his face, and he freezes, his hands up. "Remove the rifle," Schneck says to Kurland, who does so and leans it against the wall of the shack. "Please, take a break," Schneck says. When Kurland leaves, Schneck laughs and says, "A Red Cross armband. Whose idea was that?"

"Franz's idea, I suppose," Voss says. Anatoly's eyes are wide with fright.

"Now," Schneck says to Anatoly, "you will come and stand under this beam." He indicates a beam just inside the doorway of the shack, and tenses the hand holding the pistol. Anatoly lets his head droop and walks into the shack, and Schneck loops the wire noose over his head. Anatoly draws in a breath sharply, as if from the coldness of the wire, and raises his hands to touch it. "No," Schneck says.

Then Anatoly's shoulders drop in weary resignation. Russians, Voss thinks. What is it about them that makes them accept it so readily? "Ask him," he says. Schneck looks at him and shakes his head with a kind of jovial disapproval, and pulls Kurland's wooden chair over behind Anatoly. Then, with the muzzle of the pistol against Anatoly's neck, he climbs up on the chair, and pulls up gently on the wire. "Tiptoes," he says. Anatoly does not understand. Voss mimics standing up on tiptoe, and Anatoly obeys, his eyes wide with confusion and fright. When he is on tiptoes Schneck jerks the wire tight and then winds it around the beam, and Anatoly is stuck there, trying to keep his balance. When he yaws off to the side he reaches up quickly to grab the wire, but it is too slippery, and the loop where the noose is made pinches the skin on his neck. Schneck steadies him. "Careful," he says. Anatoly is straight again, balancing unsteadily. Schneck draws out the other piece of wire and winds it first around one of Anatoly's wrists, then, pulling the hands behind, around the other, like handcuffs.

"Ask him," Voss says. "Please ask him."

"He'll lie," Schneck says. "Won't you, Anatoly?"

Anatoly concentrates on keeping his balance. Tears are now running down his face, and his huge ears are a bright red.

Schneck goes into the back of the shack and looks around, then comes back with a rag, which he balls up and stuffs into Anatoly's mouth, never changing his expression away from the look of a kind of businesslike nonchalance. Then he picks up the hedge clippers and without pausing steps to Anatoly and, before Anatoly can even try to look down to see what is going on, works the heavy, curved blades around the smallest finger of his right hand, and closes the handles shut. Anatoly comes out with a muffled scream and falls backward, and Schneck catches him and stands him up straight again. Fluid runs from Anatoly's nose, and he is trembling so badly that he cannot keep his balance.

Airy and almost faint, Voss looks at his hand. The finger dangles there, still attached by tissue. Schneck jerks the finger off and flings it toward the fire pit, then jumps back when he realizes that the blood dripping quickly from the finger stump has hit his polished, black boots. He pulls the rag from Anatoly's mouth and wipes the blood off his boots, then wraps it around the stump and ties it once, loosely.

"Where are the stamps?"

"A birch stump. I'll show you." His face is ashen, and he appears to be in a kind of calm shock. "Take the wire off."

"Excellent," Schneck says, and climbs back up on the chair. When he jumps back down, he says, "There you are, a free man." Anatoly pulls his fists around to the side, gripping the rag covering the finger stump. Schneck unwinds the wire, and throws it into the shed. "There," he says. "Now you'll take us to your loot." Anatoly presses the wrapped fist of his right hand to his chest.

Voss has calmed down, and now has the sensation of all this being more or less normal. He is amazed that Schneck's expression never changed during the torture procedure. The man has surpassed all human feeling apparently. And even Anatoly, holding his hand and wincing, then groaning from time to time, seems to harbor no bitterness toward either of them.

Their march to the woods has the atmosphere of a chummy afternoon walk, Schneck from time to time noting the surroundings: Say, I notice there are birds here and none around the camp. Is it the smell? Or, Anatoly, I understand you have a girl out here somewhere. What is her name? And Anatoly answers, still hunched around his injured hand.

The loot is a bag that weighs at least a couple of kilograms. Voss stoops down at the base of the huge birch stump, just in front of the dry-rotted hole where Anatoly stored the bag, and lifts out a piece of rag with the wad of stamps inside. They are in reasonably good shape, considering how they got there. "Here they are," he says.

Schneck looks carefully, studying the fine engraving. "American," he says. "Why would a Pole have these?"

"Collectors are collectors," Voss says.

He looks into the bag, draws out watches, rings, jewelry. Some of the jewelry is imitation, and most of the watches are common. "A good deal of this is trash," he whispers to Schneck, as if in deference to Anatoly's taste.

"Let him keep it then," Schneck says. "Say, Anatoly," he calls over his shoulder. "Why don't you keep the rest of this?"

The look on Anatoly's face shows suspicious disbelief. He snorts softly, and then his face twists, as if by a mechanical act of will, into an ashen, obsequious smile.

"Here," Schneck says. "A little nest egg for Anatoly."

They turn back to Anatoly. The look on his face has changed into a fatalistic resignation, which Schneck seems to recognize. "No no no," he says, "we're not going to shoot you."

"No?"

"Of course not. We'll be friends."

Voss carefully puts the stamps in his tunic pocket, and wonders if Schneck is telling the truth.

"I'll accept any responsibility for consequences here," Schneck says. "You've had an accident, isn't that right? Go to the Revier, and they'll fix you up."

Anatoly thinks, then says, "Yes."

"All right," Schneck says, patting him on the shoulder. "We'll leave it at that. Everything is now in order. And after all, what's one little finger in the grand scheme of things anyway?"

GAS CHAMBERS, CAMP NUMBER TWO, TREBLINKA

MID-APRIL 1943

When the gas chamber doors slam open, and the workers manipulate the heavy rods that hold them open, the bodies topple out as if they had crowded at the door waiting to be released, and the dentists go to work looking in their mouths. A second and third chamber are opened, and the workers begin to run around, carrying bodies on wooden stretchers toward the roasts.

Janusz Siedlecki and Waclaw Gitzer grab the body of a woman and throw it onto the wooden litter, Janusz holding a beautiful ring he found at the edge of the ash pit. He has not had the chance to put it in his shoe, and it would be visible in his pocket. It is covered with muck and bits of rotted tissue in around the stones, which look like diamonds, so he keeps it on the end joint of his little finger, which remains crooked into his palm. They carry the woman off, Waclaw stumbling with fatigue and a kind of mindless joviality. They dump their body, and run back, Janusz in front pulling Waclaw, who hangs onto the handles and flops along, barely able to keep his feet. When they load the second body, another woman, Janusz sees Schneck coming down the high dirt bank that separates the Death Camp from the Reception Camp. He holds his hand up. Janusz stops, and the ring squirts from his fist.

"You dropped something," Schneck says. Janusz looks at the ring, his mind suddenly captured by an airy bewilderment. He puts down his end of the litter and picks the ring up. "Just put it in your pocket," Schneck says. He does, watching as the ring falls down, making a little lump on the fabric of his pant leg. Then he feels his heart slamming in his chest.

"What's wrong with your friend?" Schneck asks.

Janusz tries to control his trembling and labors over the creation of a German sentence. Then he says, "He has a sore tooth." He walks around the litter toward Waclaw, again working on a German sentence. "He's a good worker," he says. "As a matter of fact, your grace, he is an excellent worker."

Schneck laughs. "'Your grace'?"

Janusz flushes with embarrassment. "No, I mean your — I mean sir."

"Let me see. I won't hurt him."

Schneck steps toward Waclaw, holding his hands up reassuringly. "Open your mouth. I was a medical student."

Waclaw opens his mouth, and Schneck looks. "Your tooth is fractured, and you have an abscess."

"He will be fine," Janusz says. "I'll help him."

"No," Schneck says, "I will help him. Wait here." He walks to the gas chamber platform, where the dentists are levering gold teeth out of corpses. "You," he says to one of them, a middle-aged man whose pliers and hands are sticky with blood. "Go and wait by those two body carriers over there."

Next Schneck goes to one of the Ukrainian guards, who appears wary as he approaches. "You," he says. "Vodka." The guard runs off toward the shed housing the gas chamber engine.

"I don't understand," Janusz says. "I don't —"

The guard returns with a bottle of vodka, and Schneck offers it to Waclaw. "Drink as much as you want." Waclaw drinks, scowls as it goes down, and drinks again. Janusz watches his shaking hand holding the bottle.

"Now," Schneck says to the old dentist, "I want you to take his tooth out." Then he goes into a strange speech in German, only a third of which Janusz understands — "must be careful of an infection, which will —" And then words that Janusz does not understand. "Please lie down," Schneck says to Waclaw, and he does, flopping back, closing his eyes because of the sun. Schneck continues his speech, and Janusz is fascinated by his strange, dead-faced expression. Finally he nods to the dentist, who leans down to Waclaw, who squints at the blue sky as if stunned by a blow to the head.

In two seconds the bloody tooth is out, the dentist holding it up. Schneck says, "Very well," and draws his pistol. Then he shoots the old dentist in the temple, making Janusz jump back, his knees weak. The man falls over on his side, still alive. He stares at the middle distance between himself and the roast, blinking thoughtfully, the little hole in his temple leaking blood. He appears to have decided something, and his legs begin to jiggle anxiously as if he is dreaming of running, as dogs dream. Then a spot of urine begins to spread on one leg of his trousers, and a satisfied rattle comes from his throat. Schneck looks at Janusz and smiles. "Isn't it interesting how people die?" he says. He nudges the still dentist with his foot. "In any case," he says, "keep the vodka, soak a piece of rag with it and jam it down on that wound. Have him get plenty of rest, eat soft foods, and drink liquids."

"Yes sir," Janusz says. Waclaw sits up and giggles.

"I have been watching you," Schneck says to Janusz. "Please, tell me if you do not understand. You started back during the body pile-up. I saw you also at the pits, carrying those rotted bodies. You are as —" He pauses, looking for the right word. "As excellent? Yes, as excellent a victim as I am a — well, whatever word you wish. Or nearly so."

There is a moment of silence, which scares Janusz, so he says, "Thank you."

"I am amazed that you could stand your own smell, that you carried those slippery corpses after they thawed."

"Yes sir. I mean, I got used to it."

"So," Schneck says. "You shall now be a dentist — a promotion of sorts, I would guess."

Janusz looks down at the bloody pliers.

"But of course you and your friend shall finish the day as body carriers, this man being your next load."

Dr Herzenberg looks down at Waclaw Gitzer, who lies on his dirty bunk with his eyes closed and his jaw clenched on a bloody piece of rag that looks black in the dim, flickering light reflected off the ceiling from the dying roast fires. "Schneck had him pull the tooth and then shot him?"

"Yes," Janusz says. "Something is wrong with him."

Dr. Herzenberg looks once more at Waclaw. "Is this the one they call the —"

Janusz nods. The Failure. And there is Izak Janka, whom Janusz thinks of as The Bully, and Bloch, whom they call The Captain. And Izak Janka has started referring to Janusz as The Patron Saint of the Worthless, because he tries to keep Waclaw's spirits up. "Yes," he says.

Janusz reaches into his pocket and draws out the ring. "I found this in the pit," he says, "just before Schneck came. I dropped it and he saw me, but he let me keep it."

Dr. Herzenberg squints at it, and looks back at Waclaw.

"I don't have much for him, I don't know." He chuckles dryly. "Alum perhaps. Salicylic acid tablets for fever."

Janusz gives Dr. Herzenberg the ring. He stares at it in his hand, and does not seem to know what to do with it.

There is a commotion over on the other side of the barracks. Two men argue over the sleeping arrangements, and lately tempers have been short. For some reason there has been a strange, growing hysteria in the air. Everyone fears the camp's liquidation, because of the reports of Russian advances in the east. It was worse before Dr. Herzenberg came from the Reception Camp. He has imposed a kind of order in the barracks, which sometimes seems like a madhouse, with men fighting, with men trying to figure out how to barter for time with one of the laundry girls, with men proclaiming wild plans for escape. Right away Dr. Herzenberg cleaned Janusz's ears. He calmed the men, told them to be patient, told them to remove the scraps of rotted flesh from their boots before coming in, that they must wash their hands, shave, keep themselves up, be men rather than animals.

At Janusz's feet, between his filthy shoes, lie the dentist's pliers. A wave of revulsion sweeps over him.

"Schneck," Dr. Herzenberg says. "He clearly saw the ring?"

"Yes."

"That is strange."

"I have seen him shoot people like that before. For absolutely no reason. Why does he do that?"

"Because he can," Dr. Herzenberg says. "I have seen men like him before. Death fascinates them. They have no use for politics or love or any of that. For Schneck, Treblinka is a paradise, a dream come true."

The commotion from the other side of the barracks moves in their direction, and the doctor suddenly has a weary, irritated look on his face. It is Izak Janka, The Bully, walking around seeming both angry and excited. "The laundry women!" he says. "What would it take to get one of them to do it?" Then he sees Janusz, Waclaw, and the doctor. "Well, isn't this a pretty sight?" he says. "There's the stupid martyr and his chum the walking corpse. It's people like you who'll get us all on the roast."

The doctor studies Izak Janka for a moment, then says, "You must remember who we are, and therefore who you are."

"Is that right?" Izak Janka bellows. "So who am I then?"

"You are a Jew. Do you remember that?"

"I remember that I am a man, and that I am a man who wants a woman. A little gold, a piece of sausage, of course to eat, not what you might think. I'll take care of that part."

"Do you remember who you are?" the doctor asks Janusz.

"I think so, yes," he says.

"Oh that's wonderful," Izak Janka says. "He thinks!"

David Schrhafta looks down at Anatoly's hand, the dirty bandage crowning the short stump of his little finger. "Schneck," Anatoly whispers. His hand shakes.

"Anatoly," David says, "we are worried about how open you are, how you risk being seen." Anatoly has been taking too many risks — stuffing cans of petrol and gun powder and cigarettes in the barracks doorway at night, useful stuff but hard to hide.

"I'm leaving," Anatoly says. "When it is time, kill them all, kill Schneck the baby killer and that drunk Voss." Anatoly's Polish has improved so much that David is amazed at the force of his expression as he speaks. Then they see her in the distance, and Anatoly turns and leaves.

David raises the ax and trims a branch off the half-rotted trunk of an evergreen. Then he squints at Anatoly's girl — he can see by the way she walks and by the subtle shape of her long skirt encircling her stomach that she is pregnant, and for a moment he feels mystified at the idea that anything normal could be going on. If she is pregnant, and Anatoly still wants to see her, then normalcy has survived despite the camp.

David raises the ax and smacks off another branch, which shatters with a brittle explosion into four or five pieces. Pine — you must watch yourself when you hit the branches, especially when they are dead. Vlodya rises from an old stump and wanders a few meters away so he can see Anatoly and the girl. He laughs, mutters something in Russian, and stretches, squinting in the bright sunshine.

"Say, Vlodya," he says.

"What do you want, Jewish shit?" he says, and laughs. He is experimenting with imitating the officers.

David snorts amiably and steps to Vlodya. "I am wondering if you'd like to make some kind of a trade."

"Gold?"

"A little, perhaps."

"I don't like teeth," Vlodya says, working on pronouncing the Polish correctly. "No teeth."

"Watches?"

"For?"

"I was thinking of — a weapon, perhaps a pistol, or a —"

"Any of that. Can you get me a nice blonde woman?" Vlodya asks, an expression of weary jocularity crossing his face. "One I don't have to rape?"

David laughs. "Could you talk to Anatoly, about —"

"He hates them," Vlodya says. "I hate them too. When it happens, will you shoot at us?"

"No, you are our friends."

"But you will have to shoot at us. Soon?"

"I don't know." Vlodya looks at him with a knowing squint in his eye. Then he looks at his watch.

"The wagon," he says. "It has to be full."

David nods and goes back to his work.

The revolt is on, then off. On, off. That it has not yet happened frustrates him as well as everyone else. David had not understood the range or degree of this underground activity until The Doll caught the officers' doctor, Choronzycki, with currency of some sort. The rumor was that it was a huge sum of money. And Choronzycki, having been caught, bit into a vial of cyanide before The Doll could interrogate him.

David heard about it one day when the *Goldjuden* were called out to a roll call, and Choronzycki's body was dragged out into the square and ministered to by some old bitch of a doctor The Doll had called for that purpose. While the men watched, trembling, they pumped the man's stomach and tried to revive him, and while this went on, the whisper of the event passed along the onlookers hiding at building edges: In the German barracks hospital Choronzycki had the money in his pocket, perhaps something to do with the revolt. He attacked The Doll with a surgical knife and The Doll escaped through a window. Then Choronzycki took the poison.

David had watched with a sensation of rubber-legged dread, because The Doll, usually so handsome and casual, now looked so disheveled with rage that he seemed to have gone insane. When it became clear that they were not going to revive Choronzycki he began to beat him with the thicker end of a whip, so that the loud thumps, some of which caused the corpse to cough flatly, resounded off the low buildings. "Count!" The Doll yelled, because those he beat had to count the blows. "Pig! Count!" He continued to beat the corpse uselessly, and David began to see the look of mounting horror on the faces of the men nearest him. Could The Doll turn his wrath on the living? But he did not. Workers dragged the corpse toward the Hospital pit, and officers marched all the *Goldjuden* there too, to stand before the stinking sulfur fire. Later on David heard that The Doll threatened to have them all shot if they did not reveal the source of the money. No one talked, and he let them go.

Vlodya is now standing away from the stump and looking in the direction Anatoly went. Then he looks at his watch. In a few moments the expression on Vlodya's face begins to change. He now has an amazed smile on his face. It looks as if Anatoly has run off. Then David wonders: What if everyone, The Doll included, becomes so sick of all this death that they simply walk away? What if every single man wakes up one morning and walks out into the Roll Call Square and thinks, this is all wrong and it's time to give it up. And then they would gather and walk out the gate, amazed that this exodus was all along such an obvious choice, so obvious that they are all a little embarrassed that they had failed to see it until now.

As Anatoly walks, lugging the heavy bag in his left hand, he feels it there, bobbing painfully, and each time he looks at his right hand, he sees that it is not there. It is a little stump with the tight depression centered by a hard scab. The ghost of his finger pains him at night, as if by cutting it off Schneck had mysteriously left its soul to itch, to close into a fist with the rest of them. His hatred of them is so powerful that he is infuriated at the workers' failure to revolt. Nothing he did, no amount of petrol or gunpowder or zlotys or food, seemed to be good enough for them to act, to walk out of their filthy barracks firing, cutting down all the way to the commandant in his white jacket.

Magda's father must not know. He will camp in the woods, wait until the right moment when he and Magda and the baby will escape. They will live someplace where there is no pain and no death, no burning children. There will be only the circle, him and Magda, and completed when he is born so as to negate the death of the boy who looked at his ears so long ago. And then home to the oceans of wheat.

The section of woods he is in is more than a kilometer from the camp and almost a kilometer from her house, and if any of them come to cut wood and find him, he can shoot them. The pistol he kept is small and light, but he has a half a kilogram of ammunition for it. And he will pray, beg the almighty, force it by an act of will, and then wait to see the sky glow red with the camp's death.

GAS CHAMBERS, CAMP NUMBER TWO, TREBLINKA

LATE MAY 1943

Using his left index finger to hold the man's jaw open, Janusz Siedlecki looks away from the vacant eyes and works the heavy, mandible-like plier jaws around a gold-capped tooth and begins levering. He feels the tissue in the jaw popping, and then the tooth tears loose, and he flips it into the tin bucket sitting to his right. Each morning when he starts his work the teeth make a resonant bonging sound in the bottom of the bucket. Later they land on the growing pile with a soft sound, as if the bucket holds a pile of wet river pebbles. Schneck stands over by the gold sorters' table watching him, then shifting his eyes to the other dentists. Janusz tries to appear casual, but the six or seven gold crowns he has stored under his tongue irritate the soft membranes of his mouth, and force him to produce saliva, which he spits out onto the filth-slicked concrete fronting the gas chamber doors. He does not want to swallow the saliva. He began storing the crowns that broke off, some with tooth parts, about an hour before lunch. Next is a pretty girl, and he feels guilty looking at her, as he does when he looks at any of the girls. She is buxom and has a chubby, attractive face, and he is momentarily captivated by her body, the breasts and belly with the fine hair reflecting the sunlight in tiny amber and gold needles. Had she lived in a house nearby just a year ago, he might have talked to her. He might have become her boyfriend. She has no gold. As he rises, feeling the teeth shift under his tongue, she is jerked away by two body carriers who throw her on a litter and run her off to the roasts.

Now another older man. He pulls the jaw open, feeling the stubble on the man's chin irritate the skin on the back of his second finger, which is folded against the chin in order to steady it. Two teeth. He works the plier jaws around the smaller of the gold teeth and levers it, and it pops out, leaving the dark red hole. He has only three bodies left, two children and an old lady. Schneck has wandered toward the roasts, and the Ukrainians have backed away toward the thin strip of shade just next to the gas chamber building. In a quick move, as if rubbing something from his nose, he puts the tooth in his mouth, undergoes the usual feeling of revulsion at the smell, and tucks the tooth under his tongue. He hates the smell of dead people's mouths — it is bad breath squared, he thinks. Rot is horrible, but the odor of something so recently alive is worse.

He thinks that everything is worse because he hears too well. Bringing that one sense back has brought a new intensity or sharpness to all his senses. He became aware it the first day he pulled teeth — the Ukrainian Ivan opened the door and the yellow bodies tumbled out, making wet slapping sounds as they hit the concrete, their mouths gaping loosely. Workers pulled the corpses away from the door, sliding them on their own filth.

He leaned down and opened a man's mouth, and aimed the pliers, and the sudden grating sound along with the sensation of the steel's contact with the tooth vibrating into his hand made his hands go numb and all the hair stand up on his head. He could barely make himself do it. And since Dr. Herzenberg flushed his ears, this intensity of the senses became the doorway to something else, a shadow of an idea he thinks of as obvious but at the same time mysterious, like a silhouette you assume to be one thing until your perception transforms it into something else — an urn becoming two faces nose to nose. But he does not know what it is.

His back aches. He leans down to look into the mouths of the two children, and involuntarily drools saliva from his mouth, and quickly wipes his sleeve across his lips and looks around. No, that was too obvious, he thinks. He spits on the dirty concrete. The gold under his tongue is heavy, seems to stretch, to scrape and infect the membranes on the floor of his mouth. Dr. Herzenberg told him that if confronted, swallow the teeth. The first child has teeth lined up crazily, as if his mouth does not have enough room for them. The second child, a girl, has an appendicitis scar. Briefly he sees her recovering, lying in bed and clutching a doll. He considers the trauma of her operation, the parents' fear of her dying on the operating table, and then their immense relief at discovering that she would live. That night after she came home, they tucked her in so that she felt warm and safe. He turns away from her. The old woman has the stumps of teeth, brown and stinking, and no gold.

There is a lull. The other dentists are finishing up the bodies from their chambers, frequently looking toward the spot where they will be served lunch. The kapos have not brought the field kitchen out yet, and for the moment, he has nothing to do but hold the teeth in his mouth and wait until he can get close to Dr. Herzenberg. Off by the roasts the excavator clanks, its cables snapping, and a black mass of corpses flops from its jaws. The teeth irritate, and he spits again. When he expels them into his hand and gives them to Dr. Herzenberg, he will smell the gummy plaque and sticky blood on them, coming off the skin of his hand, and that smell will stay with him.

He believes he sees the pretty girl partway up one of the roasts. She had a boyfriend, who could barely control himself when they were together. Once she allowed him to put his hand under her blouse on her breast. The softness of it, the warmth and liquidity, made him nearly faint, and she promised him that when she was a little older and they were married he would be able to do all that he wanted with her. The boy went home tramping across the rye fields, seeing his life as a journey into a fantastic future, with rewards of such lusciousness that his legs became rubbery at the thought of it.

They wheel out the field kitchen and his stomach begins to churn, saliva bursts into his mouth, and the gold teeth scrape together, heavy with a metallic tartness. At one of the three mounds of bodies on the roast, Waclaw Gitzer jams a section of wood between two corpses, turning once to listen to Tadellos, who points repeatedly inward. He has recovered. That the infection did not kill him is amazing in itself, considering the hectic pace of the work. Janusz believes that it was the advice of Dr. Herzenberg that made the difference: You must keep the wound clean, you must eat, rest when you can, you must keep your faith, believe that God will protect you.

The wheels of the field kitchen squeak with faint, metallic friction that makes his skin shiver. One of the gold sorters comes to him and picks up the bucket. Now he sees Dr. Herzenberg, and gathers saliva and spits. Immediately more saliva oozes into his mouth, absorbing the infected slime of the dead mouths, and he smells the odor of the teeth hovering around his face.

Sound. Now that he is not listening to the subtle sound of tissue breaking under the pressure of the pliers, or the strange, sucking sounds he sometimes hears when he opens mouths, the exhalation of poisoned air, the passing of gas, popping of joints when bodies are jerked away, he hears everything, a blending of every sound within a hundred meters or more. Beyond the roasts the officers have a table set up with a white cloth and wine bottles, and Janusz sees the boy, Edek, who sometimes plays an accordion while they eat and drink. The men begin to gather. He moves toward Dr. Herzenberg, spitting once again. Janusz discovered the possibility of storing the teeth in his mouth and told Dr. Herzenberg. The doctor got a slightly nauseated look on his face, and then agreed that yes, it would be an excellent service to their cause. In pockets the teeth would show and would amount to a death sentence if they were discovered.

Now. His eyes meet those of the doctor, who nods his head and then looks away nonchalantly. The engine of the excavator dies down to an idle, and the operator steps down out of the cab. Janusz spits the gold into his fist, and it lies warm and sticky in his hand. When the sound of a ladle banging against the lip of a soup pot draws everyone's attention, Janusz steps next to the doctor and drops the gold into his hand.

"Good," the doctor whispers. He drops the teeth into his jacket pocket, and then, as if remembering something, gestures apologetically and walks back toward the barracks.

Tadellos is happy with their output, and gives them each a cooked sausage to go with their soup and black bread. Janusz holds the hot soup in his mouth until it cools somewhat, squirts it around under his tongue, and spits it out onto the ground. He is joined by Waclaw Gitzer and Isodor Nussbaum, who came to Treblinka with his family in April. They do not talk at first, because they concentrate on eating their food. Nussbaum has survived the initial shock of Treblinka, has bypassed suicide and the propensity for error that would get him shot, and has settled into the daily challenge of survival, and the cultivation of hope. A little wiry man with very thick glasses, each lens centered by a tiny eye, he has pinned his hopes on God, and maintains his prayers and his devotion in a manner that seems at times to be fanatical. He is less concerned with why the Nazis kill the Jews than with why God allows it to happen.

"More gold today?" Waclaw asks.

Janusz looks around, then says, "You're not supposed to know about that."

"Word gets around," Waclaw says. "Listen, be careful with this. Why do you take the risk?" He takes a bite of sausage, then closes his eyes with the pleasure of its taste. "I know it has something to do with the revolt. But then we've been hearing about the revolt from the beginning."

"Revolt is insane," Isidor Nussbaum says. "Pin your hopes on the Russians. Pray for a sudden attack."

Waclaw chuckles. "God uses the Russians for His aims?"

"Why not?" Isidor Nussbaum says. "Egypt is to the west of where we stand, Assyria is over there to the east. Judah shall outlive the great powers."

"I think your geography is suspect," Waclaw says. Janusz eats his sausage, and off past the roasts he can hear Edek playing a polka on his accordion. And behind him, along with that sound, he hears the next group of the day's transport screaming in the gas chambers.

The fires are lit after lunch, and Janusz stands and watches the flames licking at the bodies, until Ivan and his friend come around the corner of the gas chamber building and work the levers of the heavy door. In a short time he has lapsed into being absorbed by his work. He spends most of his time squatting, his left index finger crooked over the bottom teeth of this woman's jaw, that old man's jaw, over the tiny, sharp teeth of this child's jaw regardless of the fact that almost no children have gold fillings. He has his orders, and various sets of eyes work at confirming that he carries them out. And as the din of activity, of barked-out orders or the shuffling feet of body carriers or the crackling of the fires recedes, he pulls into himself and funnels his attention in on the faces of the corpses. For many of them, as he had done now since becoming a dentist, he invents pasts and identities: This old man was a teacher, feared by his pupils because of the size of his nose and ears and because of the emaciated look of his face — he smoked, drank too much coffee. But all of his pupils, in later years, realize how much they learned from him. This girl, and he accidentally runs the heel of his hand across her breast, making it bounce voluptuously, this girl wanted to be a dancer, but for her weight. Her parents and her teachers all watched the magnificently endowed body move, but alas, there was always too much of her, too much in the hips and buttocks and chest, and she was always sad, walking down the village street. Unknown to her, all the boys in the village watched, their hearts pounding. She danced her sadness away in the woods, and one day a boy — This man with two gold teeth, and Janusz pops the smaller one into his mouth, this man with the dead eyes gazing into some strange infinity, had spent his life working on a perpetual-motion machine. The pale, scholarly look of his face shows his genius and his solitude. When he is not working on the machine he writes poetry in which he tries to give name to the very infinity that has tortured him all his life.

And it is in this mesmerized state, opening mouths and pulling teeth and secretly popping every twentieth or thirtieth into his mouth, that he understands what it is that has been bothering him since he became a dentist: Each of these corpses is a person. Each has a past that is at least as complicated and abundant with memory as his own. And if he can remember every day of his life, every trivial or major experience, everything he has ever seen, then surely they can too, or could.

The abstraction of that thought vanishes, because he is nearing the end of this chamberload of corpses, and becomes aware of the smells of vomit and urine and feces and teeth. He steps over a pregnant woman who has expelled the head of her baby in the chamber, one of the two-headed ones, they are called, and is aware that a couple of guards he does not know stare disgustedly at her. They must be new, awed by what they see, and reeling at the nightmare they are stuck in.

He tries to count the teeth in his mouth by using the tip of his tongue, which is so irritated that he is afraid that it is bleeding. It is either nine or ten. The fires have become huge, and the workers have backed away from them, the reflected heat making their faces orange. Janusz moves to the doorway of the next gas chamber to help Rosengart, an older dentist who came to Treblinka in December. As Janusz bends over a corpse, he sees activity over by the fires. The officers and guards have brought in a group of people, naked women and children, who have already been beaten and are screaming with fright at the sight of the fires.

"Don't look," Rosengart says to him, without turning his head from his work.

They are Warsaw Ghetto Jews. Janusz has heard of them, heard stories about their resistance. Because they fear these people, the officers and guards, especially Ivan, who runs the chamber engine, are particularly brutal to them. As Janusz works he peeks at the activity, his legs shaking. Schneck pulls a baby from one of the women and hurls it in a pinwheeling arc into the fire, and Ivan prods her with his rifle. Then Schneck invites her to the fire, apparently taunting her for her cowardice. Rosengart levers a tooth out, and throws it into his bucket, concentrating on his work with a studious focus. Janusz tries to do the same, but finds himself looking up once more. The little crowd of women and children have bunched together, clutching at each other for protection. Schneck and another younger officer approach, deciding who is next.

Janusz is shocked awake by something, a sound. No, not a sound. It was a dream. He was a child held in his mother's arm. The arm was huge because he was so small, and he looked over the huge, pale shoulder at other women and babies standing in a group. Somewhere Edek played "Where Are You Going Mountaineer" on his accordion. And then a huge hand pulled him from his mother's arm and he was flying. When he spread his arms he saw that he was flying toward the fire, and it swept up at him, its heat rushing at his face. He landed in it and the heat increased with a powerful shock. Then he woke up.

It must be past midnight, and beyond the snoring of the men is a humid silence lying like a vapor over the barracks. He swings his legs over the edge of the bunk and then climbs up on it to look out the little window high on the wall. The camp is bathed in an ashy moonlight, and beyond the fence surrounding the barracks he sees the roast grates fifty meters away, the low gas chamber building, and off to the right at the camp perimeter the location of the burial pits, those that have been emptied filled with dirt and human ash mixed with crushed bone, and planted with vetch. Superimposed on this is a kind of movement in the air, and a subtle sound that is just beyond the threshold of his hearing. He squints, concentrates on his hearing.

"Go to sleep," Waclaw says. "What are you looking at?"

"Why are you awake?"

"I was thinking."

Janusz sits down on his bunk. In the reflected moonlight he can just see Waclaw lying with his hands clasped behind his head.

"I know what it is," Janusz says. It is simple, a matter of mathematics. "Do you know what a thousand is?"

"Of course."

"I don't mean zlotys. I mean a thousand of anything."

"Of course."

"I don't think so," Janusz says. "A thousand zlotys is commonplace." He labors over the concept. "If I pile up a thousand stones, or toy blocks, then I have a lot of blocks."

"Brilliant," Waclaw says.

"I mean, a thousand blocks lying on the ground is ten lined up by ten lined up ten times over. It is a huge quantity."

"Too many, I'd say," Waclaw says. "Go to sleep." He rolls over on his side and draws his knees up.

"When I back away, I see all these blocks, different colors, some with those pictures and letters —"

He listens. It is still there, a sound he cannot yet hear.

"Then I walk away a few feet, and there are another thousand, do you know what I mean?"

Waclaw is silent, either thinking or asleep.

"A thousand more, let's say piled up only a couple of meters away from the first pile. Ten by ten by ten, a huge pile." His father explained this to him once. How do you get a million of anything? "I look at that pile, and then walk a few meters to the next. The same, all kinds, ten by ten by ten. But by this time I have only seen three piles. More than I have ever seen in my life, but beyond the third I see a fourth, a fifth, a sixth, and then the piles keep going, right out of sight, let's say down a road." He looks at Waclaw's dim form. "Waclaw, do you know what a million is?"

Waclaw grunts in a kind of semiconscious agreement.

"A thousand a thousand times over. I don't mean blocks or zlotys. I mean a thousand in a pile, and then nine hundred and ninety-nine more piles." The understanding washes over him like the moment of discovery of the solution to a long-lasting and cryptic mathematics problem. It is simple. "We killed our millionth passenger today," he whispers.

He climbs up on the bunk again, and looks out the window. The millionth was the child they threw into the fire. And what he heard before with his improved hearing, what he hears now, is whispering. He squints out over the moonlight-silvered landscape of the camp, and as he could earlier hear and not hear at the same time, he thinks he can now see the faint shadows of all of them. They are like images on glassine superimposed on one another, or fading through one another as they walk. There are so many that multiple images fade against one another in an almost innumerable superimposition. Somewhere in there stand his grandmother, Zygmunt, and the girls. Somewhere in there a woman's spirit cradles the spirit of her child who was thrown into the fire. Clearest of all to him now is the subtle hissing sound of a million people whispering, so that no single voice is discernible. It is like wind rushing over a rye field.

He stares out at them, listening.

NEAR WOLGA-OKNAGLIK, POLAND

AUGUST 2, 1943

The man standing above her as she sits by the bush has black hair, and his face and clothes are dirty. Magda Nowak works herself into the bush, backing away by pushing with her heels. "Don't," she whispers. "Please, don't."

But he stares. Now, with the pain receding into a tense trembling in her back, she sees the look of fright on his sweat-streaked face, and with each sound coming from the brush, his eyes dart around.

"I know you," she says. He is one of the workers. All year she saw him in the woods, cutting, dragging a cart.

The man stoops to his knees, looking around. "Excuse me, but I need to know something." She smells him — sweat, petrol, a sulfur odor. "I don't know where I am," he says. "They're every-where, and I don't know where to go."

"That way," and she points toward the setting sun, "is the Malkinia railway and the gravel quarry. Back toward the camp there are village people and police."

He looks in both directions, then settles wearily. He is gaunt, and his eyes are sunken. "I don't know," he says.

"Do you know Anatoly?"

He squints at her. "You're Anatoly's girl," he says. "We saw you all year." He looks briefly at her belly. "I see."

"Where is he?"

"Well —" Then he tenses, looking around.

"You're not supposed to say?"

He listens, staring at the ground, then says, "No no, it's just that I haven't seen him. He may have been transferred."

"Did you know they cut his finger off, for stealing?"

"Yes." The man becomes impatient, his eyes again darting around. "I need to know where to go."

"My house is across the road," she says. "If you cross and go along the road, you'll be going north. That is toward the Ster-dyn Woods. Far away up there is the Bialowieza Forest."

She feels another pain open up in her rib cage, and laces her fingers under her belly and closes her eyes.

"You're in labor," he says.

"Yes," she whispers.

He remains silent as she concentrates on it, trying to will the cramp down into her thighs so that it will be over, but when it reaches its peak she feels herself unable to control it as it overcomes her, pressing powerfully downward into the center, into the space where it wants to open, the first one she had felt that is clearly pushing the baby down. She finds herself strain-ing against her will, holding her breath until she feels her face bloat with pressure. Then she lets out a long breath, and opens her eyes. The man watches her as if hypnotized. "Do you see?"

she says. "I have to get across the road and home. But the soldiers — The midwife is supposed to come."

"All right," he says. "The longer I stay here the more likely it is they'll find me. You say the woods are —"

"Across, and then north. You'll see the bigger trees."

"Can you walk?"

"Until the next cramp. Then I have to sit."

The man helps her up, and they work their way through the brush, the man walking in a cautious stoop. Magda cannot stoop, and walks with her fingers laced under her belly. Then the man gets down on his knees and peeks around a bush, and when she gets to him, she sits, waiting for the next pain.

"One more cramp, and then we go." They must cross about fifty meters of open space, and the man looks up the road and down, up and down. "When did you last see Anatoly?" she asks. "Do they do that all the time, cut a finger off?"

"I don't know," the man says. "The Germans — you have no idea what they can do. I saw him in early June, I think."

"And now he is gone, and the baby will have no father."

The man looks at her, thinking. "Anatoly is a friend to us, and we set fire to the camp partly because of that. The baby has a father, but you know how things are these days."

"Where would they transfer him?"

"I don't know, but if he can, he'll come back for you. He told us. I recall him saying he would never leave you."

He looks again. There are no sounds now, no gunfire or motors. The man puts his hand out to her. "We've only been here a minute. How about having your cramp on the other side?"

"All right," she says. Then she squints into the distance. "See there, way off — that is our well sweep, past the rye."

The man pulls her to her feet, and they step out into the open and walk toward the road. It seems magically easy. Within thirty seconds they enter the brush on the other side, and the man stops, wipes his hand across his forehead, and says, "This way, you said?"

"Yes."

"Well, when you see Anatoly, tell him you saw David."

"David, yes. But do you think he'll come back?"

"You know how things are. With things the way they are, there's no saying, but he would not leave you. Let's hope."

Then he holds his hand up, and is gone into the brush. Magda waits for the signals of the next cramp, staring through the haze at the tall well sweep next to her house.

MAIN GATE, CAMP NUMBER ONE

EARLY JUNE 1943

For Joachim Voss, the sensation of passing through the ornately decorated gate out into the countryside for a purpose is so exhilarating that he experiences a sudden, powerful recognition of the perversity of his last eleven months. He turns in the car seat. Surrounded by open space and then evergreens, the camp looks like a quaint village, or a spa.

Dietrich drives the staff car slowly, fearing damage on the bumpy road. It is the car The Doll uses. Voss chuckles. Franz has now become The Doll even to his men. Although it is mid-morning, he feels a heavy alcoholic swoon, and wonders if he drank too much before leaving with Dietrich. When he found that he would go on this mission, he drank as much as he could as fast as he could for two or three minutes, in effect filling his tank for the day.

With the excitement somewhat worn off, he tries to understand objectively what it is that has happened. Like the rest of the men, he has become so used to the camp that he has regarded as more or less acceptable all the peculiar improvements The Doll has instituted. In the evenings they sit and listen to classical and popular music concerts, they watch boxing matches between the inmates, they even make bets on the outcome. And they do all of this without any amazement, without any speculation about the obvious.

The Polish countryside is lush but nondescript — patches of forest with sprinklings of birch trunks showing through the darkness of evergreens, and here and there, large areas of collected rainwater. Anatoly is probably out there with his girlfriend. Any attempt to return to his homeland would be problematic, because the frequency of passable roads decreases as one moves northeast toward the Pripet Marshes and the Bialowieza Forest. If he tried to hide in the woods, partisans would get him, and Voss has heard the tales of partisans: torture, mutilation, death. Especially for a Ukrainian. Even these woods, he thinks, scanning the trees slowly sweeping by, probably hide them. No, Anatoly would have to have a means of traveling, and if he attempts to take his whore with him, the difficulty will be magnified.

"We'll try Wolga-Oknaglik first," Dietrich says, the veins on his neck bulging with the effort of speaking over the sound of the motor.

The desertion has made Dietrich livid, as if he held some position that rated such irritation. The Doll becomes irritated, even infuriated, and this seems proper. After all he runs the camp, seems in fact to own it. But the sadist Dietrich — his righteous anger seems silly and embarrassing. He said a number of times, "This is an unacceptable breach of security," until The

Doll's anger at the situation turned into a kind of chagrined puzzlement at the obviousness of Dietrich's artificial concern.

Then Voss understands: Anything normal is jumped at with an excessive zeal. With the staff car bouncing over the country road, Voss feels the horror wash over him like a hot, foul vapor. They are killing people, women and children, every day, half of them for the pure, lurid joy of it. And at night they listen to Mozart. It is no wonder that when Voss found out that they were to hunt Anatoly down, he felt a perfect, simplified exhilaration at this gift of unexpected normalcy. They would catch him and ship him off to a proper court-martial.

They approach a crossroad on which inches a convoy of some sort, heading east. "Wehrmacht," Dietrich says.

"Why aren't they on the railway?"

"Partisans, probably. Damaged rails or something."

Dietrich downshifts, and Voss leans up in his seat to get a better view. The convoy is a series of canvas-topped trucks interspersed with motorcycles, some with sidecars. As they approach the road, some of the men in truck cabs and on the motorcycles turn and look, but do not wave. Of course they hate the SS, they turn sour at the appearance of the black uniforms. Voss feels a sensation of bleak envy looking at them. They are regular army on their way to the front. As the convoy passes on, the last truck crossing before them in the dust cloud made by the other vehicles, Voss sees three figures on the other side of the crossroad. It is Schneck and Kuttner, with that big stupid fool Anatoly standing between them wearing civilian trousers and an ill-fitting velvet smoking jacket.

Voss has never been in the little cellar near the Ukrainian barracks. He has heard it referred to as a punishment cellar. It is dank and moldy, and Schneck has brought with them a kerosene lamp so that they can illuminate the proceedings of Anatoly's punishment. The little room seems crowded with the three of them standing around Anatoly, who sits on a creaky chair with his hands tied behind the chair back. On his face is that fatalistic acceptance that seems to Voss so Russian.

"Where is the deputy commandant?" Voss asks.

Dietrich and Schneck show a blank lack of concern.

"He's in Warsaw, I think," Schneck says.

"You are sow fuckers," Anatoly says.

In the silence that follows the bizarre statement, Schneck looks from one to the other with a jaunty puzzlement.

"Did I hear that, or is your German faulty?" Schneck asks.

"You are Nazi worms, and filthy sow fuckers," Anatoly says.

"Shut up," Dietrich says.

"Sow fucker," Anatoly says.

"This is ridiculous," Voss says. "Obviously he is out of his mind. Let's ship him out of here."

"We can't," Schneck says. "He's to be executed."

"On whose authority?"

"Kuttner. He said do with him whatever you want."

"Shoot me," Anatoly says.

Voss understands. The insults were to hasten his execution. Anatoly knows Schneck, and wants his execution to be quick.

"Life up there is going smoothly," Schneck says. "We can't shoot you, Anatoly. We must execute you silently."

"You are sow fuckers. Your mothers fuck donkeys."

"Anatoly," Schneck says. "That's juvenile."

Anatoly begins to weep. His face twists into an expression of such childish devastation that, along with the crimson ears, he could be an overacting clown. Schneck pats him on the shoulder. "Let's get this over with," he says.

Voss begins to tremble. It is apparent that Schneck is serious, that they intend to kill Anatoly here, now.

"I want no part of this," Voss says. "I thought we were going to interrogate him and then ship him off to trial."

"So, interrogate him then."

Schneck leans down, and picks up something else he had brought with the lamp, a length of electrical wire. Voss feels the hot alcohol roil up, burning toward his throat.

"Anatoly, where is your loot?" he asks.

"The same place," Anatoly says.

Voss's heart flutters a little. Could there be more?

"What loot?" Dietrich asks. "This is property of the Reich."

Schneck laughs, and Anatoly's head droops.

The laughter seems to make Dietrich angry. "We must recover what he stole," he says. "It is property of the Reich."

"Sow fuckers," Anatoly says.

Dietrich draws out his pistol and points it at Anatoly's face, and Anatoly cowers back, his eyes wide. Then he seems to think a moment, and says, "You bugger each other in the night. You are Nazi poofs." The strategy backfires, because Dietrich holsters his pistol and scowls with wonder at Anatoly.

Anatoly weeps. "Excuse me," Voss says, "but something about this procedure makes no sense to me."

"Why?" Dietrich asks. "Are you afraid?"

Voss glares at him, then shakes his head. You stupid child, he thinks. "No, I am not afraid," he says. "It is only that something about this procedure makes no sense to me." He is aware that he is slurring his words somewhat.

"Well, I'm not afraid," Dietrich says. "Give me that," he says to Schneck. Shrugging casually, Schneck hands him the length of electrical cord. Dietrich walks around Anatoly, whose head follows him until he can turn no further. Anatoly says, "I —" and then giggles. As he is about to say more Dietrich quickly loops the electrical cord over his head, and Anatoly drives his chin down into his neck so as to protect himself from it. It does no good — Dietrich winds the wire ends around his fingers and jerks up and pulls, his wrists crossed, until his arms shake from the effort. Voss stands to Anatoly's right, and, as if in a dream, circles slowly to his front. Anatoly grits his teeth, his body trembling, his eyes wide with shock, as if he is concentrating fully on the feeling of being choked.

"Excuse me," Voss says, "but —" He is then mesmerized by the expression on Anatoly's face, and is barely aware of it when Anatoly's knees begin to pump up and down, making Schneck quickly reach out to hold them down. Dietrich continues to struggle with the effort of holding the garrote, his pudgy face tensed up.

"I am not sure about this," Voss says, and Schneck looks up at him with irritation. Anatoly's chest surges with powerful convulsions, and his face is swollen and purple, his tongue crowding his mouth. His face is streaked with tears, his hair seems to stand up on his head. Voss begins to shake, his knees weak. "I wonder if this is —" But as before, he cannot finish the sentence. The air in the room is suddenly boiling with the stench of Anatoly's having voided his bowels.

"That's enough," Schneck says. Dietrich lets go of the wire, then looks at his hands, which are dented and red in lines across the flesh of his fingers.

"My God," Schneck says, "let's get out of here."

He goes up the crude wooden staircase, which is more like a ladder, and Dietrich follows, shaking his hands. Voss looks once more at Anatoly, then follows them out. He rises into the mercilessly bright morning. Everything is flat and absurdly dense in color, and squinting, he stumbles away from the cellar to the road along the Ukrainian barracks and ends up standing inside the little zoo, where he can see the pretty little fox watching him from inside his birchwood cage.

Then he remembers: He stumbles toward the main gate. He must make his way to that old birch trunk before anyone else does. He must get Anatoly's loot, and check it before taking it to the *Goldjuden*. He becomes winded because of the pace of his walking, his face pulsing and turgid with a hot, anxious delirium. The watches — he must check the watches.

Julian Sussman and I climb down the ladder into the smell of shit, and see Anatoly on the chair. I stop for a moment, and remember the winter and before that: Anatoly standing in the woods with his rifle on his shoulder, me with my armloads of pine boughs, my hands sticky with sap. "Anatoly," I whisper.

In the dank, foul air I feel my heart beating, not out of the fear of death but because of the revolt that has not happened. Soon they will dig up the last ditch in the Death Camp and it has not happened. And Anatoly is gone.

His face is smeared with fluid, and his mouth is full of swollen tongue. The redness is gone from his ears.

"We'll get him off the chair," I say, "and figure out how to take him up."

"He's too heavy," Julian says.

"Schneck ordered us to do it. If we don't, then someone will come and carry three of us out."

Julian has that look — an expression that has fixed itself, as if cemented. Fright, a kind of weary fatalism, all because the revolt won't happen. Those who run it have a better chance of surviving anyway, so they are casual about time.

"Grab his other elbow."

We lift Anatoly by the elbows, and his upper arms slide over the chair back, and he topples toward the floor. We stop him from hitting it, and his head dangles, the ends of the wire sticking up like beetles' feelers. "That's Anatoly's antenna," I say. "Anatoly, what do you hear?"

We drag him, his knees scraping the dirt floor, and wedge his head between two of the stair rungs. As he hangs there, fluid drips from his mouth, then extends into a string that dangles and glitters in the shaft of sunlight coming down through the stairwell.

"They are killing their own," I say. "Galewski must make up his mind."

"David, no one tells me. How will we know?"

"Let me explain," I say. "The fewer people who know, the better the chance of success. Everyone will know, the whole camp, even those in the Death Camp. Of the million or so who came to Treblinka only a few survived. Most of them died, leaving a thousand or so. Of those, about fifty know. It is best that way. Let the tiniest minority do their job."

We go partway up the stairs, then each reach down and grab the crooks of his elbows, and begin pulling. He comes slowly, his head scraping the stairs, the string of sticky saliva swinging and getting longer. In the strong sunlight I can see that the wire is buried in the flesh of his neck. When we get him to the top, panting with the effort, we crawl partway out onto the ground and then heave the upper part of his body out of the hole so that he is lying facedown with his legs still in the stairwell. We pull him the rest of the way out and roll him over. His face is covered with dirt.

"Good riddance," Julian says.

"No," I say. "He didn't confess. Anatoly was our friend. Why didn't you squeal, Anatoly?" I say, touching his bristly head. "Did you hate them that much?" Beyond him and the buildings I see the black smoke. I wonder if Janusz is still alive. Probably not. They said they were getting close to the last ditch. When that happens, there'll be a liquidation, but how many? Half? I am tired of considering mathematics.

I picture those who run things. Galewski, the Czechs. Masarek, the secret staff. How many know? It seems to me that the air has a kind of electric current, the explosion about to happen, but it does not happen. I sit next to poor Anatoly's stinking body and see Julian coming through the boiling heat with a cart. I didn't know he left. I reach out and touch one of Anatoly's huge ears — it is cold.

GAS CHAMBERS, CAMP NUMBER TWO
LATE JULY 1943

When Janusz Siedlecki sees the look of suspicious curiosity in The Doll's eyes, he prepares to swallow the teeth. Then he waits, looking through the fence at the orange sun rising over the brush and evergreens to the east. Maybe he is mistaken. How could The Doll see him drool in the dim light of the bulb strung above the gas chamber landing? He gathers saliva at the front of his mouth and spits on the concrete.

They began at four in the morning rather than eight, and the heat is so intense that they will finish at noon or one in the afternoon. The work becomes almost intolerable after the sun comes up, and that brings on a kind of mental laziness. More than once he has found himself brazenly studying a gold tooth before putting it in his mouth. He continues his habit of assigning identities to some of the corpses — this man is Karel Zetnik, a rich banker who gave money to the poor of Krakow, only to have one of them buy a pistol and rob his bank. This woman had five children, all of whom died, but their ghosts pestered her every day to the point that she had to move out of her house. And this handsome man had many mistresses. Janusz briefly studies his genitals, and decides that he had made his way into fifty or sixty of the most beautiful women in Warsaw, each of whom at the moment one of his gold teeth is yanked out feels a powerful shock of pain in her jaw.

He thinks that the atmosphere of the camp has put everyone to sleep. As summer wore on, they were allowed greater liberties — they milled around the Roll Call Square in the evenings, and even the laundry and kitchen women came out. The next day the men would talk about them while they worked. On Sundays they heard the concerts from the lower camp, where, he was told, The Doll arranged dramatic performances, boxing matches, and had music played by the best musicians he could find from the transports.

He spits, pulls an old man's head around into the light so that he can peer into his mouth. Stumps. He pushes the old farmer away and turns to what appears to be a jewel thief.

The Doll ambles toward the fire grates that still hold a square, blackened foundation of logs and railroad ties with the middle burned out, the ties' ends white with ash. Janusz works carefully, assuming that he is being watched. He revises the jewel thief's identity: My God, he is an important German spy they arrested, whose story seemed to them so stupid that they gassed him without knowing that he was the man who held the secret of invisibility. He had left the vial of chemicals that would have saved him back in his apartment in Paris.

Szyman Landau, one of the body carriers, pulls the old man and a child off the concrete by their ankles, and he and another carrier Janusz does not know run the two light corpses toward the roasts on a filth-stained litter.

Janusz counts the teeth with his tongue: seven. No full caps. He pushes them around so that the sharp edges point away from the softer tissue in the base of his mouth.

"Don't move."

He remains absolutely still. The Doll steps around in front of him, and he smells boot leather.

"Spit them out."

Janusz remains still, his eyes watering. He is dead.

"Stand up."

He stands. He has never been this close to The Doll. He feels dwarfed in his presence, and begins trembling. When he realizes that he has been holding his breath since The Doll first spoke, he leans down and spits the teeth out on the concrete. Schneck approaches, and then nearby workers pause to look.

The Doll moves the teeth around with the toe of his boot, then looks at Janusz with a kind of good-humored disappointment.

Landau and the other body carrier trot to the concrete to pull another body off, and stop. Janusz remains conscious through his trembling and shortness of breath. If he is not shot he will be beaten to death, or he will be tortured for information. It was good that he spat the teeth out, because they would have gone for them with a knife had he swallowed them. He sees Dr. Herzenberg walking from the roast toward the excavator. Dr. Herzenberg looks in his direction, talks to the excavator operator, and then returns to the roasts.

"Out," The Doll says.

He means the square. Janusz stumbles ahead of him, aware that a guard now flanks him on one side, Schneck on the other. He shrugs amiably, and Janusz thinks, after all this time he still likes it. He still has not seen enough. He feels his trunk become hollow and then lift, as if no organs bounce there. His heart pounds high and light as if pumped full of helium, and his vision is jerky because of the trembling.

The Doll yells, and the workers turn, then approach, because he has beckoned. Janusz is momentarily stunned by the event: The Doll gives an order, and all the ants, or sheep, or mindless robot slaves turn and come to him, a god in black, beautiful and sharply dressed, his boots and insignia glinting.

"One of your compatriots has stolen gold teeth," he yells. Then he turns to Janusz. "Why did you steal the teeth?"

"I wanted to buy a woman."

In the silence after he has said this Janusz looks down, wondering why he gave that as an answer. In the effort to speak proper German he had ignored what was most important. He looks up, trying to think of something else to say.

The Doll's eyes show his search for comprehension, and then he bursts out laughing. "You?" he says. He looks at the workers and guards in mock astonishment. "How many gold teeth would it take for this one to buy a woman?" The workers laugh. The Doll appears both confounded and sympathetic, as if the absurdity of the idea rated some compassion.

"You will be beaten," The Doll says. Janusz's vision becomes flat and stark, as if he is in a dream, and he thinks, with what? Shovel, whip, club? A guard behind prods him with a gun butt, and he stumbles toward one of the two-wheeled corpse carts. "You may count in Polish," The Doll says. "Numbers are, I suspect, difficult for you anyway."

Janusz removes his shirt, as he has seen other victims ordered to do before they were beaten, and looks at The Doll, who studies his pitifully thin upper body with a cordial skepticism. Janusz then turns and lies facedown on the cart bed, smelling the odor of vomit and carrion in the rough planking. He feels around for something to hold, and worms his fingertips between two of the planks.

A powerful convulsion rips his fingers from the crack between the planks, and in his cheek he feels a large splinter. His brain has been reduced to a bright pea of mindless perception, and he keeps his cheek on the plank so as not to drive the splinter further in.

When the second shot hits him he remembers: "Two!" and his cheek comes up from the plank, the splinter breaking away with it. He runs his tongue along the hard ridge on the inside, and his fingers find the gap between the planks. The third strike — "Three!" — causes him to urinate a little, and for a moment the pain envelopes him so that he sees himself as a tiny, soiled ball of some inert protoplasm, hunching with a fascinated concentration inside the immensity of the pain.

"Four!"

He is a pair of eyes and ears, and his hearing singles out The Doll's grunt as he brings the meter of thick whip-base down. "Five!" Then he emerges from the confusion and studies the planks of the low cart wall. With his tongue he pushes the inside of his cheek and feels the ridge of flesh around the long splinter.

"Six!"

But he no longer feels the pain of the splinter. He is numb, but so alert that he finds himself blinking, wide-eyed, at the amazing complexity of the cart's planks: lines that sweep toward darker circles that resemble comets, objects moving through some thick, visible air, others smaller, which all together form a swirling galaxy sweeping around itself in long, graceful parabolic arcs. He is aware that he counts the blows, but the counting is mechanical. "Twelve." He thinks that beyond The Doll's woodchopper's grunting he hears the wooden planets spinning with that perfect positioning, each one an exact, antimagnetic distance from the others.

"Seventeen."

Each shot vibrates his body, and now the beating seems only a mild irritation because at the edges of the area of dead tissue some remains alive, prickling with a morbid electricity.

He waits to count twenty-six. Nothing.

"Jews!" he hears The Doll say, "the next of you caught with as much as a coin will die. Don't jeopardize your privileges. Now get back to work."

The Doll walks off. "Well, I guess you will continue work," Schneck says with languid indifference. "Sorry."

Hands pull at his upper arms. He feels himself being lifted, and turns to look. It is Dr. Herzenberg.

"We'll all be fine," Janusz says.

"Here," Herzenberg says. Janusz feels the splinter shoot out of his cheek. Dr. Herzenberg looks at it and drops it in the dirt. It is four or five centimeters long.

"Put your shirt on."

Janusz can barely lift his arms to get his fists into the sleeves. As the shirt touches his back, he feels a wetness.

"I'll fix you up later. Right now you've got to work or they'll kill you. Try to make it to the morning break."

"I want my pliers."

"On the cement."

He stumbles back to the gas chamber landing, feeling so tired that he doesn't really care if he dies. But Dr. Herzenberg wants him to work, so he will work.

The bodies are cold, their saliva and vomit pasty and rank. The third one, Mr. Jagiello Reymont, a man who has spent his life trying to live up to the names of a king and a great literary artist, has two gold caps. Janusz whispers, "You with so honored a pair of names, why are you here?" He levers the teeth out, puts one in the bucket and the other under his tongue.

Dr. Herzenberg works on his back, using a salve that smells like alcohol and roasted peanuts. "The statement about buying a woman was brilliant," he says. "You tripped The Doll up, and it saved your life, and probably mine."

Janusz holds on to the post of the bunk, staring at Waclaw, who looks on, from time to time wincing with vicarious pain.

"But collecting more gold teeth was stupid. You'd surely have been killed."

"I forgot."

"Forgot what?"

"I forgot why I was beaten."

"Janusz," Waclaw says, "are you trying to leave us?"

"No, I want to live."

"You're only the second man I've seen who counted the whip," Dr. Herzenberg says.

Janusz thinks, I am not a man, I am a boy. His back has stiffened, so that the skin feels like loose plates scraping against one another.

"How did you do it?" Waclaw asks.

"There was almost no pain," Janusz says.

"He put himself into shock," Dr. Herzenberg says. "It's a talent — I could see that he was completely relaxed."

"It felt like a dream," Janusz says. "Will I die now?"

"There are lacerations, but they're not as deep as I thought at first," Dr. Herzenberg says. "The Doll apparently likes you."

The sound of chamber music sneaks in the window. Dr. Herzenberg cocks his head, listens. "Mozart," he says.

"Why does he like me?"

"I don't know, but he likes you as he likes others of us. It's the little bit of human being in him, the joker, the good beer-drinking chum." He listens to the music for a few more seconds and then moves around to look at Janusz's face. "This wound isn't good," he says. "The planks are filthy. It's like a hypodermic injection. You must keep it clean, and if it swells or runs with pus, I'll cut it for you."

Dr. Herzenberg then looks around and leans in a little to Janusz and Waclaw. "You'll need to recover quickly, because the revolt is on. I don't know the exact date, but we're going."

Waclaw shakes his fist with a kind of exultant expectation. But Janusz thinks, we'll all die. He is about to say that, but notices that Dr. Herzenberg has turned back to the window, to listen to the music coming from the lower camp.

JEWISH BARRACKS, TREBLINKA
AUGUST 2, 1943

We sit here sweating. The handle of the insecticide sprayer is slick in my hand, and the smell of petrol billows up around my face. "There is no wind," I say. It is so hot that my skin prickles. I will not sleep in my bunk tonight.

Galewski nods, looks out the window at one of the guard towers. There are five of them, each with a machine gun. "Leave the towers alone," he says. "That would give you away."

"I will do only the building sides away from the German barracks," I say. "None of them have any reason to —" Soon it will be three o'clock, then four — The guns are on a garbage litter by the arsenal, covered with trash. Our pockets bulge with money, and none of us will sleep in our bunks tonight.

"Lichtblau will blow up the garage," Galewski says. "When that happens, no one will be in the dark."

"Where is Julian Sussmann?" I ask.

"The kitchen," Galewski says. "Chaskel has him cooking." Then he says, "David, remember to work normally and wait for the signal shot. Five o'clock. The weapons distribution should be complete by then." He looks out the window, then up. Across the barracks other men are gathered at windows, whispering.

"Some day I will open a leather shop," I say.

Galewski shakes his head. "Don't think about the future," he says.

I get up, my knees shaking, and pick up the petrol-filled insecticide tank. "I'll go," I say. "Besides, sitting around in here will arouse their curiosity. We should be working."

I carry the tank out into the boiling heat, feeling the petrol slosh, and walk along the barracks wall. This morning before ten o'clock we came back from the woods, our cart loaded, and already the landscape shimmered like a molten lake. Beyond the arsenal a ten-man work crew is building a water boiler, and at one of the windows of the arsenal there is other activity, the men who oversee the hiding of the weapons on the garbage litter. There is Masarek, who looks at me and smiles, then nods. The trembling in my limbs increases, and I can't hold my head still. I reach down and push the tank plunger a couple of times, and aim the nozzle at the base of the barracks. When the petrol comes out the smell billows up around my face, and I begin to giggle, the wand with the nozzle shooting the iridescent stream of petrol shaking so much that I wonder if some tower guard will notice.

It is so hot I am afraid the petrol will ignite. Above the pools and the wood absorbing the petrol the air boils with fumes. Men pass by carrying wood, the tension on their faces obvious. I work my way around the barracks foundation and come into view of the square and the German and Ukrainian barracks, and go to the stables and the textile storage. Men rake gravel that does not need raking, and an officer rides by on a bicycle and waves at them. In the shade by the Ukrainian barracks five guards are engaged in a card game. As I begin squirting petrol on the foundation I see Chaskel out by the zoo watching a boy who walks toward the Jewish barracks. Chaskel speaks to Kiwe, who despite the heat has come out to keep an eye on things.

Something is wrong. Kiwe has approached the boy, and after some conversation, the boy pulls something from his trousers pocket. Kiwe strikes him across the face and yells back toward the barracks. Julian Sussmann approaches him, and then Kiwe takes his pistol out and points it at Julian, who puts his hands up. They have been found out — the revolt has been found out. The gravel rakers pause. The guards put their cards away and stand up. I squirt petrol, leaving wet lines like ocean waves on the textile storage wall. Then I turn back toward the Jewish barracks, to tell Galewski. The boy, perhaps Julian, will now be shot, and it remains only to see if they talk — if they don't and are shot, then we have a signal shot and a revolt, premature by a couple of hours.

As I approach the barracks I get closer to Kiwe and his prisoners, and Julian looks at me once, shakes his head "no" very subtly. Kiwe strikes the boy across the back of the head with his pistol, and the boy wilts to his knees, then rises up again, walking toward the road that leads to the Hospital.

There is nothing to do but squirt more petrol. Nothing to do but wait. Tonight none of us will sleep in our bunks.

Sitting on the edge of his bunk Joachim Voss stares into the small cardboard box of valuables he has collected in the past month. The best of Anatoly's loot is there — a few gold coins, a heavy gold watch of Russian origin, along with two marriage rings and some jewelry. The only interesting objects are two diamond-studded lockets. He suspects that Weyrauch or Liebner harbor plans to rummage through his stuff, and frequently goes to his bunk to feel for the box through the fabric of his bag. He works the box into the bag, settling it in with gold coins and jewelry he could not carry out on the last leave, a week ago. The thought of his leave sends a wave of nausea throughout his flesh, and after a moment of wondering if he should have another drink, he decides not to.

He rises from his bunk and walks a little unsteadily out toward the mess hall, thinking of the schnapps bottle under his bunk, two-thirds of it already gone and the sun high and merciless in the sky. Through the window he can see workers carrying things, tending flowers, and hunched in small groups over improvement projects. In a guard tower, a shirtless Ukrainian leans against the tower frame, apparently sleeping.

There are only two in the mess hall, Weyrauch and Schneck.

"Another of those who appreciates Mondays," Weyrauch says.

"No transports on Sunday," Voss says. "Death's day off."

Weyrauch pours himself French wine, and drinks delicately.

"Superior," he says. "Would you like some?" Voss nods, and Weyrauch fills one of the glasses from the middle of the table. Voss takes the glass, and drinks a sip.

"That is good," he says. "So, where is the deputy commandant and his following?"

"They went off, swimming I think, about fifteen of them," Schneck says. "Or Franz went to see that girl of his in Ostrow. Let the boys swim by themselves. An awfully hot day for a fuck, though." Voss laughs, and turns to the door. "Kuttner just arrested a couple of workers," Schneck goes on, and then says in a seductive tone, "I think they had money."

Voss snorts and steps to the door. Outside, the heat hits him like a powerful drug, and he is not sure if he is so obviously staggering that he will draw the workers' attention.

His leave comes back to him once more. The day he arrived from Treblinka, Petra told him that an old friend of theirs, Gerd Seidel, had been visiting, on leave from his duty in the south of France along the seacoast defense lines. In the evening he came, and they ate dinner and drank, reminiscing about their old times in Berlin. Voss had the understanding clarify drink by drink, that the expressions on their faces and their gestures showed more and more clearly that they had already made love before Voss returned. And as the night wore on he understood more and more clearly that he should have found other hiding places than the one in the basement, that Petra and Gerd had been involved longer than Voss had at first thought, that as they sat there, they could barely mask their intent: The moment Voss left, perhaps before he was three or four blocks from the house, Gerd would be driving his face between her legs, and she, sighing with relief, would be opening them to receive him.

Partway through the evening Gerd went to the downstairs bath, and Voss could easily hear him urinating with an irritating assurance. That sound seemed to confirm his suspicions: Petra sat there calmly drinking her wine with that sound making its way into the room, and she did not alter at all her look of domestic casualness, because that was the same kind of sound Gerd made upstairs cleaning himself up after having spent himself in her body.

Voss now feels the anger reddening his face. He sniffs the air, and smells nothing except petrol fumes. He does not see Kuttner. A worker pushing a wheelbarrow goes past him, nods obsequiously once, and goes behind the Ukrainian barracks. As Voss walks, the buildings shift and tip crazily, and the bright sunlight hurts his eyes. He wanted to ask her straight out, did you allow him to put it in your mouth? Did your bodies slide against each other with mingled sweat? And when I did it, did you make your womanly comparisons? Was it the same? Or did you like the soldier better? Oh, he could see it, could picture them so vividly that he almost vomited sitting there watching them talk. He had always liked Gerd Seidel, but he also knew him, knew that his rules of sexual behavior came from the old days in Berlin: Two adults, good friends, why should they not enjoy this act? Was it an insult to the husband? Of course not. If anything it was an act that sealed a soldierly comradeship. And the woman must feel the same, that she loves, in her own way, these two men.

The evening the three of them spent together remains in Voss's mind as a dark blur. He cannot remember what they talked about. He watched them, and he can remember in ugly, pinpoint detail the visions he had invented of them, of his crawling on her in broad daylight, shaking her so that he could see her breasts bounce, of his lewd pumping, making sure to plunge as deeply as possible each time, of his turning her over, having her on top, of other more perverse things done with a kind of vigorous sexual release. In Berlin years ago he had at first disliked her for her liberated attitudes, and now that dislike that he had buried with their marriage has bloomed into a bitter hatred.

At the garage on the corner of the Railway Station Square he stops, and thinks, what shall I do? Across the Roll Call Square an inmate sprays insecticide against the base of the Undressing Barracks. In the intense, shimmering heat all seems a dream. He has wanted to go and try sifting through the ash pits at the roasts for gold. Today he will do it. He turns to his left and walks through the Roll Call Square toward the road that leads to the Death Camp, which, like the other roads, has an idiotic name, "The Street of the Deportees." Again that smell of petrol wafts across his face, and he wonders if that big idiot Ivan is fooling with the gas chamber engine.

He hears a pistol shot far away, from the direction of the Hospital, turns, and sees a man running past the garage he has just left. Another man runs past the garage, and he feels the shock of an explosion. Above the garage a thick billow of black smoke bulges up, swirling around into itself.

An accident. He walks back toward the garage, feeling light-headed and half-conscious. Fire races up the wall of the Undressing Barracks, and as he walks, he sees the air above the Sorting Square warehouses boil with heat and sparks. More men run across the space between the Undressing Barracks and the Jewish barracks, which now appear to be on fire. He is not sure if he has been hearing the gunfire for some time or not, but now he is aware of gunfire. The figures of guards in the towers move, aiming machine guns and rifles. In the burning garage he sees the figure of a man approaching the fire-choked doorway, but he cannot get out.

Then he sees men hacking, bringing tools down on an officer. It is Liebner, lying on his back trying to protect his face while three inmates chop at him with flat shovels.

He pauses, and is instantly so terrified that he almost urinates. His heartbeat pounds in his neck, and he cannot hold his head still. A revolt? He reaches for his holster, but it isn't there. Then he sees more men pass before the garage, which is engulfed in flames. A huge explosion there causes a hot wind to blast across his body. Then he is running.

Liebner's prone form sweeps toward him in a jouncing plane and he looks once at the face, caved in on itself and crisscrossed by wide lacerations. One of his forearms is shattered into a right angle. He continues running, wailing with panic.

Gasping for breath, he pushes his way into the barracks. Schneck and Weyrauch are at one window, pistols drawn, and on the other side officers look out the windows. "They've called the penal camp — they'll send men in a few minutes," Schneck calls to him. Then he laughs. "My God," he says, "I didn't think they had it in them. Isn't it strange?"

"What do we do?" Weyrauch asks. He steps toward Voss, gesturing with both hands.

"You," Voss says. "Try being nice to them now."

"What can I do?" he moans. "What could anyone ever do?"

"You're a fool," Voss says.

"Look," Schneck says, "here come Kuttner and Suchomel. We'll gather our forces and go out." He turns, his face lit up with excitement. "Finally, something to do," he says.

Voss runs into the sleeping wing of the barracks. There on the post is his pistol belt. His hands are shaking so badly that he cannot put the belt on, and when he draws the pistol out, he realizes that his fingers are so numb that he will not be able to pull the trigger. He sits on the bunk, then leans over and vomits on the floor. When he gets his breath, he feels his teeth grate together and tastes the bitter foulness of hot stomach fluid. He hears more gunfire, then what sounds like jubilant shouting. His hands still shake badly. He picks up the schnapps bottle and takes a large mouthful, and swallows, the heat of the alcohol searing his throat.

Through the corner window of the barracks he sees the commandant in his white jacket standing in his doorway watching, a glass in his hand.

We are stuck between the burning garage and the burning bakery, our faces hot with reflection from the flames. I smell the bread burning along with the petrol.

"How did you get away?" I ask. "I saw you taken off."

"Kuttner shot the boy and I ran. My God, how much petrol did you spray on? Look at this!"

I laugh. "I was worried it would dry too much, but yes, look at this." No, it was not too dry. "The tracks," I say. "Let's go."

Julian looks at me. His eyes are wild, distant.

"Did you see Masarek?" I ask. Masarek stood on the chicken coop in the smoke, spraying the machine gun. Then he waved us away — get out. "He stayed. He stood there shooting. The chicken coop started to burn but there he stood."

We tried the fence beyond the firewood piles on the other side. Twenty or thirty men were working their way through, and the machine-gun fire hit them. Flesh blasted away from heads and torsos. Galewski died there. Three ran out to the low brush. One fell, and sat there until the bullets hit him.

The gunfire is at a lull. I know the Germans are bringing in men to kill us. We have three or four minutes.

"I'm going," I say. "We're roasting here." I feel my pocket. The money and jewelry are still there. "Kuttner took your money," I say. "I'll give you some. You know, we always worried that you'd squeal."

He looks at me. "They killed my family."

The sky is black, boiling with smoke, and the heat from the fires nearby is burning our faces. Julian looks confused, waiting for something to shoot at. "Come," I say. "We've got to get out of here. They're getting things together."

I pull him along. There is so much smoke from the store-houses in the Sorting Square that we can make our way to the tracks without being seen, and from there we need only to cross the tank traps and make it to the woods.

"David, look," Julian says. We see smoke from the Death Camp. "They're in it too."

We begin our run across the Station Square on the side where the coal is piled. The coal is not burning. By the time we get to the coal my throat is dry, and the money has pulled my trousers down over my hips. I pull them up, and Julian looks around again I suppose for something to shoot at. I hear gunfire all over, now mostly from the Death Camp. By the coal pile we breathe, getting ready for the tracks and tank traps. Then Julian drops the rifle. I turn, and Schneck stands pointing a pistol at my face. I wait.

He looks at us, grinning, and then scratches his chin. "Actually, why don't you go," he says, and laughs. "You haven't time. Take the rifle. Remember me to your chums at home." Julian picks the rifle up, slowly. Schneck nods. "It's all right. It really makes no difference to me."

When we turn and run, we hear him laughing behind us, making strange hooting sounds as if he has been told an excellent joke.

The perimeter fence is draped with bodies, but there are holes through which we can crawl so we aim for the biggest hole. As I dive through, the wire rips one of my pant legs. Julian follows, and when we are standing again we run out, between the steel tank traps browned by rust and intertwined with barbed wire, and running, we see the low brush jouncing ahead of us, and beyond that, the pines.

"Janusz, the camp is on fire," Waclaw Gitzer says.

He tries to process the statement. Lying on his side, his face swollen and pounding, he thought that they were executing at the Hospital right over the dirt bank from the barracks. Or the sounds were his heart, the thunderous *whoosh*ing of blood through his veins and arteries, the sustained explosion of his infection. So the camp is on fire.

"Janusz!"

The camp shall become a huge roast, with all of them dripping fat into the dirt, their faces sweating fat, then slowly surging into smiles, or grimaces, or open-mouthed tragedy masks.

Dr. Herzenberg cut his face and bandaged it, but it leaked pus and blood. His cheek crowded his mouth so that when he closed his mouth he bit the inside of it. Glands under his jaw turned into stones. Each day during work whenever he leaned down his head felt as heavy as lead and everything rushed into his cheek. Then Dr. Herzenberg cleaned his ears and it hurt so much that he thought his brain was being washed out in bits. He opens his eyes and sees orange dancing on the high windows, and hears more gunfire.

"Why are they burning the camp?"

He says it without slurring. He reaches up and touches his cheek. It is numb but not as big as before.

"Who is burning the camp?"

Janusz feels a twinge of irritation. If he wants to find out what is happening he must get up. As he rises, his head feels lighter, not as bloated. The thought that it might be healing makes a little current of hope race through his flesh. Now he hears more gunfire, and feels the heat from the wall adjacent to his bunk. They are burning the barracks!

"Excuse me, but what is —"

He walks toward the door, and Izak Janka comes in. He is ashen, sweating. "The fools!" he says. "Captain Bloch and his men! We'll all be killed!"

Janusz steps outside, and through the fence surrounding the barracks he sees first the roasts, which are not on fire, and then the rest of the camp, which is. He hears shouting, then sees a guard in the tower overlooking the center of the camp hanging partway off his box, dripping blood. He puts his hand to his face and feels the swollen spot, then runs his tongue along the inside of his cheek. There is less of that metallic taste of infection there.

He sees men crouched behind the engine room for the old gas chambers, firing up at the guard tower above the vetch-planted corner of the camp. Then a dotted line of dusty explosions sweeps across the open area toward the engine room.

Smoke now comes from the door of the barracks, and he turns and goes back in. His bunk! Izak Janka stands against the wall, his face still ashen and slick with sweat. "You idiot," Janka says. "Get out of the doorway."

Janusz steps to the side and peeks out the door. The men still crouch behind the engine room, one pointing a rifle. The rifle jumps but Janusz cannot distinguish the report from the other gunfire. Then he sees Waclaw near the bushes at the corner of the camp along with other men lying facedown, their bodies aimed at the fence. Gunfire also comes from the other side of the camp, at the corner of the new gas chamber building where the tube comes in from Camp Number One. Figures move there, a group of guards and one officer. They are advancing on the group hiding behind the engine room.

Janusz walks out of the barracks and through the wire gate into the Roll Call Square, and waves at the men by the engine room. Waclaw screams out his name, and something pings off the wire gate. That was a bullet, he thinks. He realizes that he should not be standing where he is, and walks out the gate and along the fence toward Waclaw and the others. When he passes the barracks he sees the laundry women cowering against the perimeter fence along with a few male workers. Dr. Herzenberg is there, his shirt bloody and his face pale and shining with sweat. Janusz turns to go to him, but he scowls angrily and waves his hand toward the fence.

Janusz lopes to the bushes. Waclaw has a wild look on his face, and waves him down with quick jerks of his hand. "Get your head down!" he shouts. "We're breaking out."

"Doctor Herzenberg's —"

"He's finished! Get down!"

A man farther into the bushes is jerking wildly at the wire, his hands bleeding. Then the bottom of the fence is up, choked with dirt and grass, and men begin pushing their way under it.

"Where will we go?" Janusz asks.

"I don't know," Waclaw says. "Can you run? There're the Spanish Horses, then the outer fence, then brush, and way out, the woods. We're going to the woods."

"All right, but shouldn't we take —"

"We can't. He's been shot in the chest." Waclaw turns to the line of men crawling toward the hole in the fence.

Across the square huge billows of smoke blacken the sky, and Janusz hears yelling, gunfire close and gunfire in the distance. His heart pulses in his cheek. The entire camp is ablaze, and he thinks of the anger of the Germans. He feels a little shock of embarrassment at all of this happening, and he imagines the look on The Doll's face at the sight of all this. His slaves have brought off an uprising. How can it be? How can sheep or chickens or mice do this? As the men force themselves through the fence, Janusz laughs, making his cheek hurt.

Waclaw turns, peers back at him, his cheek against the ground. "Most of them don't even make it to the Spanish Horses. We're going to be killed."

"The men at the engine room have all been shot!" someone yells from behind Janusz. Then the owner of the voice scrambles over him, bruising his back where the whipping scabs formed. It is Szyman Landau, struggling toward the hole in a violent panic. He has left a rifle on the ground.

"Shoot at the engine room!" Waclaw yells.

The engine room is just visible under the legs of the guard tower. Janusz sits up, and takes the rifle in his hands. He aims through the guard tower legs, the stock against his swollen cheek, and pulls the trigger until his finger hurts.

"Get down!" Waclaw yells.

"I can't make this work."

"The bolt! Throw the bolt!"

He swings the bolt up and pulls it back, and a shiny cartridge flips out onto the ground next to him. When he closes the bolt the next bullet goes into the chamber. "Oh, I see," he says. He aims at the engine room and pulls the trigger, and the stock punches his shoulder, jerks his cheek.

"Get down!" Waclaw yells.

"I can't. I can't see."

He throws the bolt and aims again at the engine room and fires. This time his eye catches a burst of rust or paint flying from the engine housing. He giggles and throws the bolt again.

Waclaw is farther away now, heading for the hole in the fence. Janusz aims the rifle and sees a form move near the engine room. When he fires the form goes backward, and at the moment it does he realizes that the bullet hit him, where, he does not know, but the movement was as if the man were jerked backward. He drops the rifle, his hands numb.

"I — I'm —" Who was it? The Doll? Schneck? Vlodya? Waclaw goes into the fence hole, and he follows.

Then he is up and running, the jouncing hurting his face, and ahead Waclaw weaves his way through the tank traps, slowing down to negotiate the wires connecting them. There are dead men everywhere, and bullets burst with metallic pinging sounds off the rusted tank traps, leaving gray swipes.

Men struggle with the outer fence, trying to cut the wire and widen a hole blocked by a corpse. Then one by one they go through, stepping on the body. As Janusz approaches, he sees far to his left other men, fifteen or twenty, breaking across the tank traps toward the fence near the old burial ditches. Waclaw approaches the hole and falls down, and when Janusz reaches him he pulls at his shoulders to help him up. But he is limp. Janusz turns him over. He has no jaw. Blood bubbles from the huge gap where it should be, and his eyes are glazed. The jaw is down by the side of his neck, and below it on the ground are bloody teeth.

He releases Waclaw's shoulders, and crawls toward the hole in the fence, the swollen area on his cheek flashing with the rapid beating of his heart.

As Magda Nowak walks along the edge of the rye field, which angles away from the road so that the narrow strip of brushy woodland separating her from the road widens, she can see the glint of a vehicle near her house. She stops. Would they shoot her mother or father? And what about the midwife, would they shoot her too? She is perhaps only one cramp away from home.

Then she sees men in the woodland near the road, three officers and one man in civilian clothes, and some distance away two guards in uniforms like Anatoly's watching over another prisoner, who sits smoking a cigarette. One officer is talking to the man close by, while the second officer stands off to the side with a strange smile on his face, and the third goes through something in a bag. While the men talk the smiling officer begins to laugh, and Magda holds her breath — something seems to be wrong with him. Finally the first officer draws a pistol and the civilian turns around, appearing unconcerned, almost aloof, as he talks. The strange officer continues to laugh, until the first one fires and the civilian flops to the ground. Holstering his pistol, the officer glares at the one laughing, but he cannot stop. He wipes his eyes, and turns toward Magda.

She feels the cramp begin, and tries not to move, because they will see her. The laughing officer walks in her direction, one hand out as if he must feel his way. Although she stands in almost full view, he does not see her. When he stops, near a bush, she feels the cramp constrict, and plans not to move no matter how hard it pushes, because she is frightened by the officer's face. He appears to be either drunk or insane.

As the pain increases, she laces her fingers under her belly, trying to remain still. The officer is less than ten meters from her, apparently trying to urinate, but she hears nothing. His face then contorts into a silent laugh. His skin is red, almost purplish, and his eyes are huge and bloodshot, and the expression is one of a deranged joy.

When the cramp rises to its peak and she begins to tremble, the man draws something from his pocket and looks at it in the palm of his hand. His face then undergoes a change, from that look of wild lunacy to a blank, mindless awe, as if he has been stunned. He remains locked in a mesmerized imbecility, as if frozen at the moment before remembering something. Then, as the cramp recedes and she is able to relax the tension in her flesh, a soft moan issues from his throat, drawn out into a slow, crooning wail, as if he is gradually remembering what had held him in that bewilderment. The sound of a gunshot from nearby makes him flinch.

When he turns toward the other officers, she works her way back along the rye toward her house, half-running, holding her belly and trembling, because the man frightens her more than even Anatoly's descriptions of the German officers. She does not know what she has seen, but it seems like a perversity stranger than anything her imagination could manufacture.

The yard is bathed in copper sunlight, and her father stands by the door talking with a man from the village. "— don't know the land, you see," he is saying. Briefly he stops to look at her, almost without expression, and then continues. "Around six hundred, and of course they want all of them. I am to advise them as to the lay of the land here."

She wants to ask him about the midwife, but instead walks around and in through the front door. Her clothes are moist and dirty, and the coolness of the house makes her shiver. In the darkness of the kitchen sits an old woman with hair so thin that Magda can see her skull through it. The woman turns and smiles. "Well," she says.

Outside, her father continues to talk with the village man. "What wealth they'd be carrying with them! I could see in that officer's face that I'll get something for this."

"Where is my mother?" Magda asks the old woman. "I have the pains, for more than an hour now."

"She's hiding. She's been hiding since the fire."

The old woman rises and moves toward her. When Magda sees the ancient, wrinkled face and the bony hands with fingers like chickens' toes, she backs away, feeling the pressure of the next cramp. "Don't hurt me," she whispers.

She breathes rapidly while Elena Stolarz the midwife presses with both hands on the top of the mount and whispers, "Hold the ropes and breathe, breathe, breathe —" She is glad for the ropes. And she flexes her toes rhythmically back and forth, back and forth. Sweat runs off her temples and drips from her wrists. When the pressure reaches its peak, she feels all the skin of her body prickle, and the surge recedes, pulling back up into her rib cage.

Elena Stolarz the midwife has reassured her now three times that it will only be a baby, but Magda feels it: Her stomach, womb, everything, will come out. The half-sphere has softened, and Elena Stolarz said that the baby was in the canal, and she pictured a deformed baby floating in a canal, being swept under. The baby will be born without hands, or eyes, or with its stomach on the outside in a purple bag, as she has heard happens. She will be alone with the soiled fruit of her sin.

"The next one," Elena Stolarz says. Blearily she looks — the old woman has a wart on her nose and no teeth, and when she smiles her lips collapse inward.

No one wonders about Magda. Her mother is petrified with fright, hiding in the potato cellar, her father talks money outside. Elena Stolarz says, "Let them burn the world. Let them run all over the place. I came here to see a baby born."

At first she slid Magda's hands through the loops of the rope and Magda said, "Are you tying me up?" and she said, "These are for you to hold on to," and now she is glad for the ropes.

The next cramp slides its fingers down inside her with a more forceful expansion and her toes worm back and forth, back and forth, and she feels the ropes chafing her wrists, which vibrate with the tension and she feels herself pushing, her face swollen, her eyelids about to explode, surely blood will explode from her nostrils and ears, but there is expansion that has held itself still, with all her organs as if at the edge of being torn loose, and then she remembers that she had been holding her eyes shut to keep them from exploding out, but sees a bluish white light for just a moment, and feels inside the peak of that expansion a sudden almost pleasurable sigh, not of breath but of tissue, and then the sigh becomes a soft rush that draws her breath and organs downward. Then there is a motionless hovering of her organs all in place, her tissue breathless while she breathes, breathes, breathes.

Her eyes swim with liquid and she removes one hand from the rope to clear them, but it flops back ticklishly. Elena Stolarz moves the baby around until it comes out with a flat, dry-sounding cough. It is splotched with yellow patches.

"A girl!" Elena Stolarz says.

Magda has no muscles. The baby is yellow, its features pinched, the blue-gray corkscrew of cord dropping out of sight between her legs.

"Baby's cheese," Elena Stolarz says. She works, using a knife and pieces of ribbon. "You did well. Here comes the afterbirth."

A ticklish sliding, more emptiness. She is now hollow.

"Look at her mouth!" Elena Stolarz says, holding her up. She is no longer yellow. She slowly flails her tiny arms, fists clenched, the little flower of her mouth sucking the air. Elena Stolarz slides her over Magda's belly and toward the right breast. When skin touches skin, she raises her hands to hold its tiny buttocks. The mouth finds her nipple, and with the beginning of the sucking, the ridges of the baby's gums clamping down on it, Magda's skin erupts in gooseflesh, and she finds herself chilled and giggling with pleasure and fright.

Outside her father and Balicki talk, while Michal and her brother listen and laugh at their bragging. Her mother hides in the kitchen because the Germans and Ukrainians and the Navy Blue Police are all over the place. Before they came back from their hunt Magda had a dream in which her mother gave her a silver spoon for the baby, and when she held the spoon it melted into a pliable glob that did not burn her hand, and when she drew the glob apart the shape of the spoon reappeared, and stretching it further, she saw that the words on the neck of the spoon got larger and larger until she could read a name and next to it a graph that told her how much the spoon cost in different kinds of money: francs, lira, zlotys.

The baby sleeps. Before she left Elena Stolarz made her drink a mixture of milk and yeast and crushed wheat and wine, to bring the milk and to strengthen the baby. The wine will help the baby to sleep, the milk will help make milk, the yeast and wheat will make her feel whole again, and the baby has nothing wrong with her — she has tiny fingernails the thickness of the skin of an onion, and little hairy buttocks and breasts and a little hairy forehead, and Elena Stolarz told her that the hair will go away, and the baby will grow up strong and well built because her mother is strong and well built, and in the veins crisscrossing the shiny, purple afterbirth Elena Stolarz saw that there was, despite everything, stability in the futures of both mother and child, that reading the veins she knew that nothing amiss hid behind the curtain of fate to trip either of them up, that she thought that she read in the little veins a future stability that went beyond the mother and child, that the way the neck of the cord branched out into the purple mass that had fed the baby suggested to her that like the roots of a strong tree, perhaps a birch, this child would be strong and would emanate stability like a glow around her as she made her way through the injured world. How can it be that a woman might have such a gift? she asked, cleaning Magda up and then preparing the drink. Because all the men have lost their way, because this war and all this killing was exclusively a man's business, and think of what possibilities there might be for a woman, this child who sucks so strongly and who has such an angry expression, in a world where all the men have gone to worship death like flies race to rotting meat. For this reason, she said, I think you should name the baby Marie. When Magda asked her why she told her that it would be best left secret, that the significance of the name would be diluted if the reason for its use were known, especially by its mother.

Magda listened carefully to everything Elena Stolarz said, because she knew the old woman had a special wisdom and also an unlikely sort of bravery, walking as she did through the woods and past the trucks and soldiers to deliver the baby regardless of the dangers, and when she left, walking out into the darkness, she cared not for the rumors of men wild on their Jew hunt. She said she would spit on their love of death and walk on home. Besides, what would they want with a toothless old woman like her?

I will come back in three days to take a look at you, she said. Then just before she left, Elena Stolarz said, Magda, the child is special. I don't know how it happens in a time like this, but the child is special. The veins do not lie.

"— lined them up, my God, and did you ever think a Mauser would do that? To throw the top of a man's head five meters?"

"Mine was half-dead when I got him," her father said. "It's lucky we weren't taken for Jews ourselves."

"Do you think the Navy Blue will keep his mouth closed?"

"He's a Pole. Besides, I gave him money."

"It was more than thirty meters," Michal Balicki says.

"It was a bigger target," her father says. "After all, these are not rabbits."

All of them laugh, and she can hear bottles being uncorked.

"Tomorrow will be an even bigger Jew hunt. If we see Germans we'll throw in with them. Maybe they'll pay us bounties, eh?"

"Pah!" Michal Balicki says. "Down goes another Jew."

Her father laughs. "I should have taken an ear," he says.

"No," Balicki says, "a nose. You should have taken a nose!"

Again they all laugh.

Little Marie squirms, then stirs with a fitful shaking of her fists.

Ivan Dubas is crushed against the doorway of
the railway car, bracing himself above their bags, his wife, Ludmila, against the wall holding the baby up on her shoulder.
The train inches along, and they are burning with thirst, their
nostrils too full now of the odors of urine and feces and vomit.
An old rabbi has died on the other side of the car, and also a
baby, suffocated by the crush of bodies as the railway car rocked
along on its westward journey from Minsk. They were rounded
up in Molodechno and taken in trucks to the train. Relocated.

Between his feet is the box that holds his books, which
Ludmila believed was a mistake to bring along: Mendele
Mokher Sforim's *Mishpat Shalom, Yudl, Masoes binyomin
hashlishi,* Brainin, the great Peretz, Mapu's *Avahat Zion,* many

thin volumes of Yiddish poetry. This relocation has interrupted his study and his goal, to become an expert in his literature. Even now, swallowing into a dry throat and trying to control his fright, he thinks that when he has five minutes, he will simply continue studying the books, that he still has Peretz and Sforim and Mapu to devour, holes in his knowledge that will continue to embarrass him until he has filled them.

The train has stopped, and he sighs with relief that now they will get the promised water. In Minsk they told them, there will be water, food, and work for all on the other end.

"You take the bag and the box," Ludmila says. "We'll be the first off, and if we're not careful, they'll push us off."

He hears someone working the latch, and the door slides open with a screech. Men wearing civilian clothes look up. "Come down," one says, "and keep your baggage with you. The men line up on the right, the women and children on the left."

The blazing light nearly drives his eyes shut, and he begins to perceive things slowly, the shell of a burned building, beyond that, huge piles of blackened planking and posts, and another burned building. Then he sees the Germans in black uniforms, the guards who have wide, Slavic faces. He works his way down onto the platform and turns to help Ludmila and the baby.

When they are off, they pull their baggage from the car and move away to give the others room. He looks around once again, wondering what happened here. A bombing? There are huge piles of burned wood everywhere, and the acrid smell of it is heavy in the windless air.

The women work their way to the left to form a line, and he drags the large box and his book box to the right.

"You are going to have a shower first," one of the civilians yells. "The women will go to that gate," and he points to a place where there seems to be a hall constructed of wire and pine branches. "There the women will remove their clothes —"

Joachim Voss watches the unloading of the transport from the earthen bank separating the two camps. Ukrainian guards prepare the engine. In the Death Camp, men run with armloads of wood to the roasts, preparing for the incineration of the corpses, who are now moving up the tube into the gas chambers.

In the middle of the roast work Izak Janka, one of the new kapos, yells at the workers and from time to time whips them with a thin birch rod he carries. In the Reception Camp work crews clear the rubble from the fires.

It has taken them two weeks to hunt down the majority of the escapees. Voss went out with Schneck and Kuttner to look for them, and each day they found another dozen or so, as did other units, so that they found all but perhaps forty of them. When they did they skipped ceremony and executed them summarily.

He hates the woods. He carries a flask of schnapps with him when they go, and at times, when he finds himself alone, the voices of the men nearby become flat and distant, and he stops, and the blankness hits him — there is a sudden airy space in which he becomes nothing but a pair of eyes, looking at the bright leaves and the columns of sunlight coming down. He does not know how long these episodes last because there is no time, there is no sense of body, of even breath, only stark, lucid vision in which he cannot identify what he sees although he knows what it is, and standing there does not or cannot think *Joachim Voss*, or even *I*. It would be the stress, he thinks. It would be the logistics of hiding the money and the watches and the jewels, some in the woods and now he has forgotten where he hid some of them. There is the problem of what to remove from his basement the next time he goes home, the problem of

Petra and what he will do with her, there is the problem of the beltful of jewels he now wears around his waist. No wonder, he thinks, that there was so little from the transports — the workers had most of it, and each time, when he aimed the pistol at the back of the neck and fired, he was already leaning down to see, yes, look at this, these men had taste, they knew what the most valuable stuff was.

Then in the lull after the executions he would stare down at the valuables, and sometimes that blankness would return, and he would stare at the little pile of glittering things, his eyes held in an airy, vacant fascination, so that for the moment he did not know who or where he was. This momentary gap of bright, hypnotic nothingness was not unpleasant. There was a ticklish delight that came with it, and it would frighten him only later, when he visualized it in full consciousness.

The women are now being herded into the gas chambers, many of them holding babies in the crooks of their arms.

He began to wonder about the stress. Perhaps it was the capture of one man, Sussmann it was, that first day. Schneck said, "Oh my, you've failed to get away. What shall I do now? And where is your friend?" and the man looked around at the brush and at the evergreens in the distance and said, "Have your fun of course, and then kill me — what else do people like you do?" Then he laughed. "My friend? He's long gone — you'll never catch him. You'll remember him longer than anyone you've killed." Voss listened to him speak, and then began to laugh. Schneck looked at the man, whose expression showed a thoughtful equanimity. "How would you like to die then?" Schneck asked him, and he snorted derisively. So Schneck told him to turn around and drew out his pistol. "Are you afraid?" he asked, and the man said, "Of you? No. Of death? Far less than I thought I would be." Voss then more or less wilted with laughter, his eyes wet, becoming weak with demented jocularity. Schneck aimed, and the man went on: "But you? You are terrified of death, and each time you kill you become more terrified. You can't stand mortality. No matter how many of us you kill, you will never make peace with —" Schneck shot him then, and then glared angrily at Voss, who could not stop laughing. Later he understood: It was merely his screaming flesh, the detestable reality of his being.

He hears the engine surge, thinks he can feel it in the ground under his feet. Below, two dentists carrying their buckets approach the concrete landing behind the chambers. Janka talks to Schneck, his face held in an obsequious smile.

Treblinka is to be closed down. Voss is glad for that, and looks forward to a change. He has been led to understand that he will be stationed at Auschwitz, in Silesia, and at first he did not like the idea. But after the hunt, he realized that he was visualizing Auschwitz with a sensation of ticklish anticipation. The wealth there would be enormous.

A long, familiar swoon of nausea surges through his flesh, and he pulls the flask out and takes a large mouthful, and empties the bottle. He throws the bottle down the bank, and it shatters on the concrete of the gas chamber landing, and he giggles at the mess he has made. A worker stops, looks up at him. Voss sees a lump in one of the pockets of his trousers. "Empty your pocket," he calls.

The man pulls the pocket out, and a chunk of bread drops on the ground. "No eating during work," Voss calls.

NEAR ZHABINKA, PRIPET MARSHES
MID-SEPTEMBER 1943

I was alive. The hunger made my mouth foam and my heart beat too fast, and I dug carrots at night, stole pumpkins and cabbages, ate rye seed and sometimes flowers. When I stole at night, I listened carefully for any sounds other than the whispering of the grasses and the odd ticking sounds of houses and trees settling in the coolness. I could hear better than I ever had.

As I walked, one day working my way into the woods away from the railroad tracks because of the trainloads of soldiers and tanks and trucks, I ended up surrounded by water in which tiny mosquito larvae squirmed, and the mosquitoes were everywhere, and I had to keep moving to keep them off me. I walked on spits of land, looking for something to eat. I was afraid of the mushrooms and left them. Then I had to wade through the water up to my thighs, waving mosquitoes away, and then there was a house with a thatch roof, two little boats in the water in front of it, pumpkins on the roof, and a tall well sweep.

I went past the house and farther into the strange landscape. In the middle of the day it became bright and hot, and it felt as if I had been thrust back in time to the formation of the earth, where lush weeds and billions of insects and steam shimmered before me, where every rotted log was wild with color, yellow or blue or red fungus, deep green mosses, ferns. Strange birds labored across the sky or perched, shoulder high, on tree branches.

My stomach was dying, being eaten by its own acids, and I became dizzy and fell down in a patch of grass on one of those strange islands rising from the shallow water that stretched off as far as I could see. I tried eating some of the grass and threw it up.

I was either asleep or too tired to be conscious, and I put my shirt partway over my head because of the mosquitoes, and then dreamed.

After that I heard thumping, which gradually came closer. When I peeked out of the shirt I saw a man in a boat. Behind him on the boat were strange nets shaped like cones, like lampshades. The man saw me and came closer. There was no place for me to run, and I knew that I would be too weak to run anyway.

I was frightened by his face. He was ugly, and looked like something between a hound and an ape, and I was shaking and nearly unable to see, and he scraped the boat into the weeds near where I was lying, and came up out of the boat.

I think I began to cry then, and pulled the shirt down to my neck, and on the ground before me, his dark rubber boots were closer, magnified in my swimming vision.

Where do you come from? he asked.

I still couldn't speak, and looked up at him, but he was back in his boat. Then he came back with something in his hand, and began rubbing something on my arms and neck.

What happened to your face?

The stuff he rubbed on my skin smelled of mint, and something else my mother used in cooking.

This will keep the mosquitoes off, he said.

I said, Thank you. Then I said, I had a splinter in my face and it got infected, but it's all right now.

You are hungry, he said, and went back into his boat. He came back carrying a piece of bread, a black, cold sausage, and a jug. When I reached for the bread my hands shook so badly that I couldn't hold it. I tried again, giggling and looking down through my swimming eyes, and brought it to my mouth, and when I chewed, my jaw erupted in a painful celebration that made me wince. Then it went away and I chewed.

In the boat, a little dizzy with the smell of the mint, I watched him row with powerful, even strokes. At my feet there was a wooden box filled with water, in which swam eleven black fish, who moved in unison with the shifts in the water level in the box each time he pulled the oars.

Are you a Jew? he asked.

I said, Yes. It didn't matter, because I had eaten. He could do whatever he wanted to, what I had seen done in the Sterdyn Woods, men hanging from tree branches, lines of bodies lying bloated in the sun, their heads blasted by rifle shots. I began to cry again there in the boat, remembering it.

The ugly man, whose name I would later learn was Tadeusz Chmielewski, poked me on the shoulder to get my attention.

He stopped rowing.

I know, he said. You believe that everyone hates you. I am going to show you that you are not entirely correct.

Then he continued rowing.

Are you going to give me to the Germans? I asked.

[253]

Tadeusz Chmielewski pulled the oars up and looked around, to his right and then to his left, with a kind of theatrical exaggeration. I see no Germans, he said. Look, is there a German there? No, there is not. Over there? Let me see, and he shaded his eyes with his hand. No, I see none. Perhaps in winter, when the marshes freeze over, we see them. We sometimes see a plane going over, sometimes hear gunfire in the distance. Partisans perhaps. But they are our friends, as long as we feed them a little when things get tight for them.

He continued rowing, and I watched the fish move when the water level tipped.

What are you going to do with me? I asked.

What is your name?

I told him, and he thought a moment. It is not a Jewish name, he said.

I am half-Jewish, I told him.

I have two other boys like you, he said. They are orphans, as I think you must be too. My old wife collects orphans, and if I told her I saw you and did not bring you home, she would not feed me.

He went back to his rowing, and I watched the fish move. I counted them again. There were eleven. I remember doing that, counting the fish. Tadeusz Chmielewski was the first person I told about Treblinka, and luckily he was one of those people who appreciates detail. We would fish from his little boat all day, and I would talk, and he would listen. And I found that in telling him, I had forgotten nothing. Then I thought that *because* I was able to tell him, I had forgotten nothing. It was a long time ago, but I remember all of it, every detail. I remember everything.

SITE OF TREBLINKA CAMP

He sits in the living room in what he perceives as an odor, and thinks that everything would have been right if only he had not learned about the bricks. He was assigned to the camp for its demolition, but arrived early enough to see a week of trainloads of Jews processed, and asked an officer, how long has this been going on? and the officer said, a year, and smiled.

He forced himself to focus his attention on his orders, that no matter who asks, he is to answer that he had been here years, no, he has heard of no "camp," yes, he has stepped to his front door all these years to gaze out upon low evergreens, a barn, the flat, brushy landscape of his home.

But at night he cannot sleep, and he waits day by day for the arrival of his wife and children from the Ukraine. Their photographs are lined up on the fireplace mantel, but he has stopped looking at them because their faces have undergone an evil metamorphosis, and now his children leer malevolently, his wife's eyes bore into him with a thinly concealed, strangely perverse contempt. At night he sometimes paces through shafts of moonlight coming in through the windows, making his way to the living room and to the front door, vaguely thinking of getting out, because the air has something in it, something tangible, not only an odor but a sound, like whispering, and a peculiar shifting density that makes him wary every minute.

When he does sleep, even if only for minutes, he awakens suddenly, terrified and unable to move, and when he can no longer stand lying rigid and breathless he gets out of bed and makes his way to the kitchen where he pours vodka, gripping the bottle neck so tightly that his arm and fist vibrate as if from lifting a great weight.

And all of it, this wariness that vodka aggravates rather than dulls, is caused by the bricks. He does not recall seeing it happen while he helped with the cleanup of the burned camp, does not remember wondering at all as they laid out the foundation. His farmhouse is not a house or a room, but a chamber. That was the succinct explanation offered by the handsome deputy commandant after he had explained the orders: "Why, your house is built of the gas chamber bricks. Where else would we get the materials?"

Every time he walks to the wall and places the flat of his hand there, the coldness shocks him. Then he becomes aware that the lewd photographs watch. Carefully ignoring them, he studies the bricks, wondering what this scratch is, that discoloration, that tiny material dried and fringed with a stain as if the material had bled an oil into the porous surface of the brick. Why do some have those off-white tiles, which feel moist to the touch?

And he is left with the silence that is not a silence, the clean air that is not clean, the strange, shifting tangibility of the space. When he walks outside to look at the house he feels it out there too, sensations that are frustratingly just outside his true grasp. It is as if any decrease in these sensations is meters, perhaps kilometers away. Perhaps if he walked away he might feel a change. But he does not walk away.

He sits. He waits. He has his orders. He must remain sane until they arrive. He carefully measures out his next glass of vodka, drinks it in two gulps so that it burns his throat. Everything would have been right if he had not learned about the bricks.

A NOTE ON THE AUTHOR

IAN MACMILLAN is the author of *Proud Monster, Orbit of Darkness,* and two short story collections. His work has appeared in *Paris Review, Best American Short Stories,* and the *Pushcart Prize* and *O. Henry Award* volumes. He is winner of the 1992 Hawaii award for literature, and teaches writing at the University of Hawaii.

A NOTE ON THE BOOK

The text for this book was composed by Steerforth Press using a digital version of Electra, a typeface designed in 1935 by William Addison Dwiggins. Electra has been a standard book typeface since its release because of its evenness of design and high legibility. All Steerforth books are printed on acid free papers and this book was bound by BookPress of Brattleboro, Vermont.